SPY CODE

A SAM TAYLOR THRILLER
BOOK 2

BEN BALDWIN

Copyright © 2025 Ben Baldwin

The right of Ben Baldwin to be identified as the Author of the Work has been asserted by them in accordance with the Copyright, Designs and Patents Act 1988.

First published in 2025 by Bloodhound Books.

Apart from any use permitted under UK copyright law, this publication may only be reproduced, stored, or transmitted, in any form, or by any means, with prior permission in writing of the publisher or, in the case of reprographic production, in accordance with the terms of licences issued by the Copyright Licensing Agency. All characters in this publication are fictitious and any resemblance to real persons, living or dead, is purely coincidental.

www.bloodhoundbooks.com

Print ISBN: 978-1-917449-9-08

For my own K.G.B

From Sheffield with love

"Berlin is all about volatility. Its identity is based not on stability but on change."

— Rory MacLean

PROLOGUE

JOSH QUINN STEPPED out of the main embassy building and into the gated courtyard. An early winter's night had now fallen, leaving the stone surroundings in an unnatural luminescent light. Josh felt a cold shudder run down his spine as he tried to pull his jacket collar closed. Yet it could not be said that the involuntary spasm of his muscles was purely down to the cold weather alone. He knew he had to keep moving.

Stepping forwards into the open courtyard, his eyes darted over the granite buildings that surrounded him. The British Foreign Embassy for the Republic of Ireland was a pillar of modern architecture. A combination of practicality and security combined with attractive, tasteful design. Josh Quinn was not yet twenty-five and was on his first international appointment; he had counted himself fortunate to have even been allowed inside its thick walls. Thick enough to ensure there was never a repeat of the destruction of the original embassy building back in the Troubles of the previous century. Coming to work these past few months in Dublin had become a blur of unmissable opportunities of the kind once unimagined by a working class lad from Durham. But it had turned into one opportunity too many.

Heading towards the iron gated staff entrance, Josh pushed his hands deeper into his pockets and tried to look as nonchalant as possible. It was just another Tuesday evening, he told himself as he joined the queue of colleagues having their passes scanned by security. The queue moved slowly in front of him and he took a moment to look over his shoulder at the white building behind. The odd office light remained switched on, sending a shot of warmth outwards from the black-fronted windows. Most remained dark. Josh's eyes were suddenly caught by what he thought was movement in a top floor window. He could have sworn he had seen a shape move away from the glass the moment he looked up.

"Stop it, calm down," he muttered under his breath.

Readjusting his backpack, he turned back to the queue. He pulled out his staff card ready to be scanned by the weary eyed security guard, whose hand reached out and took it from him. The guard squinted down at the picture and looked back up at the younger man. The short brown hair, the narrow face and slim frame matched the image on the card.

"Got any plans this evening Mr Quinn?"

Josh stuttered a reply. "No, nothing at all. Just going back home."

The security guard barely registered his response, her small talk skills already pushed to the limit after a ten-hour shift. She waved her hand and let him through the gates. Pushing through the bars, Josh Quinn left the safety of the thick high walled compound of the embassy and stepped into the streets of Dublin. Not that the leafy Ballsbridge suburban streets of Dublin could be called threatening. With its residential villas, tree lined streets and busy main road into the city centre, most people would have felt perfectly safe.

Josh Quinn *had* been one of those people, that was until the email had arrived. An email sent to his work account containing photos of a previous evening's encounter had changed everything. A few simple sentences made up the rest of the content.

Did you know she is just 14?
What would your ambassador say?
How much would you pay?

The photos had been the final proof. Images which clearly showed him and his companion in positions that would condemn him for the rest of his life. He had known he was in deep trouble the moment he'd clicked on the email. Who would believe him that he had been told she was twenty? That she had whispered it to him in the crowded room in Temple Bar? It would be impossible to prove. More emails had followed, each one posing an uncomfortable question masking an unspoken threat. Eventually, he had cracked and replied, asking what they wanted to make it go away. He had pooled all his savings and even asked his brothers for help. Now it was time to pay up.

Following the main street for a few hundred yards, Josh's feet were in autopilot having already made the journey that day. The blackmailers had chosen the Merrion Cricket Club on the edge of the weaving River Dodder with the large Herbert Park on the opposite bank. He had used his lunchbreak to check it out, to somehow try and find any kind of an advantage. But the grey concrete pavilion, with its deserted car park and hibernating sporting facilities, provided nothing but despair.

Quickly checking his watch, he felt relieved to see he was still on time. Leaving the main road, he headed left and took a small road lined by bare trees. He knew in his heart this would not be the final payment. Men like this did not release their prey when their foot was on its neck.

Further down the street he passed a large sporting arena, home to one of the local rugby teams. He had been there only a month ago with his colleagues to watch a game. That memory now seemed to belong to someone else. The road then ended at a T-junction; to his right stood a stone church. Its sharp tipped spires pierced the night sky. Across from the street in which he stood, a large green sign welcomed visitors to the Merrion Cricket

Club. A quintessential English sport hidden within the Irish capital. Two dark iron gates stood open and Josh crossed the road to pass through them. The driveway took him between two red brick houses and into the main carpark.

The instructions had been precise, directing him to walk towards the main building before turning left to follow the rear walls further into the cricket ground. The whitewashed wall seemed to glow oddly in the darkness and Josh used it as a guide to the second set of parking spaces. All of the bays lay empty as the members of this club preferred the warmth of their homes to this January night. Leaving the tarmac of the carpark and stepping onto the damp grass of the playing field, Josh walked on into the darkness.

Walking slowly, careful not to lose his footing on the wet grass, Josh tried to find the steel framed outline of the all-weather nets – his final meeting place. Situated at the far end of the field, these four artificial playing surfaces would be full of aspiring teenagers come summer. Now they stood deserted, their netting rolled away and tied up for the winter. His tormentors had chosen the spot well, the furthest point from any possible interruption from the rest of the city. There were only a few trees separating it from the river beyond.

Josh Quinn now stood there alone. Where for some it would be a place of enjoyment, the field seemed to suck the life from him. He was a lone figure in the darkness, watching, waiting for the coming of his fate… a coming that was precipitated by the appearance of two headlights growing ever bigger as they drove through the green iron gates. The two beams shone across the green grass of the cricket field before being suddenly cut off as the car drove behind the pavilion.

Still standing amongst the cold steel poles, Josh's heart began to beat ever harder against his chest. It felt as though his breath was catching in his lungs. Screwed up in his coat pockets, the palms of his hands grew clammy. He wanted to run. He felt a sudden urge to dive through the small line of trees behind him and into the dark waters beyond. His head screamed at his body to move, but his feet were failing to act on the message. He was frozen to the spot.

The unknown car reappeared from behind the pavilion. Josh expected the vehicle to stop and for its occupants to travel the remaining distance on foot. Instead, the vehicle came onto the sports field, the lights rising to the sky as the wheels mounted the curb and drove onwards over the wet grass. Josh was blinded by the headlights, his whole vision flooded. For a wild moment he thought he was about to be run over. Instead, the vehicle stopped when it neared him. Blinking against the glare, Josh could see the outline of a van parked a few yards ahead of him.

For a moment, nothing happened; the lone figure stood staring at the immobile vehicle. Josh hesitated. Fear gripped him and the urge to run away still tugged at his stationary feet. Without warning, both doors flew open as two figures climbed out into the darkness. Moving in tandem, their figures blocked out the headlights, giving Josh a chance to see two tall men dressed all in black moving towards him. Both wore balaclavas.

Josh's feet finally came back to life. He began to swivel away from the approaching figures, but by then it was too late. The righthand man simply increased his speed, then took Josh by the scruff of his coat.

"I hope you're not thinking of leaving us, Mr Quinn." Josh tried to mutter something, but no sound came out. Instead, he mutely shook his head. "Good. You see, Mr Quinn, we had been looking forward to meeting you in person." The stranger spoke in a deep Irish accent. Two dark eyes looked down from within the woollen mask.

The grip released and the stranger patted Josh's coat down. He turned to his companion. "You see, he's a good lad, our Josh Quinn. An Englishman with an Irish name is always going to be good craic."

The second new arrival remained silent.

"We have some business to attend to don't we, Mr Quinn?"

"Yes."

"Good. Shall we get on with it then?" White teeth flashed against the dark mask.

Shaking, Josh began to reach for his bag and the envelope of euros. As he did so, a voice came floating out of the darkness behind them, singing out to the night sky.

The men turned to look at Josh. "Who the hell is that?"

"I don't know!"

"We told you to come alone."

"I did!"

The singing drew nearer. Josh suddenly recognised the song, a Beatles melody, its familiar tune breaking the silence.

"It's coming closer," the second of the two masked men finally spoke. "From over there." He pointed behind the van.

The pair of them reached into their jacket pockets and pulled out flashlights. Together, they pointed the torches in the direction of the singing. The two beams broke the darkness past the parked vehicle. In their twin lights, a new figure could be seen.

All three of them stared in amazement at the person in front of them. A man was staggering across the cricket field. Josh wondered how he was even able to keep upright as he made his way clumsily towards them. Every so often he would pause and sing more.

No one else moved; all eyes were transfixed on the newcomer who lifted a can of beer to his lips.

"He's pissed up."

"Stupid bastard."

The newcomer seemed to hear them and increased his unsteady pacing.

"Hey you, get lost!" The first masked man shouted.

The newcomer was now alongside the van. He looked at the three of them all standing staring at him. A demonic smile split his face before he twisted and fell against the van.

The first of the masked men swore. "Go get rid of him," he ordered his companion.

"You do it."

"Jesus, let's just do it together." He turned back to Josh and once again grabbed his collar and dragged him with them.

The three of them walked towards the van with the newcomer sprawled backwards against its metal bonnet. Josh, still shaking, allowed himself to be pulled along. Moving closer to the drunken arrival, Josh saw more clearly now the figure, his face hidden as it hung down to his chest.

"Come on fella, up we get." Josh watched as the second of the two masked men went to grab the arm of the newcomer. It happened in a flash, so quickly that Josh would have trouble remembering it afterwards. The newcomer's face darted upright. The demonic smile was now replaced by a cold, stern look. Josh's blackmailer stopped in surprise. The newcomer began to rise, slowly at first. His right arm came up with him, but instead of a beer can, he was holding a black pistol, its muzzle covered with a suppressor. Flames spat out of the end of the suppressor, mere inches from the stomach of the masked man.

Wounded, the blackmailer fell to the ground, groaning in pain. His companion barely had time to register what had happened, when the newcomer was onto him. Josh could see the newcomer was tall, broad shouldered and well built. Within seconds, he had the other masked man against the van, one arm across his throat and the pistol thrust painfully into his stomach.

"Who *are* you?" Josh's blackmailer choked.

For a moment, the newcomer did not speak. Instead, he looked over at Josh, who was by now cowering behind the car.

"Mr Quinn?"

"Yes?"

"Are you hurt?"

"No."

"Good."

The newcomer spoke in an English accent. Now in the light of the headlamps, Josh could see a round face half covered in dark brown stubble. Two dark eyes studied him for a moment before turning back to his captive.

"Rory Collins?"

"Yes, how do you know?"

The newcomer forced the pistol harder into Rory's stomach.

"I'll ask the questions, unless you want to end up like your brother over there." They all looked down at the twitching figure at their feet. The wounded man convulsed and groaned. "If you answer my questions, I'll let you help him. Do you understand?"

Collins nodded.

The newcomer nodded towards Josh. "Did you take any of his money?"

Collins shook his head. The eyes set within the balaclava were wide with fear.

"Apart from you two and the girl, who else knows about this?"

"No one."

"You sure?"

"Yes, I swear it."

The injured Collins brother groaned again. The newcomer ignored him.

Rory Collins continued. "Look, I'm sorry. We will forget this ever happened. I'll delete everything, I swear it."

"Ah, top man. That's good to hear. Makes this a lot easier." The newcomer's shoulder's visibly relaxed. Stepping back, he used his free hand to brush down Collins' coat.

"We didn't want to hurt anyone." Collins stammered, rubbing his throat. "She's not even fourteen; she's eighteen."

The newcomer nodded. "I know and you will be glad to hear she's currently on a plane back to her home country."

Rory Collins, sensing the worst had passed, seemed to relax a little. He looked at the newcomer. "That's good to know." He paused and looked down at his brother. "He needs a doctor… if I can just get him some help?"

The tall newcomer looked from one brother to the next. "Go on, get him out of my sight."

"Thank you, I'm so sorry again."

Collins turned and bent down to pick up his wounded brother. As he did so, the newcomer raised his pistol and without flinching, shot both of the Collins brothers dead.

Josh Quinn could only stand there watching in horror as the newcomer bent down and checked the fresh corpses. He watched as the hands expertly searched through the pair's pockets. In the half-light, Josh could see more of the face. An ugly scar ran up from one cheek into an ear clearly mangled from an old wound. Looking down, he could see the round head almost looked small compared to the man's muscular frame. Even in the darkness, Josh could see the strength in the man.

Standing again, the newcomer turned to Josh, who was shaking. Now at his full height, the newcomer towered over him. The dark eyes scanned over the frightened embassy man.

"Who are you?" Josh managed to whisper into the night air.

"You can call me the caretaker."

ONE

THE FLASHLIGHTS SPRAYED the room once again as the camera took another round of photos. To John Travers, watching the scene play out from the edge of the office space, the whole episode seemed to be an enormous distraction from other priorities. Not that you could have told the Ambassador that. Travers, in all his thirty years, had never quite seen an occupant of the post of British Ambassador to the German Republic enjoy the publicity side of the job as much as the slim woman in front of the cameras did right now. Dressed today in a bright blue suit and white blouse, she did at least *look* the part. Only thirty-eight, Angela Cooper had risen far quicker than most to take one of the most desirable diplomatic jobs in the entire Foreign Office. A darling of the Conservative Party back home, Travers knew this current posting was only the stepping stone to far grander titles.

The camera flashed again, its soft white lights illuminating a narrow, hawk-like face whose smile seemed slightly on the sly side, to Travers' mind. A politician's smile, which could be switched on at a moment's notice. She was perched on the edge of her desk, a Union Flag to the right of her and the Berlin skyline behind. Her pose was a textbook power pose, her jet black hair perfectly styled to rest on her shoulders. Travers caught a glimpse of his own features in the dividing glass wall that separated the Ambassador's private office from the wider rooms in which he stood waiting. A tanned weather-beaten face stared back at him, pale blue eyes set under thick blond eyebrows. Unlike the refined dark hair of his ambassador, his own blond hair was wavy and receding ever further up his lined forehead.

"I think that will do, Ambassador," the lead photographer announced.

Ambassador Cooper looked almost disappointed. "Are you sure? You wouldn't like some more in our atrium?"

"No, we've got the ones from this morning beneath the gate."

Travers chuckled to himself. They must have spent over an hour in front of the Brandenburg Gate this morning, Cooper insisting on yet another angle. The glossy magazine's press team members had certainly earned their fees today. He sighed and stepped back into the open office to wait for the publicity people to make their exit. The extra lighting, camera equipment and reflectors all had to be dismantled then packed away. It all took time, which in his mind, neither of them had. He flicked through the cardboard file in his hands for the hundredth time, then finding nothing new, looked down at the empty desk in front of him. The plain white desk with its dark computer screen was the ever present reminder of the problem at large.

Back inside the private office, the teams were finishing and preparing to leave. Travers steeled himself for another round with his boss. For over thirty years he had been stationed in Berlin. From back in the old days, where every shadow was likely to have hidden a Russian spy in the final death throes of the old Soviet Union, through to the bright new age of liberalism at the turn of the century, the ever present Travers had seen it all. As the British Embassy's Head of Security, John Travers had spent more time in Germany than in his own beloved Scotland.

People were now leaving the private office and making their way through into the outer office. The magazine team was being led by the embassy's media officer back towards the exit. That was yet another job role this new ambassador had insisted was needed to ensure that Britain's best interests were projected across this most crucial of European partners.

"She will see you now."

Travers turned round to see the ambassador's personal assistant staring at him. He nodded. "Thank you, Eleanor. I'll be right in."

He patted the file once more before giving the empty desk a final glance, almost in a last fleeting hope that its owner may have somehow reappeared at its empty chair.

Stepping into the private office, the assistant adjusted the blinds, giving the room complete privacy from any onlookers. The blinds dropped into place and the young assistant finished by pulling the sliding door closed. The three remaining occupants were not to be disturbed.

Ambassador Cooper smiled as Travers entered, in a gracious attempt to make him feel welcome in her presence. After nine months of the same routine, Travers had become immune.

"John, come in and take a seat. Thank you for being so patient, these press types do like to make sure they get their money's worth." Travers simply smiled in agreement. "They have promised me I'll be on the front cover in this weekend's magazine."

"I'm pleased to hear it, madam."

Cooper smiled, flashing her perfectly white teeth. "It will be in the hands of the public at the same time as the Prime Minister is signing the deal."

"Does that mean the Prime Minister has actually signed it off now?"

"The article? No good gracious no, I don't need him to approve it. I may let him and the Foreign Secretary have a copy in advance if I'm feeling generous." She smirked and clapped her hands down on the table.

Christ she was intolerable, Travers thought. To think he meant her little media interview rather than the biggest trade deal in recent times.

"No, I'm sorry Madam Ambassador, I was referring to the trade deal. Have we had word back yet from London or the German Chancellor?"

Cooper frowned, taken aback that her Head of Security could be interested in anything other than her front-page weekend spread. "No, not yet, but it's only a matter of time. The rest of the EU will march along to whatever the Chancellor here decides and he's, well… Let's say he's easily persuaded."

Travers groaned inwardly. To hear an ambassador speak of the German Chancellor as if he were a member of her fanclub was incredible. The arrogance of the woman was beyond belief.

"I'm pleased to hear it. I for one will be glad when this deal is completed and out of our hands."

Ambassador Cooper smiled blankly back at him. "You will?"

The actual impacts of the much vaunted North Sea Deal between the United Kingdom and the European Union, like most things which required detailed attention, had clearly bypassed the Ambassador. It had not been her concern to worry about the security surrounding it, or the secrecy of the actual terms and financial arrangements. Nor did she have to consider the endless climate protesters outside the embassy's gates, all determined to stop the growing use of fossil fuels. Then, of course, there were the Russians. While no longer the ringmasters of a divided Germany, they were the biggest losers in the new deal. Once the ink had dried on the paper, fifty per cent of the Europeans' natural gas requirements would be supplied by Britain. New pipelines would be laid throughout the North Sea and into mainland Germany. In a single stroke the European community would no longer be reliant on Russian gas.

"Yes, the protesters outside in particular have made themselves most unwelcome." Cooper smiled her sickly smile once more and leant back in her chair. "The deal is almost done, John. Please don't worry about it anymore. This time next week our country will be a far wealthier one than it was when we left it."

"I'm pleased to hear that. But we need to talk about Miss May." He leaned forward and pushed the file over the desk to her.

The Ambassador looked at the offered folder, but did not take it. "Ah yes, poor Kate. Is there any news?"

"None. I spoke with the German police before I came in and they've seen nothing of her. We've had all her cards checked and she's not used them. Her phone was found in a waste bin just outside the embassy, so it's been impossible to track her. As of this moment, Kate May might well be on another planet, for all we know."

The Ambassador sat back and sucked in her cheeks as she contemplated Travers' words. She twisted in her chair to look out of the window and into the city. Without turning back to face him, she spoke. "Tell me, John, does this have anything to do with the North Sea Deal?"

Travers considered the question for a moment. He himself had been thinking about the very same possibility.

"I don't see how it can be. But with the timing of everything, I worry it just might be. We've checked her computer and she had access to nothing that could even be remotely compromising, though."

The Ambassador turned round to face him. "What do you think has happened to her? People don't just go missing."

"I'm sorry madam, but I can't tell you. It could be one of a hundred things. A young pretty girl in a large foreign city, she'd only been here three months before this happened. It's damned hard to even know where to start. I personally checked her flat, which was empty, almost devoid of any signs of a social life. We've interviewed all her colleagues and none of them claim to be on friendly terms with her. All we know about her right now is that she turned up for work every morning and went home every evening."

The narrow face frowned, the small beady eyes studying

Travers for a moment. He knew that the debate inside that hawkish head was not about the girl's safety, but whether the disappearance posed its owner any risk to her cherished reputation.

"I think it's time we spoke to London once more." Travers nodded. She thought for a moment. "Tell me everything again, everything we know. I don't want to miss anything out when I speak to the Prime Minister."

For the third time in two days, John Travers told his ambassador the tale of the missing Kate May. How the attractive dark-haired girl had last been seen on CCTV leaving this very meeting room late two evenings ago. That the external cameras had filmed her exiting the building into the cold January night air. After that, she had simply disappeared. No one at her apartment block had seen her since that morning. She had not called the embassy personnel sick line. The local police had started their search, but had found nothing of interest. Travers' own investigations had turned up nothing, either. Kate May was nowhere to be found.

"That settles it then, we need to make sure we have done everything we can in case she is found dead."

"You mean that we've done everything we can to ensure that she's found safely?" Travers reprimanded gently.

"Yes, yes of course."

Travers could tell the Ambassador was wanting to ask him something. He decided to put her out of her misery. "Is there anything else I can help you with before you ring London?"

"What do you think I should say?"

Travers sighed. "You need to tell them the truth – that at the moment, she's missing and we have no further leads. That the local police are stumped and that there is a risk that it could be to do with outside interference on the North Sea Deal."

She bristled at the reference to the North Sea deal. "You said that it was unlikely to be related to that."

"I did, but do you really want to risk it? I'm not sure it would look good in the newspapers if there was even the slightest possibility the two could be related." Angela Cooper still looked unconvinced. Travers sighed. "Ring up the Prime Minister and tell him you want a repatriation officer sent over immediately. They are part of Emma Read's team in the Foreign Office, they will be used to dealing with this type of thing."

"I've heard of them. Sir Jeff Doyle's old team?"

Travers nodded. "Yes, they were set up by him but now Read is running that show. They will be able to help. From what I hear, they like to get their hands dirty."

The Ambassador smiled wanly and stood up.

"Thank you, John. I will get on it right away. If they are as good as you make out then I'm sure Miss May will be back at her desk in no time."

Travers could see he was being dismissed. He went to take back the folder.

"No, leave it. I'll have another look through it this evening."

The Head of Security took his leave and left with the personal assistant to allow the Ambassador some privacy. He looked over his shoulder as he reached the glass doorway, to see the beady eyes already flicking through the pages. The speaker on the desk phone was sounding out an international dialling tone.

"Oh and John," Cooper called out to him, and he turned around, "if the Repatriation Office can't find her, there's always the Caretakers?"

Travers stared at the black-haired ambassador, the hawkish face looking at him intently. He thought he saw a flash within the dark eyes.

"If the Repatriation Office fails then yes, there's always the Caretakers."

TWO

"BUT THEY ARE SAYING there's no more room on the plane!" pleaded Lucy Marsh.

"Right, and have they told you when the next plane is due?"

The exasperated analyst nodded her head. "Yes, the next direct flight out of Bogota isn't for another two days."

"Right."

"And they are saying there's nowhere left to store the body and it's the middle of summer."

"Ah, and you're worried our dearly departed adventuring grandma may not last long resting in her coffin whilst roasting in the middle of the Colombian summer?"

"Yes!" The analyst pleaded with the senior repatriation officer.

Sam Taylor stretched back in his chair and ran his fingers through his light brown hair. He looked to his right, where his colleague Hannah Pearce sat watching the conversation unfold. His friendly, handsome face was etched with concern as he turned his attention to the new analyst. Lucy Marsh was a recent graduate to the Foreign Office's Repatriation Team and she was still trying to find her feet in this strange new world. In the few months since she had first joined the team, she had been involved in the day-to-day challenges of returning Britain's citizens back home. Whether missing, wrongly incarcerated or deceased, she was now part of the team that had to somehow get them back.

Now she was standing in front of the imposing figure of Sam Taylor: the one case officer whose reputation was ingrained in the very walls of the department. His friendly face with its single dimple hidden by stubble had always seemed welcoming, but if even half of the stories of his previous exploits were true then Lucy knew there was an edge to his character. Tall with broad shoulders, his frame had always drawn her eye as he made his way around the office.

"Well, what did you say?" Sam asked her.

"I said I needed to speak to my superior."

Sam laughed. "Don't look at me! I'm not in charge here."

"Shut up you miserable dick, you're the duty officer today," Hannah Pearce chided him.

Lucy looked to the pretty brunette. Hannah Pearce was, apart from his superiors, the only person in the whole office who seemed not to be awed by this Yorkshire man. Seemingly, she and Sam had worked together for too long now to be worried about upsetting the other's feelings. It was a common topic of gossip amongst the rest of the team as to when the two of them would actually get together. The fact that Hannah was currently living with a boyfriend only added to the sense of expectation.

"I am?" Sam asked her.

"Yes, you know you are."

"Fuck," Sam swore. "Okay, this is what I want you to do. Go back out there, and in your best Spanish, tell them they have to find a way to get that body on that plane today. Don't take no for an answer." Hannah and Sam watched as the nervous analyst gave a weak smile and turned away to walk back to her desk. "Oh, and close the door please," Sam called out as Lucy left the meeting room.

The large glass window splitting the meeting room from the rest of the office gave them a direct view of the whole team.

Across from where they were sitting, Lucy had reached down for her phone and began to talk.

The speaker phone on the desk in front of them blared back to life and Lucy's Spanish speaking voice filled the room. "Hello there, I've spoken with my boss and he insists we need the body on the plane today."

Sam eyed Hannah mischievously, unpressed the mute button and then in his flawless Spanish, replied, "Okay, okay, I've spoken to my supervisor and we have an idea."

From across the room they could see Lucy's body language relax at this news.

Sam continued, "What we can do is cut up the body and pack her in round the rest of the cargo hold. We think if we chop off the feet, legs, arms and then the head, we can fit in the cabin."

"Oh my God, no."

Hannah had her hand over her mouth, trying to stifle a laugh.

"Yes, yes it is no problem, we cut her up and then when we land we stick her all back together."

Out in the main office, Lucy had gone pale.

"I... You can't do that, her family will be at the airport collecting her."

"Oh no it is easy, we do this all the time, I myself have done it with one man's horse. So yes, yes leave it with me; it will all be okay. Your Mrs Parker will be home tomorrow."

Sam hung up and the pair of them watched as Lucy put down her handset. The young girl looked on the verge of being sick.

"You're a bastard, you know that?" Hannah told him.

"Yeah, but it's good for her development."

They watched as she slowly made her way back to the meeting room where the two of them sat waiting.

"Sam, I'm sorry, but you need to speak to them."

"Going to chop her up?" Sam asked her.

She looked at him in surprise. "Yes they are, how do you know?"

Sam winked at her and Lucy couldn't help but blush. "Ah,

don't worry about it, happens all the time. Let me ring them up and sort it out."

He directed her out of the meeting room, closed the door and turned to grin at Hannah. "Okay, you're right. I'm a bastard."

Hannah shook her head. "I'm going to make sure she gets you back for this."

"What are you actually going to do about Mrs Parker? She still has to get home."

Sam smiled, a twinkle in his eye. "She landed at Gatwick this morning; it's all been taken care off."

"You bastard."

"Don't worry, I'm sure karma will be making amends soon enough."

Hannah's eyes were distracted by movement on the open room floor. "Looks like karma's working quickly these days."

Sam swivelled to look out as two figures strode through the main office. At the rear marched his boss, Emma Read. She seemed agitated as she followed the man in front. Ahead of her, his face flustered, was the Foreign Secretary. Sam was not used to seeing their supposed leader in the office. Usually, Emma had to deal with one of the private secretaries dispatched to oversee whichever case had reached their master's current attention. Now, however, it seemed something had caught more than just his passing interest.

"I wonder what's caused his highness to come down to mingle with the commoners," mused Hannah.

"God knows."

"Ten quid says you're going to be dragged into it."

"No bet."

Emma caught Sam's eye as she walked past, indicating that he should follow her.

"Bugger."

"Karma works in mysterious ways."

Sam left Hannah to gloat and entered Emma's private office. Emma allowed her boss to take the chair behind the desk and went to stand on one side of the room. The Foreign Secretary looked up at Sam and waved his hand to the empty chair in front of him.

"Take a seat, man; don't just stand about looking lost."

Sam began the mental process of dealing with superiors, a skill already well refined by his years in the military police. Time to roll out the army rules. Keep it short and sweet, leave no room for further questioning.

"Thank you sir, it's nice to see you."

The Foreign Secretary grunted and studied Sam. "Emma says you're a pretty useful man to have around, Mr Taylor."

"Thank you sir, I do my best."

Emma added, . "He was on hand to help with the Galahad rockets in Amsterdam."

Sam raised an eyebrow at his superior's attempt at tact. Without him being 'on hand', the aforementioned rockets would have been in the hands of terrorists at this moment in time. To say he had been 'on hand' conveniently left out being shot, beaten and kidnapped while in the line of duty.

The Foreign Secretary grunted again. "So you're a man who can handle himself."

"I try my best, yes, sir."

"Have you ever heard of Angela Cooper?"

Sam considered the question. The name seemed familiar. He searched the recesses of his mind before the cloudy image of a black haired politician came into focus.

"Ambassador Cooper?"

"That's the one. Angela Cooper his majesty's government's Ambassador to the German Republic." He said this with unrestrained scorn.

"I think I know of her, sir." Sam was enjoying the minister's apparent dislike.

"I wish I didn't. Angela Cooper, the darling of the party members, the darling of the press, the darling of the Prime Minister and a pain in the arse. The bloody woman has only gone and lost her goddamn secretary while we are trying to tie up the biggest trade deal with the EU."

"The North Sea energy deal?"

The Foreign Secretary slammed his fist down onto the table. "Precisely! Here we are trying to finalise the finishing details and that bloody women loses her personal secretary."

Sam looked from the minister to Emma. "And how does this impact the deal?"

"On the face of it, it doesn't," she answered. "But the timing isn't great. We know there's a large number of parties who would quite like this deal to fall through before completion. The hippies want us to stop using fossil fuel, plenty of countries don't like the thought of a more independent Europe, and of course our friends the Russians will be losing one of the few aces they still have in Europe – its energy supply."

"So you're saying either Greenpeace or the Russians have kidnapped the ambassador's secretary in an attempt to… what? Stop the contract being signed?"

"That's what we are worried about. The embassy in Berlin has found no links between the girl and the deal, but Cooper has kicked off and ruffled the PM's feathers."

"And that's where you come in," the minister interrupted. "Angela Cooper has personally asked the PM to send over a member of your team to help the investigation."

Sam groaned inwardly. A missing person's case in the midst of an international game of politics was not his idea of a good time.

"I'm really not sure I'm the best choice. I'm not one of the department's German speakers–"

"You're going, Sam," Emma stopped him.

"Yes boss."

The Foreign Secretary pulled a cloth from his jacket pocket and began to polish his glasses. "You will need to catch a plane over to Berlin first thing tomorrow morning. I've informed the embassy to be expecting you."

"Taking the politics out of it for a moment, what's actually happened to this secretary? Who is she?"

The minister sighed and looked to Emma to explain the details.

She pushed a cardboard folder towards Sam. "Kate May, twenty-seven, five foot seven inches, medium build, dark brown hair. She was last seen leaving the embassy late on Monday evening. The CCTV captured her just outside the embassy building where she disposed of her phone in one of the public bins. After that, it seems she simply disappeared."

Sam half listened as he flicked through the file. He paused at the official staff photo, which must have been taken at the embassy. A pair of deep-set eyes looked up from underneath her hooded eyebrows. Her face was narrow, with high cheekbones on her pale unblemished face. An attractive woman, Sam thought.

"How long had she been working at the embassy?"

"Three months."

Sam raised an eyebrow. "That's not long."

Emma shrugged. "I can imagine there's a high turnover when you have to work with Angela Cooper."

The minister let out a bark of a laugh. "Be careful Emma, you're probably talking about your future boss. If the papers are right, which they usually are, she's looking to become an MP this year and a cabinet member by the end of it. With her diplomatic experience, I'll give you three guesses as to whose seat at the table she wants."

"International development?" suggested Sam.

The minister laughed again. "I'd like to see the PM try and tell her that."

"Moving back to Miss May," Emma chided them both, "the German police have done the usual checks and have flags on all her cards and bank accounts. Our embassy's security team searched the girl's apartment. There's no close family on her records and none of her colleagues can ever remember hearing her talk about any friends."

Sam chuckled and ran his hands through his hair. "So what am I supposed to do? By the looks of it we are chasing a ghost."

"You probably are. The girl's either run off with some bloke or is dead in a Berlin crack den," the minister said dryly. "But either way, you're going out there to – at the very least – make sure no shit comes back my way."

Sam looked up at Emma, still standing to one side, who shrugged. He turned back to the minister. "So do I get any extra points for actually finding the woman?"

"No," the minister retorted.

"Yes," Emma contradicted him. "Of course we would like to actually find her as well as ensuring that the North Sea Deal goes off without a hitch. The timeline for the project is tight. There's a public announcement scheduled for next week."

The Foreign Secretary replaced his glasses and stood up. "Of course you should try to find the bloody girl. Just keep that Cooper woman away from me."

Sam stood as the minister moved round the desk and towards the door. "Yes, sir."

"Just keep Emma here informed of what you're up to and she in turn will keep me informed." Glancing back at Emma, he added, "Don't worry about the usual channels. You have my number. Good luck, Mr Taylor."

They waited for the minister to close the door behind him, leaving the pair of them alone. Emma sighed and slumped into the now vacant chair in front of Sam.

"What a mess."

Sam pointed his thumb to the door. "You know I'm rubbish at keeping you informed. What are you going to be telling the soon to be ex-Foreign Minister?"

"I'll do what *you* usually do – lie and tell him everything is fine," she laughed. "Soon to be ex? You'd better hope he's wrong."

"You know her then?"

"Barely, but she came to a women in diplomacy day we had last year. She spent the entire day telling every speaker how wrong they were. By the end of the day she'd pretty much pissed off everyone in the room."

Sam bit his lip and mused over the file again. "What about the missing woman?"

Emma shrugged. "What else is there to say? She's a missing person, like the rest of them, and it could be for any number of reasons. I can't imagine the local police being so incompetent that we are really needed. Just go over there, make the Ambassador happy and then come home."

They fell silent for a moment. Both respected the other beyond words. Both had been protégés of the renowned former diplomat Sir Jeffrey Doyle, who had overseen their respective careers.

"When's Sir Jeff back from his holidays?" she asked him.

"He's currently cruising in the Caribbean, doesn't get back for a week or two."

"It's all right for some. Perhaps one day he can get me an ambassador role in one of those islands."

"Too hot for me."

"Typical northerner. I presume you will be wanting Hannah on support?"

Sam was about to answer, then paused for a moment, overcome by the irrational urge to buy off the karma forecasted by Hannah earlier. "Actually, you can give it to Lucy Marsh."

"The recent graduate?" Emma was surprised.

"She seems pretty competent. Get Hannah to watch over her, but she'll do all right."

THREE

SAM, not for the first time that morning, cursed the name of Lucy Marsh. He also added in the names of both Hannah Pearce and Emma Read. Standing there in the departure lounge of Luton Airport at 6am he would have been quite happy to have shot the bloody lot of them. What had been his last words to the miserable pair of analysts? Whatever happened, to book him on a mid-morning flight. Yet here he was, half asleep, waiting for the first flight of the day to leave for Berlin.

Moving further into the departure lounge, he headed off to find a drink. He looked on enviously at the groups of men drinking at the bar. Instead, he went for a large black coffee. Letting the caffeine start its work, he walked on until his eye was attracted by a display in the bookshop window. A hawkish face smirked out at him from the neat pile of books.

"Bloody hell," he grumbled. "She gets everywhere."

The alert part of his mind was curious to see what the famous diplomat had to say. Picking up the book, he studied the cover. Turning it over, he read how only by following her vision of a better future, embracing the traditions of "old Britain", could a new future be established.

He dropped the book onto the nearest fantasy fiction table.

Landing a couple of hours later in the German capital, Sam stared out of the small oval window at the snow covered airport. The pilot announced over the intercom that the local weather forecast contained yet more snow to come. Sam thought enviously of his old mentor enjoying the Caribbean sun. The pilot continued on over the speakers, advising the passengers of the time difference. He looked down at the green ringed watch on his wrist, the new Rolex still seeming alien on his arm. It had been a parting gift from his last trip abroad. That had been a case in Amsterdam that had seen him dragged into a murderous chase across the port city. At least this trip should be less eventful, he mused as he manually changed the time on the dial.

Heading into the arrivals lounge, he was surprised not to find anyone from the embassy waiting for him. His mood was made worse as he stepped out into the icy air. He adjusted the straps on his backpack and shoved his hands deep into the pockets of his arctic parker coat. The train journey into the centre would at least give him a chance to study the old city. Lucy Marsh had planned a route for him which took him through the southeastern side of the city before crossing the River Spree and hooking round the city centre.

Sam had been to many cities during his time with the Repatriation Office. All had their unique quirks, landscapes and atmospheres. Berlin's history seemed to live all around its citizens. The scenes of countless major events in the world's history were actual living memories. It was the political centre of modern day Europe, a melting pot of East and West.

In the distance, the imposing outline of the Berlin TV tower, or Fernsehturm, reminded Sam of his last visit to the city. A weekend's leave from his final posting in the army had been spent exploring the museum island before returning to barracks to be confronted by his senior commanders. Less than two weeks later, he had been out of the army altogether. Now, he was back in the

German capital and staring up at the communist landmarks that dominated the eastern side of the city.

Eight years, he had spent in the army. From Sandhurst all the way through two tours in Afghanistan. Then, on his second tour, he had implicated the son of a general for selling arms to the locals. Promotions and medals had not been the order of the day for the man who had embarrassed the army. Captain Sam Taylor had been politely told he had no future in Her Majesty's armed forces.

"Bastards," Sam muttered to himself and tried to push the memories from his mind.

Sam also had a brother serving in the army. Whereas Sam had joined the military police, Jake Taylor had become a Royal Marine. Their paths had crossed a couple of times in uniform and Sam thought about his brother for a moment as the Berlin skyline continued to blur past him. It seemed strange to think that the last time they had met, it had been in the middle of a warzone. Now in peacetime, where the mere sight of a firearm felt out of place, the two brothers had all but lost contact.

The train pulled into the station and Sam left the train to catch the Berlin U-Bahn. This final stage of his journey would take him to the heart of the city and close to one of his favourite landmarks.

Climbing out of the U-Bahn station his eyes grew accustomed to the natural light amplified by the patches of snow all around him. Ahead, at the end of the wide Bundesstrasssse, stood the Brandenburg Gate. Its six archways supported by the twelve pillars all holding the bronze Greek chariot and its rider aloft. The eighteenth-century monument had stood throughout the city's rich history.

Sam wandered along the street, amongst the tourists who cluttered the pavement. To his left stood the US Embassy and Sam envied the view given to its employees. Above him the imposing statue of Victoria, the Roman goddess of victory, surveyed the scene. He had to step aside as a family of four wandered past, the two small girls looking up questioningly at him, their long blond hair tied tightly back in a ponytail. Sam gave them a friendly smile but it only resulted in them hurrying even quicker to catch their parents up. Shaking his head, he was again thankful not to have that hassle. Give him missing secretaries any day.

Sam turned on his heel, a full 180 degrees towards the British Embassy. Taking the righthand street, he walked through a set of bollards onto the traffic-free Wilhelmstrasse. The lone Union Flag hung from the embassy wall, the red, white and blue flickering limply in the wind. Ahead of him, just at the front of the stone building, a large crowd had gathered. Protesters waved flags, held up placards and chanted slogans in both German and English. Walking closer, Sam heard the chants aimed at stopping the North Sea gas agreement growing ever louder.

A bearded protester accosted Sam as he stepped towards the entrance of the embassy building.

The man shouted at him again and moved to block his path. More of his fellow protesters stopped their chanting and joined their comrade in surrounding the bewildered new arrival.

Sam stopped walking and looked at the man blocking his path. He had no idea what had just been said to him, but guessed it was not a warm welcome. The protestor continued accosting him. The German's words lost to Sam's understanding, he shook his head and pushed his way through the protestors, and onwards to the embassy.

Switching his mind back to the job in hand, he looked up at the embassy building. The entrance was guarded by three burly security guards, none of whom smiled back at Sam. A strong arm reached out and blocked his progress into the building.

"Business?" a deep voice asked.

"I'm here to see the Ambassador."

"Isn't everyone?"

Sam gave a dry laugh.

The three guards eyed each other and then let out a grin. "Who *are* you here to see, mate?" The tone was somewhat lighter.

"I told you – the Ambassador. I'm Sam Taylor from the UK Repatriation Office."

One of the guards pulled out a tablet and checked his screen. "He's on the list."

Sam flashed his passport to the guards and was finally allowed in to be told to wait in the atrium. Moving on through, he found himself at the foot of a grand staircase which led into the depths of the embassy. Two white pillars rose from the ground to meet a red roof. To the left of him, a glass fronted reception awaited, where two receptionists paused their typing to flash warm smiles.

"Sam Taylor?" a deep Scottish voice called out.

Sam swirled around to see a tall man walking down the sweeping staircase.

"That's me."

The approaching man studied the new arrival. The tanned lined face gave nothing away.

"Thank you for coming, I appreciate it must have been short notice."

"It generally is."

"I'm sure, when did you arrive?"

"About two hours ago now."

The Scotsman smiled in an attempt to appear slightly more friendly. "Early alarm call then?"

"Too early for me."

The tall Scotsman stuck out a hand. "John Travers, Head of Security."

If you're ready, I can take you straight up?"

"All good to go here, I wouldn't want to keep the Ambassador waiting."

Travers gestured for Sam to follow him up the staircase.

"Have you been in the city before?"

"A few times, mainly as a tourist."

"It's changed a bit since I first started here. In those days we were in a different building. Back then, we could say publicly that anything that went wrong was the Russians, now it's all political politeness."

Sam struggled to keep up with the older man's long gait as he took two stairs at a time.

"So you think Miss May's disappearance is to do with the Russians?"

"No, just pointing out how things change. In those days it was looking out for men in long coats, now it's keeping the anti fossil fuels lot out of the building."

They had reached the end of the stairs and emerged into a wide open winter garden. Its wide expanse was filled with people.

"Take this place, for instance. It was once open to the public. Now, with the threat of terrorism, it's all locked down. We can still hire it out for functions and events, but even then it's ticketed."

"You almost sound like you miss the old days?"

Travers shrugged and continued onwards into the main building. "When you've seen the things I have in this city then all you long for is that retirement package and somewhere hot in which to spend it."

The Head of Security tapped a button for an elevator and they both waited.

"Have you any thoughts on the disappearance?" Sam asked gently.

"Plenty, but none of them have proved fruitful." They stepped inside the metal doors of the elevator. "The truth is that we, like the local police, are just perplexed as to what could have happened to her. Nothing indicated she would have gotten involved in anything suspicious. Everyone who worked with her said she was an efficient but shy colleague."

"What have the police said?"

"They have done the usual routines, but that's drawn a blank. What few acquaintances she did have, we've checked with, and no one's seen her."

The elevator doors pinged open and the pair of them stepped out onto a new floor.

"How's the Ambassador taking it?"

Travers eyed Sam. "Have you ever met Angela Cooper?"

"No, but I've heard of her."

Travers stopped walking and pulled Sam to one side of the corridor. "She's not your usual ambassador, I will say that."

"Did she and Miss May work much together?"

"Plenty, Kate was Angela's secretary. Took care of most things for her."

"Did she enjoy working for the Ambassador?"

Travers thought for a moment. "No one I spoke to ever mentioned anything otherwise. I mean, Cooper can be a pain in the arse, but I never heard about any issues between them."

"What about the day in question? Did anything different happen? Anything out of the ordinary?"

Travers scratched his neck. "Not really... We checked her computer and found nothing unusual from that day or before it. Everyone was pretty rushed though, as the final trade agreement for the North Sea Deal had been delivered for review, so everyone was too busy studying that to have paid any attention to the secretaries."

The North Sea natural gas agreement again, Sam thought. If there was a connection to the disappearance then he could not see it just yet.

John Travers seemed to have read Sam's thoughts. "I can't see how she could have had anything to do with the North Sea agreement. It was well above her clearance level. This disappearance is probably just a personal issue we don't know anything about. I bet she doesn't even know the trouble she's caused."

"There's still the matter of her disposing of her phone and going completely off the grid." Sam grimaced.

"I know, and like I said, I have plenty of thoughts... just none of them have proved fruitful." He looked at his watch. "Come on, she will be waiting for us, no doubt one of her assistants will have told her you arrived."

"Any last minute tips?"

"How many public figures have you dealt with?"

"Plenty."

Travers started walking. "Then remember the one thing they all like to be told – how great they are."

FOUR

JOHN TRAVERS LED Sam through into the Ambassador's main suite of offices, where the now empty desk of Kate May stood as a constant reminder of the missing receptionist. Sam asked if he could take a look while they waited.

"Go ahead. I've been over it a dozen times already."

Sam walked over to sit at the unoccupied desk, trying to imagine its owner at work. He started by going through the three fitted drawers underneath the work surface. The usual mix of stationery, snacks and small personal items were stored across all three of the drawers. Their placement neither spoke of a tidy and organised owner, nor one who was happy to leave their possessions in a state of chaos. But the lack of anything really personal caught Sam's attention. There were no photos of loved ones, no randomly kept mementoes or keepsakes connecting the owner to a life outside of the workplace.

"Anything interesting this time?" Travers asked.

Sam ignored the question and pointed to the blank screen. "Did she use a desktop or laptop?"

"Laptop."

"Did she take it with her?"

"No we have it in IT. It's been checked and there's nothing suspect on it."

"Nothing at all to do with the North Sea Deal?"

Travers shrugged. "The only possible link she had was access to the Ambassador's diary."

Sam thought for a moment about whether that information would be useful to an outsider. Possibly to someone who wanted to track Cooper's movements?

"And you're confident that's not a security threat?"

"We've changed the Ambassador's travel routines and moved some of her appointments since Kate disappeared. I've also doubled her security detail, but I still think its low risk."

"This case just keeps on giving, doesn't it?" Sam said dryly.

Travers waved his hands. "Are you saying the official verdict of the Repatriation Office is that we are screwed?"

Sam laughed aloud and pointed at the older man. "Not on your life, I've only just arrived and I'm ready to continue down all the dead ends you have lined up for me."

The glass door to the Ambassador's private office slid open and an assistant called them in.

Travers gave Sam a final glance. "Good luck."

The pair of them walked into the office to find the Ambassador standing to greet them. Travers took a seat towards the back of the room, leaving Sam standing alone in the middle of the office with Angela Cooper, Ambassador to the German Republic.

"Sam Taylor, thank you for coming to help us." The hawk faced woman greeted him, stretching out a bony hand.

Sam took it and found his hand gripped tightly as it was wrung up and down. "Thank you Ambassador, I only hope I can help."

She waved Sam to one of the seats nearest her glass topped desk. Sam watched as she walked back round to her side of the workspace. She was dressed in a tight fitting black dress, which Sam guessed was designer and expensive.

Taking her seat, she placed her elbows on the desk, clasped her hands and leant over towards him. "I trust you've been briefed on the situation?"

"I believe I have a good understanding of things."

"And you appreciate the… delicacy of the timing?"

"Yes madam, it's been over forty-eight hours since the missing person was last seen and statistically, that is not good."

It had not been the answer Angela Cooper had been expecting. The small eyes narrowed and stared at Sam. Behind him, Sam could have sworn he heard John Travers move in his seat. Whether out of concern or amusement, he could not tell.

"Of course, yes, time is not on poor Kate's side. Whatever has happened to her must be very serious, she's never missed a day's work since I've known her."

"How well would you say you knew her, Madam Ambassador?"

Ambassador Cooper shifted in her chair, looking towards both her assistant and Travers in the corner. "Well enough. I always thought we had a good professional relationship."

"Has she ever given you cause to suspect she'd do anything like this?"

Sam could tell the Ambassador was not enjoying his line of questioning. Within moments of their introduction, he had moved the topic of conversation away from protecting her and the North Sea Deal to the actual disappearance. Not that it worried him, he was not concerned in the slightest if the bloody woman felt uncomfortable.

"No, nothing. Kate was a perfect employee, always on time, produced a high standard of work and was willing to help with anything."

"If I may ask, what do *you* think has happened to her?"

The Ambassador looked uncertain for a moment, unsure what to say. "I really don't know, Mr Taylor."

"But if you had to make a guess, humour me, as by the sounds of it we've got little else to go on."

Ambassador Cooper glared at Sam. "Like I said, I really don't know, Mr Taylor. I thought it was your job to find out?"

Touché, thought Sam. "Of course. I'm sorry Madam Ambassador, I had hoped you may have been able to provide some insight." He decided to retreat a little and went back to a more comfortable topic of conversation for the rattled ambassador. "I guess this is quite a stressful time for you all, what with the North Sea Deal being so close to completion?"

Cooper's body language relaxed a little and she sat back in her chair. "Yes, I'm afraid it's rather taken all of our combined efforts to have reached this far. It's a very exciting proposition for our country, which I'm sure you are fully aware of, Mr Taylor."

"Was Miss May involved in the deal at any stage?"

"No, Kate was never involved with the deal. She organised my diary around it, but at no point will she have had access to anything that was confidential in relation to the actual discussions."

Sam rubbed his chin, debating his next line of questioning. He was wary of the Ambassador. His instincts told him that this was a woman who kept back far more than she was thinking. There was a calculated act to her persona, he felt that that the politician facade was in full swing.

"Let's say for a moment that her disappearance was related to the North Sea Deal. What would be the worst case scenario in terms of it impacting on the final talks?"

Angela Cooper thought for a moment and looked towards her Head of Security.

Travers shifted in his chair. "We've given it some thought, run a few scenarios and we can only think of two. One would be to hold her for ransom to stop the trade deal."

"There've been no demands or contact from any possible kidnapper. Even the most optimistic kidnapper couldn't really believe we would cave and accept those kinds of demands."

"Exactly, we do not negotiate with terrorists." Said the Ambassador without a hint of sarcasm.

"The other would be to try and extract some sort of information from her about the negotiations or something personal about the Ambassador." Travers' face was grim.

Sam considered this hypothesis for a moment and then dismissed it. "Then, why did she go willingly? We saw on the CCTV that she voluntarily disposed of her phone."

"She may have been blackmailed? Either way, this is the one thing that worries me most as it wouldn't have taken long for them to have realised their captive couldn't give them anything of value."

No one spoke for a while. Everything they had just said was based on pure guesswork. It was time to try and find something more substantial.

"So, what is actually happening in terms of a search?" he asked the room.

Travers answered. "You know most of it from the report. The local police are giving us all the help they possibly can. I spoke with the lead detective this morning and he's got people watching her apartment twenty-four-seven. They've got alerts out on all of the airports in the country, but without her passport it's unlikely she will be flying anywhere."

"Her passport was found in the apartment, yes?"

"Indeed, but I've taken the liberty of storing it in the embassy safe for now."

"Fair enough. What about the other low hanging fruit? Local criminal activity?"

"Not that we know of, although I'm not sure the police would share that kind of intelligence with us."

Sam turned his attention back to the Ambassador. "Then what about our local Russian friends? I'm guessing they still have a presence here?"

"They've been rather quiet recently. I raised it with the Chancellor when we met to discuss the North Sea Deal. We are both very aware that this arrangement will be upsetting our friends in the East."

Travers interjected. "The German security services have been watching all known Russian agents closely for the past six months. I've seen all the most recent reports and they've been keeping their heads down."

That was one bit of good news, thought Sam. He did not fancy having to deal with a bunch of FSB agents chasing him.

"So it's a case of wait and see?"

"Pretty much," Travers admitted. "At this moment in time we've run out of ideas."

"That's why we need you," the Ambassador interjected. "We want someone with a fresh pair of eyes to have another look and see if there's anything we've missed. With everything that's going on here in the embassy, it's not hard to imagine that something could have been overlooked."

Sam highly doubted that John Travers would have missed anything. The grizzled Head of Security seemed pretty efficient to him. Plus, the German police force was not some amateur set-up like some Sam had encountered.

"Have you got any preferences as to where I start?" he asked the Ambassador.

"None at all, you have complete carte blanche. You have my permission to access to everything we can possibly share. John here will be happy to provide you with anything you need and if you'd like, I can arrange for you to meet with the police officers involved in the search?"

Sam was not quite ready to meet with the local police teams. He wanted some time to get his own thoughts together on the case first. At the moment, a number of questions were pulling at him. The fact that Kate had seemingly willingly disposed of the one thing that could have tracked her movements made him uneasy. But he had to balance that against the fact that they were talking about a secretary who apparently had access to nothing of interest. He wanted to know more about the missing woman. The folder in front of him had given him nothing more than the basic details. While everything he had heard had suggested there was nothing remarkable about the missing Kate May, there was something about the woman which piqued Sam's interest.

He reached over to the desk, where a copy of the case report lay untouched, and flicked to Kate's staff photo. Her pale face stared up at him with its pale blue eyes. The lips were poised in an almost sultry look. Privately, Sam could not quite imagine the woman in the photo as a secretary.

The rest of the room's occupants watched as he flicked through the report's pages. John Travers sat back in his chair, silently staring at Sam. The Ambassador had begun fidgeting impatiently, her movements increasingly frenetic with each passing moment. The assistant remained to one side, completely forgotten by all.

A few pages in, Sam arrived at a number of photos seemingly taken at the girl's apartment. He tapped the images. "Who searched the apartment again?"

"I did," Travers answered gruffly. "As apartments go, it was very ordinary. Certainly nothing of interest. I went through the entire place and found absolutely zip which could have been of use."

Sam knew his next words would risk upsetting the Scotsman. But what had the Ambassador said? He had carte blanche, so why not? Back in his detective days in the military police he would have started any case by building a picture of the suspect or victim. What better place to start than the person's home?

"Would you mind if I had another look? Just to get a feel for the place?"

Travers' body language clearly said he *did* mind, but he shrugged.

"If you must, but I think you're wasting your time."

"I think it would help me get a better understanding of the missing girl."

The Ambassador beamed, glad to have found a way forward. "John will be able to arrange for one of his team to drive you over to the apartment block. I believe she rents one of the rooms in an embassy owned housing block where a number of our staff members live."

"That works for me. I can go straight away?"

Angela Cooper stood up and placed her hands on her hips. "We have a plan. I trust you will keep me informed of any developments? I did promise I would keep the Prime Minister fully up to speed with everything."

Ambassador Cooper walked round from behind her desk and gestured to Sam to follow her out of the office. John Travers had remained seated and was not even attempting to hide his frustration.

"Madam Ambassador, I really think we can find a better use of Mr Taylor's time."

"Look, let Mr Taylor spend some time feeling his way into the case. For God's sake we've had to live it for the past few days, so why not let someone else suffer it?"

Travers looked like he wanted to continue his protests, clearly Sam had insulted his professionalism. But instead the Scotsman shook his head, rose and followed the two of them. They moved back into the reception area of the Ambassador's office with its empty desk. Sam's belongings remained on the chair.

"I trust the North Sea discussions are going well?" Sam asked as they made their way out.

"Positively, we have just a few small details to iron out with our European partners and then it will all be ready."

"I'm glad to hear it."

Angela Cooper gave him her best politician's smile. "Indeed, this will be a major moment in our nation's history. If you help me find our missing secretary and avoid rocking the negotiations then I can promise you a lifetime's supply of goodwill. Who knows, I may be working in the Foreign Office myself one day and I'm always on the lookout for good people I can trust."

Sam looked into her dark beady eyes, alight with the glint of political promise, and felt his stomach lurch. She had never looked more hawk-like.

FIVE

AMBASSADOR COOPER RETURNED to her office, her assistant closing the door behind her. The moment the glass sliding door came to a close behind them, a furious John Travers turned to face Sam.

"You know you're wasting your time, don't you?"

Sam shrugged as he bent down to pick up his coat.

"I personally went over that place with a toothpick and there was nothing out of the ordinary."

Sam ignored the older man's grievances, if the Scotsman didn't like having his work double checked what was it to Sam? For a moment Sam wondered if Travers didn't want him looking for another reason, was the old head of security hiding something? He pushed the thought to one side, it was probably more that he didn't like having his work questioned. But still the defensiveness seemed strange.

"Give me an hour or so at her place and we can head off and see the local police teams. I'd quite like to know what they think of everything."

Realising he was not going to win the argument, Travers surrendered. He pulled out his phone. "Fine, I'll have Hendricks drive you over."

They found Hendricks waiting for them in the underground car park. To Sam's eyes, he looked barely old enough to be behind the wheel.

"Hendricks, this is Sam Taylor," Travers introduced the young man. "Hendricks is one of the embassy drivers, he may look like he's not old enough to shave but he will get you to where you need to be."

Hendricks smiled up at Sam. "So, what takes your fancy?" He waved his hand round the parked cars. "Jaguar or Land Rover?"

Sam chuckled. "I'm easy."

Ten minutes later they were weaving through the Berlin traffic on their way to Kate May's apartment block. Sat up front with his driver, Sam watched as the city passed by. The freezing January air had not yet driven the population inside. But the hardy locals were thickly wrapped up against the elements.

"So has there been any news on Kate?" asked Hendricks.

Sam turned his head to look at his driver. "Nothing, it seems we have a vanishing act on our hands."

"Ah no, that's not good to hear."

"Do you know her?"

Hendricks nodded. "She lives a couple of floors above me at the embassy apartment block."

"Do you like her?"

"Yeah, she seems nice enough, a quiet one but each to their own."

"Do you know if she has any friends locally? Everyone I've spoken to said she kept to herself at work. Did she ever have any visitors to her apartment?"

Hendricks held back his reply as he navigated an upcoming turn. As the vehicle settled in its new course, he answered Sam's question.

"I saw her come and go pretty regularly, but never really with anyone else."

Sam sighed, resigned to having nothing else of interest on his missing person.

Then Hendricks spoke again. "Oh I tell you what, I did once see her with a man. In fact, I saw her with him a few times when she'd just moved in."

Sam twisted back in Hendricks' direction. "A boyfriend?"

"Possibly."

"Embassy staff?"

"Maybe, but I didn't recognise him."

"When did you last see him around her place?"

Again, Hendricks paused for a moment, considering his answer. "About two months ago."

"Ah," said Sam, deflated. It would be highly unlikely that this man had anything to do with the disappearance, having been out of the picture for two months.

Hendricks drove them further away from the city centre and towards the more built-up suburbs. He had chosen a large black Land Rover for the journey and Sam was impressed with his handling of the bulky vehicle as he weaved his way through the tight traffic.

"Have you been here long?" Sam asked him.

"About two years now. My old man used to work for Travers when he was my age. He managed to get me this job and I've been here ever since."

"So you know Travers well, then?"

Hendricks laughed. "No one knows John Travers well. I mean, everyone knows *of* him, but I've never known anyone say they know him well."

A common trait amongst all the embassy's staff, thought Sam.

"But the guy's a legend around here. It's like... he knows everyone in the diplomatic circles. The amount of time he's been here means he's got contacts throughout the city."

Sam kept quiet and let the younger man talk, he was interested to know more about the Scotsman.

"My dad used to tell me all sorts of stories about what they used to get up to over here. During the Cold War days, they used to get themselves into all kinds of scrapes with the Russians and

East Germans. Travers must have dealt with more spies in his time than anyone in the service. Think about it, he's spent his entire career in the capital of espionage. Yeah, sure he's not a spook, but as the head of security at an embassy like this one, who do you think is the biggest threat?"

"Spies?"

"Exactly, the guy's seen it all."

Sam thought of his own mentor Sir Jeffrey Doyle and his chequered past. The rumours of his blurring of the lines between diplomacy and espionage were well established in the office.

"You guys don't get up to much of that now though, do you? I thought everyone was friends?" Sam pretended to be naive.

"We still have our moments. This North Sea Deal is driving up the tensions."

"How has Travers taken it all?"

"Another day in the office isn't it, for him? I'm sure he will have seen worse."

Sam thought for a while. It wasn't completely unheard of for someone in the Foreign Office to spend their entire career in one posting. But still, how long had the old timer actually spent in this city? How long can a person be close to his enemy before he begins to no longer see them as such? It was only human nature to try and reason with a view alternative to your own, to see things in a different way. Could all these years stuck in the same posting, no doubt watching other men being promoted around him, have been enough for a man like Travers to become more open to the other side?

Hendricks pointed out of the window. "There's the apartment block."

Sam followed Hendricks' gaze and looked up at a drab looking set of apartment buildings rising from the street corner. The frontages were clad in white granite, with dark rectangular windows symmetrically placed along the walls. The corner apartments all had small balconies, their design strangely curved compared to the square architecture of the rest of the building. The block was of a plain design, a suitable home to the apparently plain inhabitant Kate May.

Hendricks turned the car into one of the empty parking lots and turned off the engine, nodding towards something ahead of them. "That's the police car they've assigned to watch over the place."

Sam saw an unmarked police car parked directly opposite the main entrance.

"They've had a car parked there for twenty-four hours a day, watching over the building. Waste of time really."

"Why?"

"There's at least three other entrances which they can't see."

"Ah, and they're not doing any sweeps?"

"Not that I've seen."

Sam unclipped his seatbelt and opened the passenger door. "You're wrong about it being a waste of time, though."

"How so?"

"They are here for show as much as to watch over the apartment. Tells the world the German police are still at least trying to look like they are searching for our missing friend."

The German police were also watching *them*. Upon recognising the embassy car, they walked over to meet the pair of them. Sam looked on as the two burly uniformed officers met them just outside the glass door that led into the main building.

"Hallo, ich nehme an, Sie sind von der Botschaft?" The first of the two asked.

Sam stared back blankly, his understanding of the German language non existent. It was left to Hendricks to respond. His German was slow, and he stumbled over some of his words, but he was able to get his message across.

"You have come to look at the apartment again?" One of the police officers replied in English.

"Yes, is that going to be a problem?"

The two officers stared at each other and then at Sam. "Who is this? He is a new face."

Hendricks, now bristling with impatience, answered. "He's with me and if you don't mind we are in a bit of a rush."

Again, the two officers looked at each other.

"You still have the keys?"

"Yes."

"You still remember the agreement?"

Hendricks rolled his eyes. "Yes, we are not to remove anything from the apartment without your permission. Now, can we get on with it?"

Finally, the two of them were allowed to enter through the glass doors and into the lobby of the apartment block. Hendricks was still smarting from their interaction with the two police officers.

"Honestly, they are supposed to be helping us, one team and all that rubbish. But instead, they like to act the big bollocks."

"Trust me, you put a man in uniform and it makes them think they have to fill it. Pushing around a couple of Englishmen after sitting in a car all day was probably the highlight of their shift."

Hendricks was still simmering as they entered the lift. Sam tried to change the subject. "What floor do you live on?"

"The first, Kate lives on the third."

The elevator doors pinged open and they stepped out onto the third floor corridor. Six black doors led away into the different apartments.

"Number two is down this way," Hendricks told him and walked towards the black apartment door.

The younger man fished into a pocket, pulled out a pair of keys and fitted them into the silver lock, which clicked open.

"So, how do you want to do this?" Hendricks asked Sam.

"I've not fully decided yet."

Hendricks led him inside the apartment. "It's a simple enough layout, one bedroom, an open living room and kitchen area. There's the ensuite, a small utility room and then there's the main bathroom. There's no balcony in these rooms, that's for the management."

"Let's start in the living room. You can have a seat while I potter about."

The living room was a simple affair. A single sofa facing the television set. There were few personal effects to give Sam any indication of the type of person who would have lived here. No family photos perched on the windowsill. No discarded books or magazines to betray a hidden interest. He was surprised to find even a television.

"Exactly the same set-up as when we move in. Minus my mess, this could have been my flat," Hendricks told him.

Sam sighed. "Come on then, let's get to it and see what old Travers has overlooked. I'd love to tell the old man he missed a howler."

"Good luck with that."

Sam winked at the younger man and began his search by diving to his knees. Pressing his head to the floor he ran his hands under the sofa. Failing to find anything he knelt up, lifted the cushions and ran his hands over the leather covering.

"What are you looking for?" Hendricks asked him.

"A hidden seam, a zip or I'll take bit of chewing gum at this stage."

"You've only just started, no need to get desperate just yet."

"True."

He looked round the living room and walked round the edges looking for anything that might suggest a hidden cavity in the walls. The floor was a thick carpet firmly fixed to the ground with no signs of a recent uplift at any of the corners. The only other furniture in the open plan room was a coffee table, which stood barren and empty.

Sam smacked his lips together. "One room down. Kitchen?"

The kitchen was small with a basic hob and oven set up. Sam quickly ran his hands through cupboards and over the shelving.

The fridge was relatively full, with produce slowly going out of date.

"Well I give her top marks on her choice of poison," Sam told his companion.

"Poison?"

Sam turned and held up a blue bottle of Tarquin's Cornish gin. "I've suddenly decided I want to find this girl."

"She lives in the heart of Germany and drinks gin? What about a German beer?"

Sam returned the bottle to its cupboard. "You would like my brother, he's into a good German white beer."

"Top man, glad one of you has sense."

"Hmmm," replied an absent minded Sam. "Hello, what have we here?"

The two of them turned and stared at a cork noticeboard fixed onto the wall. A cluster of pins were placed in the bottom righthand corner. Only one was in active use.

Sam pointed at the board. "I guess this is standard issue across all the flats?"

"Yes, well there's one in mine. What's pinned up?"

Sam reached out and unpinned the cardboard attached to the cork board.

"What is it?" asked Hendricks.

"An invitation to an art gallery opening. And as luck would have it, its tonight."

"Did you want me to ring Travers and see if it's been looked into?"

Sam shook his head as he recognised the name on the invite. "If I remember rightly it says in the report they've already interviewed the actual artist Otto Schafer."

"Ah yes, both us and the police. I actually drove Travers to the guy's apartment. Bloody expensive apartment, I can tell you."

"What did Schafer say?"

Hendricks waved his arms around. "That he had not seen her

for a couple of weeks. The last time they had spoken was when she'd met him for dinner one night."

Sam flicked the cardboard invite over and whistled. "I was not expecting that."

On the back of the invite was a handwritten note, written in loopy English. 'My darling Kate, my love, this achievement I dedicate to you.'

SIX

SO KATE MAY was human after all. He had started to think she had been some robot sent out to see if it was possible to live the most boring, uneventful life imaginable. But now there was some life in the mystery woman.

"So we may have a love interest on our hands," said Sam triumphantly.

Hendricks looked back at him. "Otto Schafer is not a love interest."

"That's a bold statement to make when you don't know the man."

Hendricks shook his head and turned back into the sitting room. "If you search Otto Schafer on your phone you will find he is one of the foremost gay artists in Europe. Most of his work is aimed at celebrating gay culture. He'd have to be the biggest hypocrite in the city if he's sleeping with women."

"Bugger," Sam swore. "Back to the drawing board."

"You crack on. I'm going to sit down."

Hendricks walked back into the sitting room, leaving Sam alone in the kitchen. He took a final look at the invite, and for reasons he was unsure of, pocketed it. At this stage he would have to cling onto the smallest of threads. He gave the kitchen a final look and decided there was nothing else to be gained from its small interior.

The next step was the utility room, which was even smaller than the kitchen. Sam tried all of the old tricks of his detective trade. There were no false bottoms in the wardrobes, the cylinder in the washing machine was fixed in place and all of the room's contents were infuriatingly normal.

"Did you want a drink?" Hendricks called from the living room.

"Just a water, thank you," Sam replied as he entered the bedroom.

He knew that here was his best chance of finding something. A person's bedroom, no matter how private the owner, always contained something of interest. The clothes would tell him how she dressed. Was she someone who was body confident or preferred to cover up? Was she sporty? What type of make-up did she use?

The wardrobes were filled with a mix of clothes, from everyday wear to a few items Sam guessed would be worn for going out. There was a mix of make-up items on a small dressing table in the corner and Sam made a mental note of the brands. Checking the drawers he found some small pieces of jewellery, nothing overtly fancy. He looked at the mirror, which the young woman would have studied her reflection in every morning before work. It would have been a pretty reflection as well, thought Sam.

The detective in him was enjoying itself now as he went around the room. There were certainly more belongings in here, enough to give him at least a picture of the girl's routines. He had even found two pairs of running shoes with a packed gym kit. This was the life, he told himself, back on the hunt for a missing person. It was just like the old days of being a military police officer. He opened up the top drawer and grabbed the clothing within as he looked back into his memories of forgotten cases. There had been some good cases, ones which he would always remember. Definitely enough to outnumber the bad cases, the ones where the crimes had been too heinous to ever forget.

Sam paused in his search and looked out of the window, taking a moment to think of the people he had met along the way. He smiled at the memories.

"One water," announced Hendricks as he walked into the bedroom and then stopped. He looked quizzically at Sam as he stood there smiling while holding onto the missing Kate's underwear. "Found anything?" Hendricks looked amused.

Sam came back to the present then looked down at the women's underwear in his hands before quickly replacing it.

"Not yet, but I live in hope."

"I can see that," Hendricks said, indicating the underwear drawer.

Sam shut the drawer and started on the next one.

"It's one of the drawbacks of the job."

Hendricks came to stand next to him, handing him the glass of water. "It is?"

"Sometimes all that is left to us poor old crusaders searching for answers long after a person has left us is the contents of their underwear drawers."

"Kate hasn't left us yet."

Sam gave the younger man an encouraging smile and clapped him on the back. "Not yet."

They left the bedroom and entered the final room within the small apartment. The bathroom consisted of a bathtub, a fitted sink and a toilet. Immediately upon entering the room, Sam's eye was drawn to a dark mark that had been scratched on the white tiled floor. Stepping further into the room, Sam started on the toilet and lifted the porcelain lid that covered the cistern. Finding nothing, he quickly ran through the drawers fitted beneath the sink, again discovering nothing of interest.

"I'm beginning to think Mr Travers may have been right," Sam sighed.

"I told you he'd been over this place with a toothpick."

Dejected, Sam sat on the closed seat of the toilet and leant back. His eye was once again drawn to the black scratch on the white tiles. Following it along the floor, he saw it ended underneath the corner of the fibreglass casing of the bathtub. At least half of the screws were missing their covers, suggesting recent use.

"Have you ever read any old detective novels, Hendricks?" asked Sam.

"I was never really into my reading. Preferred playing with my cars."

"With your driving I can see why. But do you know what those books would have taught you?"

"How to get away with murder?"

Sam chuckled. "They would have taught you that there is a nice big gap inside a bathtub's external cladding. Perhaps big enough for a body."

Hendricks eyed the seemingly normal bathtub nervously.

"Do you know if Travers searched under the bathtub?"

"I don't think so?"

"Then why are all of the screw caps missing from the front panel?"

They both looked at the front panel and its missing screw covers.

Sam pointed at the black mark. "You see that? I'm willing to bet that it's from the corner of that panel."

"Surely Travers wouldn't have missed it?"

Sam raised an eyebrow. "I think we'd better check for ourselves just to be certain. Do you have a screwdriver in your apartment?" Hendricks nodded. "Run down and grab it. Don't let the police see you doing it."

Hendricks hurried out of the flat, leaving Sam still sitting on the toilet seat. He studied the bathtub casing and wondered what could be inside such an unremarkable object. The mark on the floor was clear to be seen by even the most halfhearted of explorers. Could Travers really have missed it?

A few moments went by before Sam heard Hendricks re-entering the apartment. The young man burst back into the bathroom, his face alive with excitement.

"I've got one here." He flashed the screwdriver towards Sam, who looked back at him flatly.

"Well go on then."

Hendricks blinked in confusion. "You want me to do it?"

"As I tell the young graduate in my team, it will be good for your development."

"What, as a plumber?"

"Fair point, but I'm not preparing you for a profession. One day there will be a Mrs Hendricks and she may have her eye on a new bathroom."

"Jesus, you're full of shit."

Sam sat back and rested the back of his head in his hands. "Or you may just need a good place to hide her body after a few years of marital bliss."

Hendricks shook his head in bemusement and began to unscrew the cladding. As he reached the halfway point, Sam knelt next to him and began to take the weight off the side.

"Nearly there," Hendricks grimaced as he turned the final screw.

At once, Sam felt the siding give way and he heaved the now free fibreglass out of the way. They both peered into the dusty interior and saw the dark outline of something shoved towards the far wall.

"It's not a body," Hendricks observed.

"You almost sound disappointed."

"You can blame yourself for that, you built it up with your crime novel crap."

Sam found himself laughing again. He reached forward and pulled the dark shape into the brightly lit bathroom. It was a black sports duffel bag.

"Strange place to keep your holiday essentials," Sam

commented as he unzipped the bag before emptying out its contents.

Both men stared in amazement at the contents now strewn over the tiled floor. For a moment, no one spoke, it was almost too hard to comprehend what they were actually looking at.

"What the hell *is* all this?" Hendricks asked him.

Sam reached down and moved the bag's contents around, trying to take it all in.

"I have no idea."

Laid across the bathroom floor were bundles of euros, each one marked as containing 5,000 euros within the banding. Alongside these were three passports, one cardboard folder, a pistol and spare ammunition.

"You can forget needing to read any detective novels, you'd be best starting with a spy thriller." Sam picked up the pistol.

"What?" Hendricks asked in shock.

"All this, you could have pulled it straight out of a spy novel."

Hendricks frowned and picked up a bundle of cash. "You're joking."

"I really hope I am. Take this." He held up the pistol. "Not your usual personal secretary property."

"What is it?"

"A Russian made MP-443 Grach pistol, this little bastard fires out seventeen nine nineteen millimetre bullets straight at the target. I wouldn't worry; it may look nice but it's a bitch to use, too unreliable." Sam unclipped the pistol and pulled out the ammunition before making it safe. He looked it over and found numerous wear and tear marks over the body. It felt like an old gun in his hands. "And you will not be surprised to know it is one of the Russian standard military issue firearms."

"What the hell is it doing here?"

"Now that is the question." He looked at the bundles of cash on the floor. "Gather all that together and see how much our Miss May has been sitting on."

Hendricks looked like he wanted to ask more questions, but Sam headed him off.

"Come on, I don't want to be surrounded by all this if those two police officers decide to come knocking. Plus, I want to know how much it costs to buy an ambassador's secretary these days."

Hendricks began counting the bundles of euros as Sam put the pistol in his coat pocket. Next, he picked up the three passports. All three were well worn, their pages thumbed smooth. In his hands he held a German, Russian and British passport all with the same photos of Kate May inside, but all three bearing different names. He gathered them together and put them in his back trouser pocket. His companion was still counting the money as Sam picked up the cardboard folder. He used his fingers to break a flimsy seal and studied the contents. The first few pages were biographies of people within the embassy, each with their own photograph of the individual stapled to the page. Sam saw both the Ambassador and her head of security on the very first pieces of paper. He skipped through the next few sheets until he came across a print-out of what he guessed was Cooper's diary for the next few weeks.

"One hundred thousand euros, split into bundles of five thousand. All brand new notes," Hendricks told Sam, the piles of cash stacked neatly in front of him. "What's that you have there?"

Sam passed him the first few pages.

Hendricks swore. "That's a picture of me!"

"You seem surprised?"

"I will be bloody pissed off if that bitch was spying on me."

"Why? Have you something to hide down in that apartment of yours?" teased Sam. Hendricks blushed. "But it does rather suggest your Miss May may not be who she claimed to be."

Sam continued reading the papers from the file. There was more embassy material, most of which he decided was probably harmless. But as he neared the end, the final sheets began to have references to the North Sea Deal. There was a map of the planned pipelines, a copy of an itinerary for a visit by the European

Parliament to an offshore rig, an estimate of the volume of gas required over the coming five years. Sam felt queasy and put the papers straight back into the folder without alerting Hendrick. This was not their fight, he decided.

He looked down at the stacks of euros. For some reason, the newness of the bank notes surprised him. Beside the worn-out pistol and passports, the crisp newness of the European currency stood out. It was like the scratch mark on the tiled floor, just too obvious for his liking.

"Come on, it's time we got out of here," he told Hendricks. "Let's fasten the bath back together then put that cash in your pocket and I'll hide the folder in my trousers. We don't want the police to see you walking out with all that cash."

Hendricks nodded and between them they fastened the bath cladding back into place, leaving the now empty bag back inside. Sam hurriedly stuffed the folder down the back of his trousers, the pistol and passports already safely away.

"I can't get it all in my pockets," Hendricks told him.

"Here, give me some."

Sam took the remaining four bundles and stored them in his coat pockets.

"I don't think I've ever been richer," Hendricks sighed as he looked at himself in the bathroom mirror.

Sam grinned at the younger man. "Hey, if anyone asks me I'll tell them we only found ninety thousand."

They left the flat, locking the door behind them before heading back downstairs. The two policemen were waiting for them by the entrance. Both officers gave the two of them long stares. Sam glared back and strode straight past into the afternoon air. The sky was a clear blue as they left the apartment block, the air seemed extra fresh. So just who was Kate May after all, he wondered? Keeps no personal possessions within her flat, but just so happens to have a bag full of cash, a Russian pistol and three passports all under her bath. But then that nagging thought hit him again as they entered the waiting Land Rover. How had Travers missed it all? The scratch on the floor had been so obvious to even Hendricks' untrained eye. He was not looking forward to telling the Head of Security about his mistake on their return. Or *was* it a mistake? He thought back to the change in mood when Sam said he was about to visit the flat. Why had Travers not wanted him to go? That idea gave him no comfort.

"Back to the embassy?" Hendricks asked.

Sam looked over at the watching police officers one final time. They would never have been able to stop anyone entering the building unseen from where they had been parked up. Who was to say when this bag had actually been hidden away?

"Yes, I suppose we should go back and share the good news," Sam paused for a moment. "Unless you want to take the cash and go straight to the nearest bar?"

SEVEN

JOHN TRAVERS WAS WAITING for them in the embassy's underground car park. As Hendricks drove the Land Rover into its parking space, Sam studied the Head of Security. The tall Scotsman was standing with his hands in his pockets, his gaze unwavering as they climbed out of the car. Throughout the journey back from Kate May's apartment, Sam had been trying to answer the questions surrounding the Scotsman. He just could not understand how, if Travers had been as thorough in his search of the small flat as he said he had been, he had failed to find the stash currently inside their pockets? It made no sense, unless he had not wanted anyone to find the hidden bag? Had he not been the one who had tried to stop Sam from going to the apartment in the first place? That thought scared him, the implications were too much to contemplate. Travers was clearly not someone to cross. What if he was working against them? Sam felt the hairs on the back of neck stand on edge at the mere thought of it.

"Have you found her yet then, Mr Taylor?" The Scotsman asked as they walked towards him.

"Not quite."

"We did find something!" Hendricks began before Sam cut him off.

"We did find something, but its best that we show you and the Ambassador together. This isn't the right place to discuss it."

Travers studied Sam for a moment, looking as if he wanted to argue the case.

"Is the Ambassador available?" asked Sam.

"She instructed that she was to be informed the moment you returned," Travers replied stiffly.

"So shall we go and see her?"

Eventually, Travers seemed to make up his mind and led the pair of them towards the elevator.

"Was there still a police presence?" he asked Hendricks.

"Yes, they were there."

"Did they give you any bother?"

"No, they just left us to it."

"They didn't want to go in with you?"

"No."

They travelled up in the elevator in silence. The door pinged open and the three of them stepped out onto the Ambassador's floor.

Travers spoke directly to Sam. "We've been asked by the local police to allow them to remove the guard from outside the building."

Sam shrugged. "I would let them, they are doing nothing to stop anyone getting in. Any political points of being a visible presence have now been earned. Keeping them outside that building is not helping anyone."

Travers chuckled. "That's what I told Cooper, but she disagrees. She insisted they stay."

"It's just something she can point to when London calls in to demand to know what's happening."

They entered the reception area of the Ambassador's office. Sam could see Cooper at her desk, with the same assistant as this morning, studying her computer screen. He was pleased to see his belongings were still left where he had placed them earlier. Again, he took off his parka, but this time he removed the Grach pistol from one of the pockets.

Travers immediately noticed the Russian pistol. "What the hell are you doing with that?"

Sam twisted the gun in one hand and held it up by its muzzle, the ammunition clip in the other.

The Ambassador had also noticed Sam holding a gun in the middle of her office. "I think you best come in here and close the door. I dread to think of the alarm you'd cause if anyone was to walk past right now."

The three of them moved into Cooper's private office and the assistant moved to close the door behind them. Travers' eyes had not left the weapon in Sam's hands.

Cooper leant back in her chair and eyed Sam. "I do hope there's a good story behind you brandishing a gun in my offices."

"If I told you that this was found in Kate May's apartment, along with a do it yourself espionage starter kit, would that be a good enough story?" He placed the pistol onto the glass desk, along with the three passports from his back pocket. Then he followed it up with the cardboard folder from the back of his trousers. Hendricks mirrored him and placed the piles of bound euros alongside them. Sam suddenly realised that he had left some of the cash in his parka back in the outer office, but the missing bundles did not take anything away from the impact of what was now on the Ambassador's desk.

Cooper, Travers and the assistant all stared dumbly at the items. All three were trying to understand what this could possibly mean.

Travers broke the silence. "Tell us everything."

Sam started to relay the search within Kate's bathroom. How he had noticed both the mark on the tiles and the missing screw caps. How Hendricks had retrieved a screwdriver from his apartment before they had searched underneath the bath. Sam described the contents of the black duffel bag, picking up each of the referenced items before passing them round.

"This is a Russian made MP-443 Grach pistol, you would expect to find one of these on standard Russian infantry rather than in a secretary's apartment." He handed it over to Travers, who studied the weapon.

"Then there are the passports, three in total. I'm not a documents expert, but I would say they seem to be a pretty good standard, possibly even real."

Cooper took the passports and flicked them open before handing them to the assistant.

"The cash, well, the cash says everything it needs to. My only comment would be on the newness. I would have thought that they would have preferred to have used notes rather than new ones."

"Why?" the ambassador asked curiously.

"New notes are easier to track, these bundles will have come straight out of a bank somewhere. The local police will be able to source it in hours."

"How strange," commented Cooper, as she picked up a bundle.

Sam picked up the cardboard folder. "Then there's this. I would recommend you save yourself some time and skip to the back pages. There's probably information on the North Sea Deal that you would prefer wasn't in the public domain."

Cooper dropped the euros and reached for the folder, her face a mixture of concern and fear. "I'm not sure I want to look inside here, Mr Taylor."

"I'm not sure you want to either Madam Ambassador, but I recommend that you do so."

The Ambassador flicked through to the pages containing the details of the North Sea Deal. Her beady eyes narrowed as her mind processed the printed words in her hand. After studying each page she handed it to her Head of Security, who took his turn reading the contents.

As she handed over the last of the pages she pulled the paper back. "How did you miss this, John?" she asked, using Travers' Christian name.

"I didn't miss it. I don't know what happened, but there was nothing in that bathroom when I was there. No black marks on the tiles, no missing screw covers."

"Then Sam and Hendricks are lying?"

Travers eyed Sam suspiciously. "I don't know, but I'm telling you I would not have missed something like that."

Ambassador Cooper looked like she wanted to continue the fight, but Sam interjected. "I can't answer for whatever search took place before, but I'm more worried about what is now directly in front of us."

Cooper turned back to Sam. "So what does this mean? It doesn't seem to me that it helps us get any closer to finding out what happened to Kate?"

Sam was bemused at the Ambassador's apparent lack of understanding.

Travers spoke. "Like Sam said at the beginning, all this here in front of us is your espionage starter kit. It would seem our Miss May was working here under false pretences."

"Oh my God, what has she done?"

Travers rubbed his face. "I don't know, but this changes everything we thought we knew."

Sam studied the collection of items on the table. Something was still tugging at him. Back at the apartment he had felt the same nagging concern. It all seemed too obvious, too perfect, as if someone had gone to great lengths to create an ideal espionage stash.

"I thought you had done all of the security checks on her computer?" Sam asked Travers.

"We did."

Sam pointed at the papers in his hands. "Could she have had access to any of that information?"

Travers studied the sheets in his hands. "I don't think so, no? We have some of the best IT security in the western world."

"That's not to say she did not get it in some other way," said Cooper. "I'm sure these people are quite resourceful."

Sam could see he had at least made a small impression on Travers. He decided to continue. "I've already spoken about the new bank notes. Most criminal activity would use used bank notes, right." Travers nodded. "Then there's this." Sam reached down and picked up the battered Grach. "This may be Russian made, but I'm telling you now there's very few FSB agents who would choose it as their choice of firearm."

"What?" Cooper asked.

"The Russian security service, the FSB."

"I know who the bloody FSB are," she snapped at him.

Sam ignored her. "Most field agents with the FSB prefer to use exported weaponry like the Glock 17 or a Browning. They find the Grach too unreliable, jams too easily."

Travers put the papers back on the desk and took the Grach from Sam. "He's right, there's always been a black market within the FSB and the KGB before it, for better western firearms."

Cooper looked at them both in confusion. "So what are you saying? That she's *not* a spy?"

"I wouldn't rule out some kind of set-up," Sam answered.

"No," Travers answered firmly. "I'm sorry, but you're clutching at straws and ignoring the facts. You're trying to look for the best outcome when the facts are telling us otherwise. If it looks like a duck and sounds like a duck…"

"Then it's a goose," Sam answered.

Travers turned on Sam, his temper flaring. "I don't know who you think you are, but I'm getting tired of your attitude. First you insist on going to visit the apartment, then you somehow manage to find all this evidence, only to tell us it's all fake. What are you trying to do here?"

Sam stood calmly and pulled himself up to his full height, squaring up to him. "I could ask you the same question! It was you who didn't want me to go in the first place, and you who somehow managed to miss the most obvious of clues. Perhaps we should be asking what are *you* trying to hide?"

"You insolent piece of shit."

Sam thought for a moment that the Scotsman was going to hit him. It was down to Ambassador Cooper to calm things down.

"Gentlemen," she commanded firmly from her seat. "This isn't helping. Now, can someone tell me what this all means."

Travers spoke first. "If we are to believe what we can clearly see in front of us then your personal secretary has been spying on us for quite some time. Now, either she's managed to get everything she needed and has gone back to wherever it is she calls home, or she was interrupted in her mission and felt she had to do a runner."

"Rubbish, why leave all the money? If she's been paid to spy on you, why not take the cash? She could easily have bypassed the police outside of her apartment." Sam practically spat his response, his chiselled jaw grinding.

Travers gave him a patronising look. "Because she thought she could come back for it later. You said yourself it was hidden."

Sam knew he was facing defeat. Travers had made up his mind and nothing he could say would change that.

"Then everything we've done for the North Sea Deal has been compromised?" asked Cooper.

Travers nodded. "Potentially. If it is the former scenario then she may have already found everything she needs."

"God help us! And if it's not?"

"Then we need to establish what it is she was after."

"And how she managed to evade such tight security," Sam added sarcastically.

Stepping back from the table, he took the same seat Travers had sat in on their first meeting, at the back of the room. He watched as the Ambassador fidgeted in her seat, her mind trying to process everything and what it must mean for the North Sea Deal or more likely, her own future. The embarrassment of being known as the woman whose personal secretary had been a spy could follow her for years to come.

"Who was she working for?"

Travers answered. "I think we have to presume it was our Russian friends."

This was crazy, thought Sam, the ageing Head of Security was making assumptions based on the most suspect of evidence.

"But how, John? How did she manage to do this? To fool us all?"

Travers swallowed and waved his arms helplessly. "I don't know, it does however sit with me, and I can only apologise. We will find out what happened."

Ambassador Cooper blinked and tapped the edge of her desk. "So, what happens now?"

"We need to completely review what she had access to and try to establish if she was able to get what she was after. We also need to tell the Prime Minister and the Foreign Secretary that their negotiations may have been compromised."

The Ambassador paled at the thought. "And the Europeans? Should we tell them?"

"That's not for me to say, madam Ambassador."

"I'll leave that to the PM," Cooper decided. "And the girl? What do we do about her?"

"I can help there. I can keep searching for her."

"No, this is not in your remit Mr Taylor," snapped Travers. "Your job is to bring people back. I'm not sure hunting spies falls under that. We have our own specialists who can handle this now."

"So that's it then? I'm to... what? Just go home?"

"Well as you're no longer useful here then yes," Travers said firmly.

Sam laughed, he could not help it. "You seem pretty confident about all this. I mean, not to question your judgement, but you were the one who felt that having another look at the apartment was a waste of time. Now you're... what? A master spy catcher?"

Travers' face turned a deep shade of red. "I've been protecting this embassy from foreign agents since before you were even toilet trained, Taylor."

A threat filled the room as Sam and the Head of Security stared at each other. The assistant and Hendricks were watching on in horror, their presence otherwise forgotten.

It was left to the Ambassador to break the tension. She cleared her throat. "Perhaps, Mr Taylor, it would be best if you reported back to your office. They will probably appreciate having you back soon."

Sam was helpless. He looked from Travers to the Ambassador. "I think I can still be of some use in finding her."

Cooper smiled, her face contorted in an attempt at pleasantness. "I'm sure you could be, but John is right, this is no longer your area of expertise." She stood and waved at Hendricks. "Hendricks here will drive you back to the airport."

Sam was flabbergasted. Here he was, being pushed out and driven away from a case that he had just thrown wide open. Before he had arrived they had been clutching at straws.

"I'm telling you both, you may be right and she's nothing more than a spy, but for God's sake try to keep an open mind."

Again, Cooper smiled politely at him. Travers just glared. Sam stood and moved towards the door, Hendricks behind him.

"And Mr Taylor…" Sam turned to look at the Ambassador. "Thank you for everything you've done here."

Sam walked out of the office, forcing his frustration to remain hidden. Grabbing his coat and bag, he gave the occupants of the Ambassador's private office a final glance before following Hendricks out. Having been in Berlin for a matter of hours, Sam Taylor had been thrown off the case.

John Travers watched the Repatriation Officer being escorted out.

The Yorkshireman had been too clever for his own good and he was not sorry to see the back of him.

"So what now, John?"

He turned to the Ambassador. The hawk-like face looked at him, willing him to solve her problems.

"I think it may be prudent to ask the German police to stop their search for Kate. It needs to be us who find her. It could cause us all considerable embarrassment if they were to find her before we did."

"Agreed… and by us finding her, you mean the Caretakers?"

That was a sad statement in itself. He resented having to call the Foreign Office's last resort, those elusive men and women who kept the diplomatic services clean and tidy. In all his years of working in Berlin, he had only needed their assistance once before.

"We need to find her, and we need to get to her before anyone else does."

Ambassador Cooper walked round her desk and looked out of the window to the city below.

"Do it, John. Make the call."

EIGHT

SAM STRUGGLED to control his temper as Hendricks led him through the embassy. The frustration of being pushed out before he had even managed to find the girl was hurting him. He hated to leave a job half finished.

Hendricks guided him into the lift before daring to break the silence. "Did you want to go to the airport straight away?"

"I'm not going to the airport."

Hendricks looked at him nervously. "You're not? But the Ambassador said…"

"Relax, I'm not going to cause any trouble, I've got a reservation for a hotel tonight so I might as well use it. I don't want to waste the taxpayers' money."

"Oh right, did you want me to drive you there?"

Sam sighed. "No, I'll make my own way. It may help to clear my head."

Hendricks hesitated before asking the question. "Do you really think Kate is being set up?"

Sam paused. *Did* he really think that, or was he just being stubborn? He had been acting purely on a hunch, one that had cost him his place on the case. Had he been foolish to have been so adamant in the face of such overwhelming evidence?

"I don't know, but I think they are being too hasty in ruling it out. I don't like the thought that someone may be playing us, especially with what is on the line."

"But what other explanation is there? Why would someone set Kate up?"

That was the question. Why indeed would someone go to such effort to frame an apparently unremarkable secretary with access to nothing that could be deemed classified?

"I don't know, Hendricks, but there are some bloody clever people out there and if you're not careful you can end up playing their games."

They both fell silent as the lift carried them down to the ground floor. Stepping out into the main atrium, where Travers had first guided Sam through earlier in the day, the pair turned and shook hands.

"I wish you the luck of the chase, Hendricks. I feel you will all need it."

Hendricks smiled and squeezed Sam's hand. "Thanks Sam, I'm sorry we didn't have longer to work together."

Sam left the embassy through the main entrance and found himself face to face again with the climate protesters. This time, no one bothered him as he walked past and headed back up towards the Brandenburg Gate. He tried to clear his mind of the day's events and to think about what he should do next. He knew he should contact Emma back at the office, but he was not in the mood to have that conversation just yet. Instead, he continued to walk in a bid to come to some sort of conclusion. Perhaps the Ambassador was right, and the case had evolved beyond his expertise. Did he really want to get involved in whatever murky world the embassy leadership had found itself in? This thought cheered him. Whatever had happened to Miss May, there was clearly some sort of involvement from the FSB. Whether as one of their own or in some sort of set-up, those intelligence agents were dangerous adversaries. Probably best to leave it to someone else, he decided.

The noise of the city helped to break his bad mood further. He was in the middle of Berlin with nearly a full afternoon left in front of him to spend as he wished. There was plenty of time for enjoying the city's food and drink offerings. Hannah had told him she had advised Lucy to book him into a hotel she knew had its own gin bar. Perhaps he could spend the afternoon in there, drowning his sorrows. He reached into his pocket to pull out his phone to set a route, but instead his fingers closed around the now crumpled art exhibition invite from Kate's apartment. He read it aloud. "My darling Kate, my love, this achievement I dedicate to you."

Sam turned it over and looked at the date. The exhibition was tonight. He wondered if any of the embassy security team would attend to follow up this, an actual genuine lead. He doubted it. Perhaps he should go and meet this famous artist for himself. There would at least be a free bar. But then his excitement was punctured as he read the dress code. Black tie. He definitely did not have anything remotely close to smart in his bag. Yet, thinking about it he did have a pretty hefty expenses budget, the 20,000 euros stuffed deeply into his parka pocket. In all the frustrations of leaving the case he had forgotten about the four bundles of euros. Sam's excitement got the better of him then. Perhaps there was still a chance to find Kate himself and prove the miserable bastards wrong. Plus, he thought, it would be rude not to at least have someone to represent the Foreign Office at Kate's friend's big night.

Lucy Marsh had picked well. A waiter smiled at him as he placed the glass of Tarquin's Cornish gin and tonic on the bar in front of him.

Sam raised his glass. "Cheers."

The waiter smiled back and left to serve another customer. Sam caught his reflection in the mirror behind the bar and admired the view. An afternoon spent shopping in the fashionable stores of Berlin had been most productive. Now dressed in a fitted designer black suit, waistcoat, black shirt and tie, he had decided being officially off the case was not as bad as he had first thought. He had even bypassed the usual boots for a more formal pair of black shoes. Across the bar he noticed two women smiling at him and he raised his glass. Now this was the world of espionage! A smart suit, a good drink and the attention of not one but two women. Feeling adventurous, he beckoned the waiter over and paid for another round of drinks for the pair of them.

"Say it's on Ivan," he told the waiter as he handed over a crisp note.

Sam knew he would have to hand the found cash back in the morning, but who was to know how much had actually been recovered? He checked the green Rolex on his wrist and decided it was time to go. Giving the two women a goodbye wink, he turned and walked out of the bar.

The brisk January night air made him shiver as his body acclimatised. He hailed a taxi, paid using the Russian funds, and sat back to watch the lights of the German capital flying past.

The afternoon call with Emma had not been easy. After soothing her concerns over the missing Kate and the supposed involvement of the FSB, Sam'd had a tough job trying to convince her to let him stay. But like most of their conversations when on a case, the physical distance between them had made it very easy for Sam to bypass her fears. He was on the ground, at the heart of the actual events. She was in London, she could wait to give him the lecture on his return.

He sank further into the taxi's back seat and began to wonder if he was wasting his time. What did he expect would happen when he turned up at the exhibition with Kate's invite? That Otto Schafer would suddenly tell him where she was? Probably not, but Sam was interested to see how he would react all the same.

The taxi turned off the main road and drew up outside the gallery entrance. Bright spotlights lit the area as guests made their way inside the square white building. Sam stepped out of the taxi and onto a bright red carpet that led all the way from the kerb to the entrance. There was a giant outdoor rectangle made of up of hundreds of letters making up the various artists' names that filled the gallery. Sam thought it resembled a huge word search. Entering through the main doors, he made his way further into the gallery. A grey concrete floor led into the main exhibit areas. Grey walls and white painted ceilings reflected the bright spotlights that gave the area a laboratory feel. Still following the main crowd, he took the stairs up to the first floor, where a door led off to a private exhibition space.

A staff member waited outside, collecting tickets. Next to him stood who Sam presumed must be Otto Schafer. He was a slim Black man who wore his long hair tied up in a bun. Schafer was dressed in a dark green suit that glittered slightly in the bright spotlights of the room.

Sam handed his ticket straight into the outstretched hand of the artist himself, who expecting a handshake, looked at the ticket in surprise.

"Otto Schafer?" asked Sam.

"Yes?"

"It's a pleasure to finally meet you. I'm Sam Taylor."

Schafer looked at Sam in confusion. "You are?"

"Yes, I believe we have a mutual friend?"

"We do?"

Sam stared intently at the artist. "Yes, Kate... I'm sure she must have mentioned I would be coming?"

Schafer paused for a moment. "I don't think she did."

Neither man spoke for a moment before Sam pressed on.

"Not to matter, let me say how excited I am to be here. I love your work."

"Thank you?"

A waiter walked past and held out a tray of Champagne flutes.

Sam took one. "I look forward to seeing your latest achievements!"

Otto Schafer looked like he wanted to question him further, but Sam clapped the artist's arm and walked into the gallery.

"Now let's see what you do after that," he muttered to himself.

Sam walked among the first of the artworks, feigning interest. All the while, he kept half an eye on the confused Schafer. In his peripheral vision he saw the artist pull out his phone and take a sly photo.

"Now, why would you want to take a photo of me?" mused Sam. "Unless you were sending it to your friend."

The decision to come was already proving fruitful. He walked briskly through the rest of the exhibits, barely even noticing the exhibits. Art had never been his thing.

Finding the bar, he pulled up a stool and motioned to the barman. Then he paused, remembering his German was non-existent. For a fluent Spanish and French speaker, he wondered why he was never sent somewhere a bit warmer. The barman looked at him expectantly.

"Erm… bitte einen gin and tonic?" Sam asked, more in hope than expectation.

The young barman grinned at him. "You're English, aren't you?"

"I asked for a gin and tonic, didn't I?"

The barman laughed. "Next time lose the and." He passed over a glass.

"So how do you like working here?" Sam asked him, taking a sip.

"I'm studying, this is just part time."

"Fair enough." Sam looked over his shoulder, back at the art gallery, then had an idea. "Do you want to earn a little extra?"

"Depends."

"Do you know the apparent creative genius behind tonight's event?"

"Otto Schafer?"

"That's the one, dresses in a shiny green jacket."

The barman laughed. "Yes."

Sam pulled a crisp fifty euro note from his pocket. "Tell me when he enters, looking for me."

The barman took the money, allowing Sam not to have to keep staring behind him. "How do I know if he's looking for you?"

"Trust me, all those people in there are here to celebrate him. If he's leaving them to come in here, it's to see me."

As Sam had predicted, it was not long before the barman was giving him a nod to warn of Schafer's arrival. The barman's simple wave gave him time to prepare himself. The artist took the seat next to him.

"How did you say you know Kate?"

Sam turned to face him. "I didn't."

Schafer bristled. "Then… how do you know her?"

"I don't really."

"Then what are you doing here?"

"Having a drink and enjoying the works of art."

Schafer grabbed his arm. "Bullshit, who are you?"

Sam looked down at the hand holding his arm. "I'm someone who's trying to help your friend. Who we both know is in a hell of a lot of trouble." He shook his arm free, and dusted off his sleeve.

The German stared at Sam with a mixture of disdain and mistrust. "I don't know what you're talking about."

"I think you know *exactly* what I'm talking about." Sam knew he was pushing his luck, and that there was an extremely high chance that Otto Schafer had been telling the truth to Travers and had no idea where Kate was. "There's more than just me searching for your friend in this city right now and I don't think it's too much of a push to say I'm the only one who actually wants to help her."

Schafer released his grip on Sam's arm and sat back. He thought for a moment, considering Sam. "Who are you?"

"Sam Taylor. I work for the British government and if your friend wants to get home safely you would be wise to tell me where she is."

Schafer shook his head. "I do not know what you are talking about. As I told your people before, I have not seen her."

"They are not my people."

That gave Schafer something to think about. He turned to face the bar and rested his elbows on the top.

"I do not know what else to tell you. I do not know where she is."

"I do not believe you, Herr Schafer. Kate is your friend and she is in very serious danger. She will not be able to hide forever and when she is found it will be her word against theirs. Let me tell you they are very confident in their version of events." Schafer did not reply. "Look Otto, you don't know me and you have no reason to trust me, but if someone else finds Kate then there's a good chance she won't even have a chance to tell her side of the story. These people have too much to lose to allow her to talk. If you want to help her then I'm your best bet."

Sam's words failed to have any obvious effect. The German artist stood up, waved to the barman and gave him a quick order in his native language. He then turned to Sam. "For the last time Mr Taylor, I do not know where Kate is. I hope you enjoy your evening, but if you'll excuse me."

Sam turned in his seat and watched him walk back into the exhibit. "You're a bloody bad liar, Herr Schafer."

"Excuse me?"

Sam twisted back round to see the barman holding a new glass of gin apparently ordered for him by the departed Schafer.

"I told him his friend was in danger and he didn't even ask why or how."

"Sorry?" the confused barman asked.

Sam picked up his glass and took a sip. "He knows where she is."

Sam felt sure he was one step closer to finding Kate May.

NINE

SAM PULLED out another fifty euro note and passed it to the barman. "I have one final ask of you."

The barman hesitated then took it.

"Are there any other exits from the gallery that someone would use if they wanted to get out of this place?"

"Not tonight, the main building's all closed up now so the only way out is through the main entrance. Unless there's a fire alarm, but you're not going to?" He looked panicked.

Sam grinned and stood up to leave. "What, and destroy all this amazing culture? Nah, not today. What time does this thing end?"

"Not for another two hours."

"Bloody hell I'm going to be cold."

Moving towards the exit he saw Schafer talking to a group of people. Sam made a big show of waving to him as he walked through the glass doors and back into the main gallery. Heading downstairs, he pulled on his thick parka and braced himself for the wintery air that awaited him. The next two hours were going to be slow, but if he was lucky, they could yet prove fruitful.

Wandering down the red carpet, he saw a bank of taxis awaiting the leaving guests. That was a good sign, as it meant that the possible routes for Schafer's exit had narrowed. He could still take public transport, but Sam guessed that Schafer would want to get back to wherever Kate was hiding as quickly as possible. That was Sam's gamble – that the artist had indeed lied to him and would be desperate to get back to his friend, and that would give Sam the chance he needed. Either that, or Schafer would just return home after a successful night and that would be the end of it. Schafer would be home, warm in his bed and Sam would be out in the cold, alone in the Berlin night.

Sam walked past the waiting taxis to find somewhere to try and pass the next couple of hours. Across the road he saw a late night cafe bar with tables outside on the street. Thick woollen blankets covered the low chairs while electronic heaters shone down on the occupants. Now that was a better option than standing around, thought Sam as he walked over and took an empty table. He wrapped himself deep into the blanket, pulled up his hood and then pushed his hands into the cold parka.

The time ticked by. Sam got colder even with the blanket's protection, and so ordered a coffee along with a burger and chips. The earlier gin and tonics started to make him drowsy while sitting under the heat lamps. He tried to stay focused by using Google Translate to practise what he would need to say to his taxi driver when the time came. He knew timing would be everything if this was to work.

After about an hour, the first of the guests began to make their way home. Sam, still huddled in his blanket, felt the temperature drop further below zero as snow began to fall all around him. He ordered another coffee. Half an hour later he was the only customer still outside. The waiting staff had conveniently forgotten about him, instead deciding to concentrate their attention on those not stupid enough to be sat amongst the falling snowflakes. By now, the guests were flowing out of the gallery to form an orderly queue for the waiting taxis. Sam was having to concentrate on watching all of the departing faces to make sure he did not miss Otto Schafer. His body was tense under the layers of protection from the cold, the suspense of what was to come driving adrenaline through his veins.

The last of the queuing guests entered their taxi and sped off into the night. The tension within Sam increased with every passing second. What if Schafer had somehow left a different way? If he had convinced a gallery staff member to open a second door for him? He swore and threw the blanket off, standing to try and get a better view of the entrance. Lights were beginning to be turned off within the white building. Sam began to walk back towards the gallery's entrance. Crossing the road, he made his way round the few remaining taxis. The red carpet had long since been rolled up. The falling snow thickened.

A small group of people pushed through the glass gallery doors and into the open air. In amongst the small group, Sam saw the tall outline of Otto Schafer and felt the weight leave him. The three men and one woman were deep in conversation, so none of them had spotted Sam, who quickly turned on his heel. Committing to his original plan, Sam hurried towards the waiting taxis and flung open the door of the last vehicle. The driver, surprised at being chosen out of line, began to speak – but Sam interrupted him in his prepared German.

Pushing over 300 euros towards the bewildered driver, he stumbled out the rehearsed phrase. The driver took a second to understand Sam's poor German, but grasped both the directive and the offered euros. Sam sat back in his seat and watched the approaching group. He had promised the taxi driver an additional 300 euros if he was able to follow whichever taxi Schafer entered.

Schafer himself was in deep conversation with one of his companions. His face was animated with excitement as he clasped the outstretched arm of the stranger. Sam studied the newcomer and saw an older man whose silver-grey hair was well oiled and combed to one side. A thick pale blue scarf was wrapped round his neck. Sam was surprised when Schafer embraced the older man in a great bear hug. A buyer, he guessed, as he watched the two of them step apart.

Sam leant forward as he watched Schafer leave his remaining companions and get into the first taxi in line. He patted his driver. "That's the one."

The taxi driver was able to bypass the language barrier and turned on the engine.

"Ja, geh, geh."

The car pulled out into traffic and began to follow Schafer's vehicle. Sam looked on intently as his driver negotiated the traffic. Now he felt like a spy, in a chase across Berlin, the snow descending around them. He thought of the cantankerous John Travers back in the embassy and what he would have made of Sam's actions that night. Whatever awaited him at the end of the journey, Sam was at least enjoying himself.

The two cars zig zagged through the night's traffic. Sam began to relax as his driver performed miracles, somehow keeping close enough to their target without being too close. Not once did he ever ask Sam why he was following Schafer, his curiosity sated by the thought of the promised financial reward. They left the city centre heading west and Sam wondered where they could be going. The route they were on took him close to his hotel before Schafer's taxi turned north and drove up into the Tiergarten Park. Sam looked through the windscreen and saw, standing above a busy roundabout, the Berlin Victory Column lit up in the darkness. The golden winged statue shone in the clear lights and Sam hoped he would be sharing its victorious feeling that night.

Schafer's car turned west again at the column and followed the main Bismarckstrabe away from the park. They were now on one of the main roads out of the city, leaving Sam to wonder if they would be leaving the city altogether. Instead, they left the road at the next roundabout and entered the Charlottenburg district. Sam's only recollection of the name was the large palace that was once home to Prussian royalty. The streets were quieter now and Sam's driver found it easier to keep up with the taxi ahead of them. They entered a brightly lit street filled with a variety of shops, their doors closed and locked up after a day's business. Schafer's taxi indicated and began to slow until it stopped in front of what Sam guessed was the artist's studio.

"Keep going," Sam indicated to the driver. He did not want to stop too close to the store.

As his driver increased his speed again, Sam watched Schafer say goodbye to his own ride and turn to his studio. The ground floor of the studio was in a shroud of darkness, but lights shone from the windows above. Someone was home. He twisted in his seat to look out of the back window as Schafer opened the gate which protected his glass door before stepping inside.

"That's perfect, *danke*, you can park over there." Sam pointed at a small car park near the end of the street and the taxi driver pulled in.

The driver brought the car to a stop and turned expectantly towards Sam. The Englishman duly paid and left the heated vehicle to once again brave the snowy night. He did not stop to watch as his ride drove off to find his next fare, which Sam guessed would be neither as fruitful nor as interesting. Sam began wandering down the street back towards where he had last seen Schafer. As he walked, he took a look at his position on the Maps app. He wanted to take a look at the satellite photo of the street upon which Schafer had his studio. A back alley ran parallel to where he was now strolling. He swiped inwards, blowing up the image segment of the studio. There seemed to be some sort of landing on the roof, a flat space with a variety of garden furniture to be used in warmer weather. Another way in, perhaps.

Reaching the studio front, Sam peered through the large window. A number of pieces blocked most of his view, but staring between them he could see the shadowy outline of the studio. There was a counter, a couple of sofas and a variety of artworks, some on the walls, others on stands. A staircase led upwards to the next floor and Sam could see a thin sliver of light cascading downwards. There was no sign of Schafer.

Sam debated with himself about what to do next. He was tempted to call it a night and return in the morning. But if he did call by in office hours it would be unlikely that Schafer would let him upstairs, and that was where he guessed Kate was. She had never been at her flat, that would have been too obvious. No one had been interested or bothered enough to do a proper job of investigating Schafer. That would have required some imagination, thought Sam, grumpily.

He knew he had to get inside the building tonight. Something told him there was not going to be a chance tomorrow. True, no one had found Kate so far, but if Sam had managed to piece the clues together inside a day then surely someone else would sooner or later. He remembered the Ambassador's comments about it not being his area of expertise. Did that mean there were going to be other searchers with that expertise on the way?

Sam studied the metal gate that protected the glass entrance and knew there was no chance of being able to pry it open. Instead, he decided to try his luck from the rear. Heading back down the street to the car park where he had been dropped off, he found the entrance to the rear alley. He weaved his way through rubbish bins that filled the narrow street. Finding Schafer's studio he was disappointed to find the rear door locked. It had been a slim chance, but a chance all the same. Stepping back, he looked up at the dark building. Two windows looked out, their light blocked by thick blinds.

Looking further down the alleyway, he noticed a shadow protruding from the wall. Walking over to investigate, Sam found a metal ladder fitted to the brickwork. A fire escape or perhaps a maintenance entry point. Either way, it would be perfect for his needs. Gripping the icy metal bars, he began to climb. In the silence of the night, the sound of his shoes on the rungs seemed to echo loudly. The cold metal stung his hands as he made his way upwards, while the snow had made the going slippery and he had to concentrate on each steady movement to avoid falling.

Finally reaching the top he climbed over the ledge, standing still for a moment to collect his bearings. To his left was Schafer's rooftop sitting area, which Sam had seen on his phone. A low step down from the roof Sam was standing on was all that separated him from Schafer's studio. A large glass panel gave him a direct view into the room below. Bypassing the snow covered furniture, Sam hopped onto the flat roof, crept to the door and peered downwards. Voices could be heard echoing through the wooden door frame: two voices, one of which Sam was certain was a woman's. His heartbeat began to increase.

Reaching out, Sam took hold of the handle and twisted. It was unlocked. He pushed the door, gently and silently slipping inside. The heat from the building hit him like a sledgehammer after the cold. He steadied himself and swallowed. A nervousness had crept in. What would he do if he was wrong? After all this, he was about to walk into Schafer's private property without a valid reason. The thought of Travers' mocking expression filled his mind, the shame of having to explain his actions too hard to contemplate. He forced the thoughts from his head and pushed onwards.

Walking down the steps, he could hear the voices more clearly. One was definitely a woman. She was speaking urgently in German, seemingly questioning Schafer. Sam's confidence grew. He reached the final step and took a deep breath before stepping out into the open space. Raising his hands palm open above his head, he moved forward. Two people – a man and woman – stopped talking and stared at him, mouths open.

Sam tried to give his most friendly, reassuring smile. "Hello there."

He had found her.

TEN

THERE WAS absolute silence for a moment as all three began to process Sam's intrusion. Standing there watching the two shocked faces staring blankly back in complete surprise, Sam would have sworn he could hear the soft falling of the snow outside.

Otto Schafer was the first to break the stillness. The artist jumped to his feet and drove at Sam, pushing him in the chest.

"What the hell do you think you are doing in my property? How dare you do this?" The man's face flushed red in anger.

Sam kept his arms up in the air, letting the German push him backwards. He knew, with his larger, stronger frame, he could easily have overpowered him… but he figured Otto had a point – he was intruding – so he chose to remain passive.

Schafer continued his rant, but now had moved into his native language.

Sam, not having a clue what had been said, replied as calmly as he could. "Herr Schafer, as I told you before, I am only here to help you both. I mean you no harm."

"And just how exactly do you intend to do that?" Kate May spoke for the first time.

Sam was surprised to see that she seemed entirely unflustered by the discovery of her hideout.

"To be honest, I don't quite know that myself yet," Sam admitted. "I had not thought that far ahead."

Sam's honesty seemed to amuse her and she spoke firmly to the still standing Schafer in German, before adding in English, "And then you can throw him out."

Schafer gave Sam a final push, gentler this time. His face was still red with anger, his slick black hair now less sculpted to his head.

Sam gave him a smile. "Glad to see the German reputation for hospitality is still very much intact."

"As is the English sense of humour, it seems," Kate replied cooly. She spoke in a soft voice, calm and measured. Her composure slightly discomfited Sam. For a woman supposedly on the run, such confidence unsettled him.

"I try my best."

He looked around the room. He was standing in a small sitting area with the occupied sofa and an empty armchair facing into a brick fireplace. A fire burnt crisply, filling the room with its warmth. Behind Kate, he could see a kitchen and doors leading off to other unseen rooms.

"A nice place you have here," said Sam, waving his hand around. "Would you mind if I sat down? It's been one of those nights, I would be glad of a rest." No one answered him, so he took off his heavy coat and laid it on the armchair. Sitting down, he leant back in the cushioned seat and crossed his legs. "And may I add, this is a bloody good hiding place. You've had a lot people very worried about you Miss May, or shall I call you Kate?"

"Kate will be fine, thank you."

Sam nodded and rubbed his chin, feeling the stubble scratch the palm of his hand. He had been wrong about one thing. The file photo had not done the girl's looks full justice. Now, sitting here in front of him in the firelight, her pale face seemed to shine. She was dressed in a red jumper and jeans. Her grey blue eyes had not left him from the moment he had first walked in and now, staring directly into them, he found them mesmerising. Even after days in hiding, this girl had a presence that made all of the searching worthwhile.

"If I may say so Kate, you don't seem surprised to see me? If anything, you seem quite relaxed to have been finally found."

"Perhaps I am."

Sam studied her and waited for her to continue.

"I'm guessing based on the conversation you had with dear Otto here at the gallery that you must be Sam Taylor."

"I am."

"And was he right in saying you work for our government?"

"I do."

"Then I'm surprised it took you this long to find me."

"I only arrived in the city yesterday morning."

"Then I'm impressed."

Schafer cut in again, speaking in German, but the tone was clear enough to pass on the message. Kate listened to him and looked back at Sam. She shook her head, patted his knee as he sat down, then turned back once again to stare at Sam.

"You can't really blame him for being angry with you."

"For breaking into his house, or for finding you?"

She laughed for the first time. "No, you ruined his big night. This exhibition has been many months in the planning and then you turned up."

"Ah, well then I'm sorry for disturbing his big night."

Schafer still glared at Sam, but said nothing.

"Don't worry about Otto, he made a big sale this evening – one that has been in the works for a few days – so he will get over it."

Sam was still uncomfortable. The conversation was very casual, as if he had simply arrived on a social visit. He decided to try to change that.

"So, what is all this? You've been in hiding all this week,

you've cut yourself off from your old life and hunkered down here above your friend's studio. You go to all that effort, but then you seem almost pleased to be found? What the hell is going on here?"

Kate looked at Otto and shrugged. "Have you ever been in hiding, Mr Taylor?"

"It's Sam, and no."

"It's not a very nice experience. You have to lock yourself away from the world, from everything you once knew. All that remains is your own mind and that is a dangerous thing. It plays games, making you think of all the possible outcomes or scenarios that may or may not happen. But at the same time, never even giving you a glimmer of a solution to your problems. Imagine being trapped knowing there's no way out and having nothing to distract you from it. It's a kind of torture until all you are left with is a desperation for a solution, any kind of solution. Even being caught."

Sam listened to her intently, feeling the pain of the past few days. His arrival had at least meant that something would change, for good or ill.

"Then will you at least tell me why you have done all this?"

"No."

"No?"

"No. I told you I was desperate for a solution to my situation. I did not tell you that I trusted you or wanted your help."

"Bloody hell."

What did you expect – a damsel in distress?"

Sam ran his hands through his hair and studied her carefully. "Okay, so where do we start?"

Kate sat back on the sofa. "You first, you're the intruder." She looked at Schafer. "Three beers, Otto?"

Otto Schafer did not look like he wanted to play the happy host, but relented. He got up slowly and walked round to the kitchen.

Kate looked back at Sam. "UK government? Only arrived today?... Repatriation Office, yes?"

"Indeed. How did you know?"

"I've worked with your office before while at the embassy. I wondered if they would send one of you." Kate reached up and took a bottle from Schafer, who then handed one to Sam. "Thank you. It's a tick in the right box, it means you don't work for the embassy. So go on then, tell us your story and we will decide whether to trust you."

Sam took a pull of the German *Weissbier*, then began. He told them how he had arrived in Berlin and met with Travers and the Ambassador. Kate snorted at the mention of Travers.

"He's a miserable old bastard, I never liked him."

Continuing, Sam described how Hendricks had taken him to her apartment and how they had searched it again. Schafer had stiffened at hearing of the search in his friend's private apartment, but Kate soothed him. Only when Sam moved on to the discovery of the duffel bag did either of them look surprised.

"You found what?" Kate was incredulous. "Under my bathtub?"

"Yes, I take it you hadn't hidden it there for a rainy day?"

"Absolutely not."

"I didn't think so."

Sam continued on, describing the reactions of the Ambassador and her Head of Security. How he himself had questioned the evidence in front of them and how he had been thrown off the case because of it.

Schafer let out a sneer at hearing Sam was off the case. "So you have no authority to even be here, then?"

"No, not really. Only a stubborn pride to prove I was right."

"Right about what?" asked Kate.

"That regardless of anything else you may have done, and the evidence to suggest otherwise, you are not in fact a spy."

Kate looked at him carefully. Sam could tell she was weighing up whether to trust him. "And are you certain of your decision? That I am not what they think I am?"

"I don't pretend to know why you are hiding here, but I do not believe you are a spy. I think someone wants us to think you are, but as to why… perhaps you can tell me?"

Kate and Schafer looked at each other. The German shook his head, but Kate just raised her eyebrows.

"I trust him."

"Why? I do not."

Kate pointed the bottle of beer at Sam. "If he was really here to hurt me he would have killed us by now. If he was going to arrest us the police would have been here already."

Schafer shook his head in exasperation. "He broke into my flat."

"He didn't break in, the door was open. Plus, I like his eyes, he has trustworthy eyes," Kate said, smiling at Sam. Suddenly, almost unbidden, he felt a thrill of excitement. This girl was far prettier than he had expected, the photo had not done her justice.

"Either way, I don't think we have much choice. He's found me now and I doubt he will just let us go without at least an explanation."

Schafer stood up again. "Then on your head be it, Kate. I know you want to get out of here, but I do not believe this man is the answer to your problems."

The German walked round the sofa and leant against the fireplace brickwork. Folding his arms, he glared at the pair of them.

"He reminds me a little of Travers," mused Sam, smiling his lopsided grin and raising an eyebrow.

Kate laughed and looked down shyly, her face flushing a little. "Yes, you're right. I'd never noticed that before."

"So I've told you my story, what's yours? I'm guessing it's a little more interesting than my own?"

The woman put her hand into her jeans pocket. Withdrawing it, she held up a small silver USB flash drive.

"My story starts with this."

She threw it at Sam, who caught it in one hand and studied the small device. The silver USB was covered in a metal case. He rolled it between his fingers, seeing a small 'G' engraved on one side.

"What's on it?" he asked.

Kate spread her hands. "I have no idea. We've not dared put it into any of Otto's computers."

"Why not?"

"Don't they teach you anything about cyber security in the Foreign Office? Surely even you guys have been taught not to use USBs anymore?"

Sam threw the USB back to Kate. She was right, everything was supposed to be cloud based now. Any digital files they used had to be uploaded to the government's secure cloud storage systems. The use of physical storage devices such as flash drives like this was strictly forbidden in any government department. The risk to data security by the misuse of one was too high to comprehend.

"What makes you suspicious about this one?" asked Sam.

"I found it plugged into the personal laptop of Ambassador Cooper."

"Ah," said Sam, beginning to understand. "I think you'd better tell me the whole story."

"I'm not sure there's much more to say. It was towards the end of the day on Monday evening. I'd been writing up the Ambassador's diary for the next morning when Ambassador Cooper and John Travers walked out of her office. It looked like they were worried about something to do with the North Sea Deal and they were deep in conversation. I don't even think they noticed me. Well, they walked out and I finished up typing the next day's rider. I printed it off and went to put it on her desk. That's when I saw this USB plugged into her laptop. I quickly went round the table and saw a countdown on the screen."

"A countdown?" asked Sam.

"Well... a transfer progress bar. I could see it was downloading files from the Ambassadors laptop and that it was already at eighty-five per cent. I could see on the screen that there were a number of North Sea Deal documents, which I knew were confidential and classified, so I panicked."

She fell back against the sofa and looked at the USB between her fingers as if it would explain to her why she had acted in the way she did in those moments back at the embassy.

"What did you do?" prompted Sam.

"I pulled it out! I didn't even think to eject it, I just panicked and pulled it out as quickly as I could so that whoever wanted the files wouldn't get hold of them."

Sam tried to picture the scene in the Ambassador's office and tried to think what he would have done in Kate's shoes. He probably would have done the same. With the transfer to the memory stick at eighty-five per cent complete, she would have had very little time to find help. The only other option would have been to have ignored even seeing it, to have turned around and left it to someone else to deal with. He wondered if she wished she had taken such a route.

"So, you pulled it and potentially prevented a cyber attack? Why did you suddenly decide to run?" Sam asked, confused.

Kate gave a sarcastic laugh and leant forward again, pointing her beer at Sam. "I heard voices coming from the side door into the Ambassador's office. Imagine the scene: the last people to leave the office were the embassy's two most important people. Between then and that moment, I'm found holding onto a USB, which just moments before had been plugged into the Ambassador's laptop. What do you think is going to happen? There's the two of them, who will swear they have never even seen the device before, and then just little old me caught red handed at the scene of the crime. As it was, they both saw me coming out of the office, so I'm sure when whoever it belonged to found it was missing, they wouldn't have had a difficult leap to make. While they couldn't accuse me at the time, they knew they could set me up afterwards. Why do you *think* I ran? And now, according to what you've told me, they seem to have framed me further by hiding that stuff in my apartment."

Now Sam could better understand the journey Kate had been on. She was right, of course. If she had remained in that office and been found, it would have been her word against theirs. She would have been outright blamed for the USB being in the laptop. She would have been accused of spying. But that left overarching questions, which hung over them without needing to be voiced. Who had actually inserted the USB? And who was quite happy for Kate to take the fall?

ELEVEN

KATE FINISHED HER STORY.

"I ran, well walked out of the embassy, and came straight here. I knew Otto would be able to look after me. I've not left since."

"I found her outside my studio just as I was locking up for the night. She was lucky because I almost missed her!" Otto added.

"What about your phone? Why did you drop that in the bin on your way out?" Sam had already guessed the answer.

"It was the only thing they could track me with. Everything else, such as credit cards and other electronics, are back in my apartment. Or they *were,* unless they've been taken. Otto here has bought everything for me since then – including food and clothes."

"And you are most welcome," Otto smiled for the first time since Sam had arrived. "What they have done to you is disgusting."

Kate gave him a warm smile in return. Sam was impressed by the way she had handled herself, both since his arrival and at the discovery of the USB. Her quick thinking had almost certainly saved her from an even more tricky situation. Not that their current situation was much better. She was still on the run and there was now new 'evidence' against her in the form of the duffel bag's contents.

"So what now?" asked Sam.

Kate shrugged. "I don't really know. I was hoping you would have an idea about how to get me out of this mess. I can't go back to the embassy, because they will have me arrested the moment I set foot inside the building. But I should tell you now, I'm not some damsel in distress waiting for you to rescue me. I want my life back and I want revenge on the people who did this. If you can help me that's great, but if not then you can sod off back to London."

Sam considered the situation. Naively, he had assumed the act of finding her would solve the rest of the problems now laid before them. There was no way he could take her back to the embassy while the weight of evidence was so firmly stacked against her. If she even tried to defend herself, those with the power to make the decisions had already made up their minds. They needed help.

"Kate, I'm sorry but there's not much I can do right now. I think you're correct that if you went to the embassy and tried to plead your case it would be a waste of time. Everyone in there now thinks you're a paid-up Russian spy. The North Sea Deal has only heightened everyone's tension."

"So wait it out, let the deal be signed in peace then show them you are not involved in it?" suggested Otto. He had moved back nearer the sofa. "You can stay here as long as you need. I can pay for a lawyer and we will face it together."

Sam shook his head. "I don't believe you can hide here indefinitely. I managed to find you within twelve hours of being on the ground. Sooner or later, they will track you down. Travers said they would be getting in extra help to find you after he kicked me off the case."

For the first time that evening, Sam noticed Kate looked concerned.

"But where can I go? I can't go home and I've no money to travel anywhere."

"You can stay at my apartment," Otto offered.

"No," Sam said firmly. "I found her through you and that means sooner or later they will look at you again. Whatever you do Kate, you will need to do it without Otto."

"So I'm alone then?"

"I didn't say you were doing anything alone."

Kate eyed Sam with renewed suspicion. "And who's going to help me? You?"

"I'm now off the case and I have plenty of untraceable funds to ensure that we can stay anywhere you fancy in the city. I have friends in London who at the very least will be able to ensure we have a fair hearing when the time comes. They may even be able to help us get out of the country."

Kate May took her time to think about Sam's offer. He watched her eyes narrow as her mind tried to weigh up the options available to her. Could she put her life in the hands of a man she had just met?

Sam tried to help her. "Look at it from my point of view. I'm trusting your version of events based purely on gut instinct. By even helping you, I'm becoming an accomplice to a suspected spy. I'm having to trust you almost as much as I'm expecting you to trust me. Right now, we are in it together."

Schafer moved uncomfortably next to her. Sam could guess where his mind was at already. But what about Kate? He failed to see what other options were available to her. In time, whoever was searching for her would eventually succeed.

"I need to think on it. Do you think we have until morning?"

"When I left the embassy they had no idea where to even start, so I doubt they'd arrive here tonight. I think we can stay the night here, and then if it's okay with you, we should move to a new location."

Kate stood up and stretched, arching her back.

"Then let me sleep on it and we can decide what we do in the morning. I think I trust you Sam Taylor, but you are asking a lot. I want to believe that you can help me, but I need to feel sure."

"I understand. I would be cautious if I was in your position as well."

"What will *you* do now?" she asked him.

It was well past midnight, and he was not very keen on the idea of travelling back to his hotel.

Kate answered for him. "I think you should stay here. You can sleep on the sofa if that's okay with Otto?"

Otto's face made it clear that he would have preferred not to have had the Englishman in his apartment any longer, but he relented.

"Good, well Otto has his own room and I have the guest room. I take it you are not going to kill us in our sleep?" she challenged Sam.

"If you don't trust me, take a kitchen chair and put it against the handle of the bedroom door. But you will be wasting your time as I'll only be fast asleep in front of the fire."

Kate May gave a wry smile. "You see Otto, he's even house trained."

Schafer muttered his opinion of Sam's house training in German, but left to retrieve a blanket.

Kate sighed. "I'm sorry about him. He can be a little bit protective of me at times. But he means well."

"It's not a bad thing to have friends like that."

Schafer returned and threw Sam the blanket. "The toilet is just round there if you need it," he told Sam abruptly.

"Thanks, I'll see you in the morning then."

The pair of them left Sam alone and retired to Kate's room. From there, Sam could hear Schafer begin to furiously debate with Kate in German. Even without being fluent in the language, Sam had no problem guessing the subject of their discussion. But she had not taken a kitchen chair to press against the door.

"There you go Sam, always making friends," he said to himself as he arranged the cushions on the sofa.

Kicking his shoes off, he lay back on the sofa and rested his head in his hands. Looking up at the ceiling he reflected on how he could have possibly ended up in such a stupid situation. He had gone from hunting an intriguing missing woman to aiding a suspected spy. Sighing, he rubbed his face, feeling the stirring of fatigue pulling at his senses. Heat from the fireplace made the blanket redundant and he kicked it to the floor. Light from the flames made shadows dance on the walls around him.

The argument between his hosts continued in earnest as he lay there collecting his thoughts. Tomorrow, if Kate agreed to trust him, he would need to escort her through the city and into a new hiding place. Various locations flashed through his mind. With the money left in his coat pockets they could stay anywhere they liked. He twisted and turned on the sofa, trying to find a more comfortable position to fall asleep in. The voices from the guest room continued their debate. Trying his utmost to shut out the noise, he concentrated on watching the falling snow, which was now swirling in the air outside one of the windows.

Later, Sam woke with a start and sat up, blinking sleep from his eyes. Sweat had made the shirt clammy and the fabric stuck to his back. The fire had died low, with embers now flickering in their death throes.

"I'm sorry for the intrusion." Sam turned round and saw Kate. Her face was illuminated in the firelight as she sat in the chair previously occupied by Sam earlier that night. The glow of the flames danced over her strong features.

There was something different about her now, her body language was tighter. She sat with her knees brought up to her chest, her arms wrapped tightly around them. Her pale face looked tired as she rested it on her knees.

"How long have you been there?" Sam asked.

"A little while. I couldn't sleep after Otto went to bed. I wanted to talk to you some more."

Sam rubbed the sleep from his eyes and sat up fully on the sofa. He checked his watch. The green ringed face showed 4am.

Kate pulled her brown hair back behind her ears.

"I'm going to go with you tomorrow," She told Sam flatly. "Otto doesn't like it, but I think you're right that there's nothing else I can do. I'm going to have to trust you."

"I agree."

She stretched out her legs and hung them out over the chair arm. "You know everything about me. I'm sure you've read my files. I have nothing left to hide. But what about you, Sam Taylor? Who are you? Why are you helping me?"

Sam looked away from her toned legs and met her eyes.

"What do you want to know?"

"Tell me something about you. Something that helps me get to know you."

Sam raised an eyebrow. "I used to be a military police officer, spent two tours in Afghanistan."

She hugged her knees more tightly.

"Tell me something else. Where did you grow up?"

"You can probably tell from my accent that I was born in Yorkshire. Both my parents are still alive, I have one sister who's married with two kids, and I have a brother."

"I never had any siblings."

"I know, you were an orphan."

"So tell me about your siblings."

"The last time I saw my brother was in Afghanistan. We did not part on good terms."

Kate looked at him with interest. "What happened?"

"I did something I shouldn't have."

"And?"

Sam's mind flashed back to the moment he had last seen his brother in that godforsaken country. The pain in his brother's eyes as he had been carried away across the sandy market town. They had not spoken again since.

"And what? I don't even know where he is. We've not spoken to each other. The last I heard he was working abroad, or something like that."

Kate twisted in the seat and crossed her slim legs. "Now the second question. Why are you helping me?"

"Why not?"

"By doing so you are only implicating yourself in something you could have simply walked away from."

"I don't see it like that. I only see it as righting a wrong."

"And to prove John Travers wrong?"

"A benefit rather than the goal."

Kate laughed. She walked towards him and crouched down. It was the closest she had been to him that night and Sam's nostrils were filled with the smell of her perfume. She took his hand and squeezed it, sending a slight shiver down his spine.

"I'm sorry Sam, but I lied to you earlier."

"You did?"

"I'm scared Sam, and I don't know what will happen to me. I feel trapped in a game I don't understand. I don't even know if I can trust you."

"Perhaps you can't?"

She warned him. "Don't mess with me."

Sam pulled his hand away and put his hands on her arms, leading her upright until they were both standing. Gently moving her to one side, he picked up the discarded parka. Reaching into the pockets he pulled out three bundles of euros. He placed all three within her palms before closing her fingers over the crisp notes.

"I can't make you trust me and I cannot possibly say anything which can give you total confidence in me. Christ, I don't even know what we should be doing. But there are 15,000 euros in your hands right now. If you don't want to trust me, and would prefer to go it alone, you can do whatever you want with it. Hide, then wait it out in the best hotels in Berlin and let Otto hire you the most expensive lawyers he can. You can wait until I'm asleep then slip out into the night. I'd have no idea where you had gone and I would not try to find you again. Or we can go together and just maybe find out who the bastards are behind all this."

Kate looked down at the bundles of cash within her grasp and stepped back from Sam. She seemed to be coming to a conclusion. Giving Sam the money back, she clasped his hands again.

"Okay, so we are in this together."

Sam smiled at her. "Damn right."

"I've decided to trust you, Sam Taylor."

He guided her back to the sofa, wrapping the blanket around her as she curled up. He sat in the armchair beside her and watched as her eyes began to close and her breathing became soft and rhythmic. Putting his head back in his hands he gazed at the beautiful woman next to him.

"Of course you do," he whispered. "It's like you said earlier. I have trustworthy eyes."

TWELVE

SAM WAS awoken by the sound of Otto Schafer moving around in the kitchen behind him. For a moment, he sat stretched out under the blanket, wishing he was back at home in his own bed, far away from the problems of this damned city. The cold light of dawn had brought home the realities of the situation. The stakes were higher than anything he had been involved in before. This was not playing off against organised crime, or even a terrorist group, this was fighting between nations – and Sam did not fancy their chances.

"Oi Taylor, do you want a coffee or are you going to continue to pretend to be asleep?" his German host called out to him from the kitchen.

Sam sighed and sat up, the blanket falling away from him. His black suit was now completely dishevelled. He reached up and took the offered mug of coffee from Schafer.

"Thank you. I could get used to this kind of service."

Sam looked around the small kitchen space. Everything was perfectly ordered across all the worktops. He noticed a small screen, which displayed images from the studio's security cameras downstairs.

Schafer scoffed and walked back to the kitchen. "Don't get

used to it. I'm still not happy about Kate leaving with you this morning."

"Ignore him," Kate called as she walked out of the bathroom.

A small towel was wrapped around her body. A second was being used to dry her long brown hair. Sam tried not to stare.

"He's just happy that he got a sale this morning. Oh, and the shower's free if you want one."

"That's him being happy?"

"He made you a coffee, didn't he?"

Kate walked past them both and stepped back into her own room. Sam stood up and folded the blanket, before carrying it over to Schafer.

"Is it a sale from last night?" Sam asked, trying to break the ice.

"Yes and no, it's a Hungarian collector who first contacted me a couple of days ago. He's coming over this morning to make the final arrangements."

"Nice, do they usually come here?"

Schafer gave him a patronising stare. "This is my studio, where else would they come?"

"You have another apartment though, don't you?"

Schafer rolled his eyes. "Yes, but again, why would they go there rather than my actual shop?"

Sam gave up and went back to the sofa to wait for Kate. Checking his phone, he saw Emma Read had messaged him for an update on his plans. He ignored her. Instead, he started to search for hotels within the city and checked their availability for the evening. While he could not book online for fear of being tracked, it would at least tell him whether there were any beds available.

Kate joined them not long later, her hair now dried and tied in a knot at the nape of her neck. She was dressed in the same pair of jeans as last night, but was now wearing a dark green hoody. In one hand she carried a pair of sturdy looking boots and in the other, a bag which Sam guessed contained her few belongings.

"So when are we going?" she asked, trying to sound upbeat.

Sam looked at his watch. It was only eight in the morning. "Soon, but we've missed the streets being quiet enough for no one to be around to notice us and it's not yet late enough for us to be able to blend in with the crowds."

"Do you know where we are going yet?" she asked, taking a fresh cup of coffee from Schafer.

"I was thinking of the Ritz?"

"London? That's a bit further than I was expecting," said Kate.

"He means the Ritz-Carlton at Potsdamer Platz," Schafer informed her. He looked at Sam. "That's a bit close to the embassy, is it not?"

"It's where they will least expect us. Living it up in one of the finest hotels in the city."

Kate beamed. "I like your style, Sam Taylor, especially if there's a spa!"

Schafer shook his head in exasperation. "Don't you know you are supposed to be on the run? You're acting like you are going on some sort of honeymoon."

"It's called gallows humour, the English are fans. When there's nothing else you can do you might as well laugh about it."

Schafer muttered something in German, and left the room to get ready for his customers.

"We should try and get away before his guests arrive," Sam told Kate.

She agreed and came to sit next to him to tie up her boots. "There's one thing we forgot last night."

"What?"

She waited until she had finished tying one boot before continuing. "We never discussed who the USB belongs to."

"It could have been either the Ambassador or the Head of Security. Does it really matter? For all we know it could even have been both of them."

Kate started on the next boot. "I don't think it could be both of them, how would that work? Plus, if it were, why did they leave the room? Surely its more likely it was only one of them and they used the excuse of the North Sea Deal problem to get the other one out of the office?"

"With that logic it must be Travers. Why would Ambassador Cooper need an excuse to have some privacy in her own office?"

"Ah, but Travers entered her office and they left only minutes later. Perhaps he disturbed her?"

"Try to think about it from the opposition's point of view. Who would be a more useful informant? A new ambassador or a long serving head of security?"

"Or perhaps it's about who would be easier to get access to?"

Sam laughed. "We could do this all day, but at this moment we have no idea, so we treat them both as suspects. We don't even know who they are actually working for. We presume the Russians, but who's to say?"

"You two are the worst agents I could possibly imagine," Schafer had reentered the room. "You are a pair of amateurs playing a game you barely understand."

"But at least we have a plan now!" Kate smiled.

"Which is to spend a night at a luxury hotel." Schafer sighed and reached into one of the kitchen drawers. "Here, these might help." He threw a pair of keys at Kate, who caught them before pocketing them.

"They are my assistant's keys. She is out of the country at the moment. She uses the studio's parking spot in the car park at the end of the street. It's a grey Seat."

Kate hugged her friend. "Thank you Otto, you've been amazing. I don't know what I would have done without you."

"I think you are making a mistake, my friend, but I'm always here for you."

Sam put on his shoes and suit jacket. "We should be getting off."

Kate agreed. "Okay, come on, let's go."

But as she moved towards the stairs to the studio below, the smart screen in the kitchen lit up and played a doorbell tune.

Schafer swore. "It's my customer from last night. They are early. I'm sorry Kate, are you okay to wait? I would not want them to see you just as you leave after all we've gone through."

Kate looked at Sam for direction, who nodded. "Of course Otto, you go and open up. We can wait."

Otto straightened his shirt and left them to go downstairs, his feet echoing on the metal staircase.

"It seems your friend does pretty good business."

"He's absolutely loaded. The guy has to only draw a stick figure and it sells for thousands."

Sam watched as her eyes narrowed as she looked closer at the figures on the screen.

"What's up?" he asked her.

She tapped the device, making one of the images blow up to fill the entire screen. "Otto's customers, I think I recognise them. Well, at least one of them."

Sam senses were heightened. At times like this especially, he did not like coincidences. He walked round and stood behind Kate. Looking at the smart screen, he could see three figures outside the store, waiting to be let in. Two of the men stood either side of an older man who Sam recognised from the night before. It was the silver haired man who Schafer had hugged on his way out.

"One of Schafer's old friends?" he asked her.

"No, I don't think so," she muttered. "But I've seen him before, somewhere..." Her voice trailed off.

The silver haired man was still wearing his pale blue scarf from the night before, but was now in a long grey coat. He wore rimless glasses, which seemed to have been squashed into his face. Sam felt the hairs on the back of his neck rise. Beneath them, he could hear Schafer moving about his store. He took another look at the two companions. Both looked burly choices to be accompanying this art dealer. Both had their hands deep within their pockets, too.

"I don't like this," announced Sam.

"What do you mean?" asked Kate.

Sam was already turning around and heading to the door that led to the store downstairs. He grabbed the handle and began to shout to Schafer, to tell him not to open the thick metal gate that protected the studio. As he did so he heard a muffled *snap* from the floor down below.

"No!" Kate screamed at the screen.

Sam turned back and hurried over to see. The screen had switched to one further inside and Sam could see the three men stepping into the store, over the body of Otto Schafer.

"They shot him!" Kate gasped. "Sam, they shot him."

But Sam's mind was already in survival mode. He grabbed one of the kitchen chairs and rammed it under the handle of the door, which led down to the stairs below.

"Come on, grab your stuff," he ordered Kate.

But Kate was frozen. The shock of seeing her friend gunned down had totally incapacitated her. Sam placed his hands on her face, forcing her to look at him.

"Kate, we have to go. There's nothing we can do for him."

She blinked back at him. "The cameras," she whispered.

"What about them?"

"There's someone else downstairs!"

Sam turned back to the screen and saw the image had changed view again, this time to the back door, where a new figure had walked in. Now there was shouting from below, the voices challenging. Then more gunshots. Someone was firing again.

"What the hell?" Kate turned to him, frantic. "Who are they shooting at now?"

"Themselves, hopefully. Now come on."

Grabbing her arm, he pulled her to the doorway that led to the rooftops, only pausing to grab his own coat. Still holding her arm, he took the stairs two at a time. Below them, gunshots still sounded. Reaching the rooftop, his eyes took a moment to get used to the bright scene in front of them. A thick layer of snow covered the area and the fresh early morning sun reflected from the frozen surface. He had to take a moment to remember the way to the car park. He looked at Kate, her face even paler than usual.

"Kate, listen to me. I need you to think, to get that brain in gear. We can get out of this, and we can get the people who killed your friend, but right now you need to work with me."

The grey-blue eyes were filling with tears and she blinked them away.

"Okay."

"Come on, time for me to start earning your trust."

They ran across the rooftop and climbed onto the neighbouring building. Behind them, Sam could hear the muffled sounds of yells. They did not have much time to find the car. The next rooftop was flat and allowed them to sprint across, but at the following one, Sam had to give Kate a leg-up. He jumped to reach, nearly slipping as his hands tried to find the ledge in amongst the snow. Finally finding his grip, he slid over and looking back he saw they had a pursuer, who had reached the first rooftop and spotted them.

"Keep going," he instructed Kate, who ran to the next building before clambering down the brickwork, grazing her hands as she went.

Sam followed and slid down, landing hard on the final rooftop before the car park. They ran to the edge, hoping to find a ladder.

"There's no way down!" Kate moaned.

Sam dropped to his knees. "It's only one storey. I'll lower you down and then lower myself."

She followed his instructions and grabbed his hand as she rolled her legs over the parapet.

"See you at the bottom," Sam said.

He leaned over the edge and when he could not reach any further, he dropped the hanging Kate to land in a heap on the ground.

"Find the car!" he shouted to her, and watched with satisfaction as she went to the only grey one in the car park.

He twisted on the ledge and began to inch down the wall. As

he did so, their pursuer appeared on the next rooftop along. Sam swore, panicked and let go. He fell with a crash onto the bonnet of a large SUV, the sheet of metal breaking his fall, leaving him with only bruising. Sliding off the now dented car, he brushed the snow from his coat and looked for Kate. She had already started the engine, the windscreen wipers clearing the covering of snow. Running, Sam reached the passenger door and slid in.

"Where do I go?" Kate asked.

"Anywhere."

She grabbed hold of the gear stick and began to reverse the car out from its spot. Further snow fell from the roof of the car and slid down the window. Free from the parking spot, Kate hit the brakes, causing Sam to be thrown forwards in his seat. Forcing the resisting gear stick into first, Kate revved the engine and Sam felt the wheels attempt to grip the snow. Turning to look over his shoulder, he peered up at the rooftop they had just jumped from, to try to see their pursuer. A head appeared at the same spot Sam had just fallen from.

"Time to go, Kate," he warned her and she began to accelerate forward then came to an abrupt stop.

"What are you waiting for?" he shouted.

"There's someone in the way."

Sam turned in his seat and stared forward through the windscreen. Ahead of them a man had stepped forward to block the entrance to the car park. He was tall and broad shouldered, wearing a denim sherpa jacket, the white fleece lining standing out against the blue. His head was round with dark brown hair clipped close. A grim scar ran up his cheek to where a mangled ear remained. In his hand, he carried a pistol with a silencer attached. His attention was broken for a moment by the appearance of their pursuer appearing on the rooftop above him. Barely pausing, he raised his pistol, fired twice and the pursuer fell, landing on the same car as Sam had earlier.

"Bloody hell!" Sam swore.

"Who is it?" asked Kate.

Sam stared at the figure ahead of them who once again turned to face the stationary vehicle. He raised the pistol to give a mock salute, then stepped back to allow them to drive by.

"Go!" Sam ordered.

Kate accelerated forward and Sam could only stare in shock as they drove past the watching figure. A pair of sharp hazel eyes followed their progress. As they moved away, Sam watched as the newcomer mouthed something as he waved them goodbye. "See you later, big brother."

THIRTEEN

AFGHANISTAN

Lieutenant Sam Taylor stared up at the tent's canvas ceiling and tried to guess what the previous occupant had thought about while lying under its protection. Did they spend their time thinking of being back home, or perhaps just how many days they had left to stare up at the green canvas? Probably how many days they had left before they would be able to return to Camp Bastion, decided Sam. No one was stupid enough to think of home when stuck out here. But counting down the days to when they could return to the main coalition base rather than this primitive set-up they currently called home would be far more mentally stimulating. The allied coalition base of Camp Bastion was practically a holiday park compared to the rundown forward operating base they currently called home. Situated half a mile from an Afghan market town that would barely even be registered on the map, Camp Duke was not somewhere Lieutenant Sam Taylor would request to be stationed again.

The alarm on his watch began to sound and he rolled off the camp bed. The air within the tent felt stuffy from the midday sun, its heat making him sweat through his T-shirt. Standing, he reached into his bag and pulled on a new T-shirt, which felt no fresher. With temperatures rising above thirty-five degrees, summer in Helmand Province was making its presence felt. Outside the tent Sam could hear the ever-present buzz that surrounded the camp during the day. A mix of vehicles and generators hummed, mixed with the constant human interactions of hundreds of military personnel living together behind the camp's walls.

Sam Taylor was a lieutenant in the Royal Military Police's second regiment, two twenty-two provost company, and he did only have five more days left. But those days would still feel like weeks. He fastened his belt buckle, a Glock 17 holstered securely to it. Reaching down, he picked up his red beret that denoted his status as a member of the MP corps, otherwise known to the rest of the army as the Redcaps. Sam flicked off the stray flecks of dust before placing it on his head and checking his reflection in the mirror hanging off one of the poles. The stern face staring back at him looked tired, older than he remembered. While maybe not as sought after as the maroon beret of the paratroopers or the sand coloured beret of the SAS, Sam would not have swapped his redcap with any of them. The rest of the army would often refer to them as the monkeys, but not many would have dared say that to Sam's face.

The red beret securely fitted to his head, he walked past the rest of the camp beds and pushed the door of the tent open. Outside, the heat seemed even worse than within the tent. The sun's rays seemed to draw out dust from the very ground, pulling it skywards into the very air he breathed. Walking briskly down the rows of tents he headed towards the north side of the camp, which housed the main operational buildings. He nodded at a couple of passing soldiers as he made his way past. A game of football had broken out in one of the open areas of the camp. How they were even able to find the energy to run in this heat was beyond Sam.

Reaching the north end of the camp he crossed the marshalling area, an open space in front of the main gates to the camp.

Opposite, he watched as a group of marines were preparing for that afternoon's patrol into the town. Officers and sergeants were checking their men's equipment and weapons ahead of leaving the camp. The local population here had at least been fairly receptive to their presence. In the time Sam had been on station there had been no attacks by the Taliban. His own interactions with the new recruits to the Afghan police force had been nothing but productive. The trainees had been receptive and enthusiastic to try out their new equipment that had been generously paid for by the allied forces who had invaded their country.

A voice boomed across the dusty ground as an officer berated an unlucky private for the state of his equipment. Sam watched on as the squaddie was unceremoniously marched back to his quarters to repair the offending item.

"Looks like someone forgot to tie his shoelaces this morning, sir," a voice called out to Sam.

He turned and saw Corporal Tim Bell heading towards him. While only a few years younger than Sam, the baby faced Bell barely seemed old enough to be in uniform.

"Marines Tim, you know they should stick to velcro when choosing their boots. Laces are far too complicated."

"Yes sir," laughed Bell.

Sam pointed to the waiting patrol of marines. "Are they the new arrivals?"

"Yes sir, they only arrived yesterday. Seem pretty eager to get out there, don't they?"

"Probably have a commanding officer who's due a promotion."

Corporal Bell crossed his arms. "Bloody officers. All the same." Sam raised his eyebrow. "Present company excepted, sir."

"Very good Corporal, what have we got on this afternoon?"

Bell passed a clipboard to his officer and fell into step as they walked towards one of the cabins that housed the camp's offices.

"We've no training scheduled for today sir, but we do have the inventory checks to complete from the cache found last week."

"How many are left now? We have the AK-47s and then there's some RPGs to pack off as well." Sam flicked through the top pages, barely skimming the report. "What about the issue with the two squaddies from the other night?"

"The fight? I think their sergeant is coming to see you about that today. I think he's going to ask for some leniency due to a special circumstance."

"You mean they were drunk under his watch."

Bell nodded disapprovingly. "Probably."

Sam sighed and walked on. They were now level with the waiting marine patrol and Sam studied the waiting soldiers. There were a couple of nervous looking young men in the patrol, probably about to go on their first outing since arriving in the country. A tall, burly sergeant was cajoling a couple of them, telling the usual jokes said when out of earshot of the officers. Sam watched on in amusement. The countryside round Camp Duke was not the worst place to bed in any new troops. They would all be back in their mess by teatime.

"Right Corporal, go make a start on registering those AK-47s. Chuck them in the truck and bring them round to the office. We can then get them sent back on the next delivery. I'll go and check the sentries on the gate before coming to join you."

"Yes sir," said Bell, and turned away.

Sam watched on and was about to follow when he heard the voice of the marine sergeant drifting across the camp. There was something familiar in that voice and he turned to stare at the figure with his back to him. The shoulders were broad, bigger even than Sam's own, and even the hefty body armour looked small on its frame. Sam knew the chances were slim that the voice was the one he remembered, but he still had to check. He walked over to the marines.

"Afternoon sergeant, are your men ready for the patrol?"

The tall sergeant gave his men a knowing look before slowly turning round to face Sam.

"Bloody hell! Jake, what the hell are you doing here?" said a stunned Sam.

Sergeant Jake Taylor barely registered any surprise at seeing his brother. The round face under its helmet stared back coldly. A pair of hazel eyes studied Sam.

"I'm here on patrol, sir."

Sam was taken aback by the dryness of the response. His shock at seeing his brother in the middle of a warzone completely bypassed the military norms and customs. He grabbed his brother's shoulder and shook it.

"Bloody hell lad, why didn't you tell me you were here? I didn't even know you were in the army."

Jake Taylor looked down at his brother's hand on his shoulder before shrugging it away. "I didn't know you were here, sir."

Sam frowned at the use of the formality. "Right, but still, you should have messaged me. Do Mum and Dad know you're here? They didn't tell me."

Jake looked round at his squad before answering. "I don't know. I've not spoken to them since coming out."

Sam was beginning to become put out by his brother's tone. His own surprise at seeing his younger brother had turned immediately to joy, but he sensed frustration in the other man. There had always been an unspoken jealousy causing distance between them, but they were in a warzone, for goodness' sake.

He took a step back. "Right, well, it's good to see you again. Do you know where you're going this afternoon?"

The younger brother seemed happy to be back on a more formal footing as he answered. "Yes sir, we are heading down to the riverbed, then following it down into the town. Up through the marketplace and back here for dinner."

Sam nodded and looked at the rest of the patrol. He noticed the more nervous faces and gave them a confident grin. "Easy going for your first patrol. But don't get excited about having a walk by the river, it's more like a bloody stream that's pretty much dried up."

A few of the marines caught his eye, most stared back blankly. Sam knew when he wasn't wanted. He guessed his presence was frustrating his brother, so began a retreat.

"Well, I think that's your officer returning so I will let you get ready." Then, speaking to his brother, he added, "It's really good to see you again, Jake."

Jake's hazel eyes narrowed. "Yes, sir."

Sam well knew when a subordinate was responding for the sake of it. He himself had given countless bland answers to senior officers to get himself out of a situation.

The two brothers stared at each other for a long moment before Sam broke off and turned back towards where Bell had disappeared to count the recovered weapons. He would wait until the patrol had left before seeing the gate sentries. The old frustrations of having a younger brother were burning up inside him and he felt childish urges to give his now taller sibling a beating.

"Bloody bastard," Sam swore.

The last time he had seen his younger brother had been the day he had left for Sandhurst. Jake had just finished college and was between jobs at that time. Years had passed since then, until it seemed that now they could barely speak to each other. Well, let the miserable bastard sulk. Putting his frustrations behind him, he walked round the large main operations cabin, where he found Bell stacking crates.

The Corporal looked up to see the stern face of his commanding officer.

"You all right, sir?"

Sam walked over and sat on one of the crates.

"Do you have any siblings, Corporal?"

Bell grinned.

"Yes sir, two older sisters."

"Do you ever want to throttle them?"

The younger man laughed and stopped what he was doing to answer. "They were both over eight years older than me when I was growing up, so would have beaten me in a fight. I was more interested in dating their friends. Why?"

Sam decided he might as well tell Bell, as everyone in the camp would know that Lieutenant Taylor's brother was on site by the end of the night. Only gossip spread faster than wildfire.

"Ah, sounds a tricky situation," Bell answered.

"He was always a stubborn bastard, one of those people with a constant chip on their shoulder."

"Youngest child syndrome," Bell chuckled. "I was the same – any time my sisters tried to tell me what to do, I just exploded. Drove me nuts."

"Is that why you joined the army?"

Bell shook his head. "No, I was told there would be so many women around that I'd be fighting them off."

Sam laughed and rubbed his face. Even that short conversation with his brother had left him drained.

"Why is family such hard work, eh?"

He stepped up and turned to the crates. Each contained weapons recently recovered from a farm on the other side of the town after the owner had traded them in for American dollars.

He opened one of the lids and picked up an assault rifle. "What do you think then, Tim? I reckon this hasn't been fired since the Russian invasion in the eighties."

Tim Bell picked up another rifle and studied it. "I've no idea. If you look, all of the serial numbers have been filed off."

The two of them continued through the crates, logging their findings to ensure the weapons were ready to be uplifted. An hour had passed when suddenly, Sam's attention was caught by a muffled bang somewhere in the distance.

Bell heard it too and looked at Sam quizzically. "Where did that come from?"

A second bang echoed over them and this time Sam recognised the sound of an explosion. The two looked about to see the cause, but seeing no telltale trails of smoke in the camp, they gave up.

"Must be from somewhere outside?" Bell pointed at the thick Hesco bins that made up the walls of the camp.

An uneasy feeling pricked at Sam's stomach. He thought of Jake and his patrol.

He tapped Bell on the shoulder. "You finish these then get a drink and a bite to eat. Are there more in the truck?"

Bell nodded. "Yes, two more crates."

"Right, leave them till later. I want to find out what that noise was."

Leaving Bell to finish up, he wandered back round the cabins and into the main marshalling area to find a buzz of activity all around him. Patrol vehicles were being prepared for departure, their mechanics passing up rounds of ammunition to the crews. Medics were hurriedly carrying over bags of equipment. Officers were shouting their orders to men who only moments before had been resting in reserve.

Sam walked to the main operations room and stuck his head into the office. Spotting someone he recognised, he asked what was happening. He knew the answer before the other officer could confirm it.

"The marine patrol, it's just been ambushed. A bloody IED, we've not had one of them for weeks and now two take out half a patrol."

Sam felt his stomach drop. "Casualties?"

The officer turned to him. "Yes, quite a few. The response team is on its way out now. We've called in air support and evacuation already. Hey, where are you going?"

Sam had left the officer in the cabin and was running towards the first armoured vehicle driving to the gate. A couple of soldiers were seated on the roof, manning the machine gun. They stared at him as he jumped up and perched alongside them.

"Hang on, what the hell are you doing?" They stared in disbelief at the military police officer.

Sam was wearing nothing but his trousers, T-shirt and red beret. The rest of the troops on board were fully armoured up with helmets, body armour, weaponry and all the other equipment expected to be worn. Sam, with his single Glock 17, was not exactly armed to the teeth.

"Seriously sir, you can't leave dressed like that."

Lieutenant Sam Taylor turned to the addressing soldier. "Private, if you speak again between now and our destination, I promise you will need a response team to come and rescue you."

FOURTEEN

JAKE TAYLOR ARRIVED in Berlin at the same time Sam Taylor was leaving his hotel for Otto Schafer's reception. Earlier, he had driven the two bodies of Josh Quinn's blackmailers across the Irish border and into one of the more unionist suburbs of Belfast. Parking the van in the middle of the unionist estate, with its Irish number plates, was a guaranteed way of ensuring the bodies were never found. Then a taxi ride to the airport, a pint of Guinness in front of him, and he was ready to return home to London. Until the call had come in.

He answered the withheld number and heard the familiar distorted female voice at the end of the line. "Good evening Jake, I have some bad news for you." The voice was soft and calm in tone.

Jake had never met the woman. It was all part of the caretaker lifestyle, to keep everything clean and tidy. Leave nothing behind.

"I take it I'm not going home, then?"

"No, I'm afraid not. You're needed in Berlin this evening. One of the embassy staff has gone rogue and has been spying for the Russians."

"Ah, not good then."

"I've changed your ticket for the next flight to Berlin. It should be with you now."

Jake felt his phone vibrate with the email's arrival.

"Are you sending a toolbox?"

"Yes," said the voice. "A courier will have arrived at the embassy before you land."

"Anything else I need to know?"

"It will all be emailed to you, Jake."

The phone call ended, and not for the first time, Jake was left wondering about the woman at the end of the line. He looked at the email and saw his flight was due in an hour's time. Certainly a good opportunity for a final Guinness.

Landing late that night, Jake took the same route his brother had taken earlier that day. Exiting the U-bahn station just below the Brandenburg Gate, he emerged into the now snowy Berlin evening. Unlike his brother, he did not stop to look at the monument, instead he walked directly to the embassy. Like his brother, he was accosted by a group of climate protesters, still outside despite the cold.

He stared down for a moment at one protester, who was barely as tall as his shoulder. Jake could have broken the man's neck without even pausing. But he firmly grabbed the man by his arms and moved him to one side. As he did so, the protester started to complain, and Jake looked down at him menacingly.

"Fuck off," he snarled and the man backed off, allowing Jake to make his way to the waiting security guards on the embassy door.

The three guards watched as Jake walked towards them, before the most senior of the trio challenged him.

"David Miller. I'm expected." He gave the agreed name to be used within the embassy.

One of the guards went to check their tablet when a voice growled from behind them. "He's with me."

The guards turned to see John Travers walking slowly out of the doorway. The tall Scotsman looked Jake up and down. Not liking what he saw, he indicated that they should move inside. Jake, like Sam before him, struggled to keep up with the Head of Security, who led him through the embassy and into the lift that would take them up to the Ambassador's floor. Travers refrained from speaking until the metal lift doors closed.

"I take it David Miller is not your real name."

Jake remained silent and so Travers continued.

"If I remember correctly, the last time you were here you were called Harry Jackson."

Jake shrugged.

"You see, I've been in this job for quite some years, so I've seen all sorts of different people come and go. Before there were Caretakers, there were many others, but they all do the same thing. Last time you were here it was to deal with one of the previous ambassador's mistresses, I think?"

"They all merge into one," Jake lied, remembering full well the mistress who would not take no for an answer.

Travers shook his lined face. "You are all the same, young men who don't ask any questions. Just follow orders."

"There's a couple of women as well now."

"Such a diverse group," mocked Travers as the doors opened.

He led Jake through the now empty corridors of the embassy, its normal business closed for the night. Entering the Ambassador's offices, they went straight on through into the private room. Ambassador Angela Cooper was seated at her desk as the pair arrived. Travers allowed Jake to pass and take a seat across from the Ambassador, before shutting the door behind them. Jake studied the dark haired woman in front of him. Just another politician looking to climb the greasy pole, he decided.

"Mr Miller, thank you for coming in such quick time." Cooper attempted to sound friendly.

"It's all part of the service."

"Yes of course, you will have to forgive me as I've never worked with anyone from your... department before."

Jake did not reply.

"I take it you are fully up to speed on events?" Ambassador Cooper asked.

"Unless anything has changed in the past few hours?"

"No, I'm afraid nothing has changed since we found the hidden materials in Kate's flat."

Jake nodded and then made to stand up. "Ok then, I will start immediately."

Ambassador Cooper and Travers looked at each other, confused. Cooper asked the question they were both thinking. "Right, of course, is there anything else you need from us?"

Jake looked at her in confusion.

"Why would I? I take it my package has arrived?"

Cooper looked to Travers, who nodded in confirmation. "Indeed. I have it with the car you requested."

"Is the car traceable back to the embassy?"

"No, not directly. Someone on my team rented it out this evening from one of the local dealers."

Jake smiled for the first time since entering the office, putting the rest of them a little more at ease.

"Then I best be off. I'm sure you'd prefer it if I was out there searching for your missing secretary."

Cooper and Travers had no choice but to acquiesce, and the Ambassador quickly jumped to her feet, her hand outstretched.

Jake simply looked at the offered hand. Embarrassed, the ambassador sharply pulled it backwards. Instead, she attempted to put on her most confident smile, which looked pained rather than friendly.

"I must say Mr Miller, I am very relieved to have you on the scene so quickly. Ever since the repatriation officer found that bag inside Miss May's apartment, I've not stopped worrying."

Jake stared at her, his body tense. "Did you just say it was a repatriation officer who found the material?"

Travers answered. "Yes, he arrived this morning and helped us uncover Miss May."

Jake now turned to the Scotsman. Travers was surprised by the look in the caretaker's eyes.

"What was he called?" he asked, slowly.

"Sam Taylor," Travers told him carefully, unsure of what to expect in response.

Jake Taylor let out a bellow of a laugh and rubbed his forehead. "Bloody hell, and where is he now?"

Cooper and Travers looked at each other in confusion, each taken aback by the strange man's reaction.

"We don't know," Travers answered honestly. "After the case took this most recent turn…" he paused and eyed the ambassador, "we thought it was best that he was taken off the case. The fewer people involved, the better."

"We wanted to ensure that you had a clear run at things," Cooper added sheepishly.

"You kicked him off the case?" Jake asked incredulously. He was struggling to keep a straight face.

"Yes?" Cooper now looked positively worried. "Why, have we done anything wrong?"

"Absolutely bloody not," Jake chuckled. "Absolutely not."

The caretaker laughed aloud, and without another word, left the pair of them in the private office.

"Kicked off the case!" he said to himself, imagining his brother's face at being told he was surplus to requirements. But knowing Sam, there was very little chance he had actually left the case. It would have become a matter of pride to the bastard.

"I'll take you to the car." Travers caught up with him. "I put your delivery in the back."

"Thanks," said Jake, curtly.

Entering the basement car park, John Travers threw him the

keys to a black Golf and then indicated something in the rear of the car.

"How did they get that here so quickly from London?"

Jake walked over and opened the car door, checking the metal briefcase was visible on the back seat.

"Who said it came from London?"

Travers began to speak, but stopped. Jake sighed and climbed into the driver's seat before looking up at the Scotsman.

"We have them stored in a variety of places. You never know when you're going to need to clean up some embassy's mess."

Travers scowled and Jake started the engine then shut the door. He gave a final friendly wave and drove off into the Berlin night. Immediately hitting traffic and grinding to a standstill, he dialled a number on his phone.

The voice answered. "Hello Jake, what can I do for you?"

"I'm sorry to ring so late."

"It's not late, what can I do for you?" Jake always thought he detected a slight American accent when speaking with the unknown woman. Sometimes, he would spend time visualising her, hoping one day the real life version lived up to the image in his mind.

"I need you to track a phone for me."

"Go on."

"Sam Taylor. He works for the Foreign Office."

The voice paused, recognising the surname. "Taylor as in…?"

"Yes."

He could hear tapping on a keyboard over the line before his phone pinged.

"I've sent it to your phone, it will be live for forty-eight hours." She paused. "I take it this is the same Sam Taylor as…"

Jake interrupted her. "Yes, does it make a difference?"

"No, not to me. Just make sure it doesn't… get in the way."

The phone went quiet, leaving Jake to muse on what he had learnt. So, the embassy had given up on Sam and sent him packing. The fools, if anyone was going to find the missing Kate

May then it would be Sam. Christ, Sam had been in the city for nearly twelve hours. Jake expected him to have found her already.

The traffic came to a stop again, giving Jake a chance to look at the tracker on his phone. Sam was stationary in the Charlottenburg district. Jake altered his course. At the next set of lights Jake saw his brother was not only stationary, but inside a studio. Schafer Studio", read Jake, recognising the name from Kate May's apartment inventory inside the report. "What are you doing there?" Jake asked aloud to the empty car.

It had been years since he had seen his brother and the parting had not been pleasant. Their relationship had never been easy. Sam, the elder brother, was always the favourite and he felt like the youngest and forgotten child. Jake had decided long ago that brotherhood was not for them.

Arriving on Schafer's street, he drove down it, slowing as he went past the closed storefront. Now he was certain his brother was onto something. He noticed the lights from the first floor and figured that was where his brother was spending the night. Deciding to also call it for the evening, he drove to the pre-booked hotel and, checking Sam's tracker had not moved, fell asleep.

Waking before dawn the next day, Jake drove back to the store, where Sam's tracker had remained stationary. He debated with himself about breaking in and settling the case once and for all. But he decided he still had plenty of time, so it was best to see what his dear brother had planned. There was no way Sam would have stayed here unless he was with Kate. Whatever else Sam was, he was bloody good at his job. Jake parked the car a few yards down the road to watch the entrance to the store. The snow had stopped falling and the cold morning was causing the temperature in the car to drop. He kept turning the engine back on to let it reheat. Reaching behind him, he picked up the metal briefcase, entered the four-digit code on the digital lock and opened it.

Inside was his toolkit. The standardised equipment he would use on any job across the globe. From passports and credit cards to a variety of weapons, including two Heckler & Koch P30s complete with extra rounds and compressors. He put one of the P30s into a shoulder holster and slipped it on. His thick denim jacket blocked it from view.

The time went by and Jake sat waiting to see when his brother would appear. Pedestrians were now walking past on their way to work. The street next to him was becoming busier. The cold and the waiting were beginning to annoy him. He was not someone with the greatest of patience at the best of times. Perhaps his brother would like to be surprised inside rather on the street? If he was with Kate May then surely they would prefer to be met away from prying eyes. That settled it, he would head inside.

Leaving the car, he decided to try the rear of the building. The front of the store had clearly been locked up. Using the Maps application on his phone, he headed down towards the car park, which he knew led to the backstreet. As he walked, he noticed four men had just left the small car park. Their leader, dressed in a long grey coat and a pale blue scarf, seemed to give an order of some kind and one of the men turned back into the car park.

Something about the group seemed off. He eyed them as they passed by on the footpath. The leader of the three barely registered Jake's presence, but his companions glared up at him, the warning clear to be seen. Jake let them pass, but increased his pace. Something was happening. Jake could recognise an ambush when he saw one. Now jogging through the car park, he reached the entrance to the backroad and pressed himself against the wall. Peering round, he could see the fourth man walking away from him towards where he knew Schafer's store to be. He decided to follow, the fresh covering of snow helping to muffle the sound of his boots.

The man ahead of him stopped and stood outside what Jake

guessed was the door to Schafer's. Jake watched as he reached into his coat and pulled out a firearm. Now this made things interesting, thought Jake – whatever this was, it seemed Sam had got himself into trouble. Time for his little brother to come to the rescue.

Increasing his pace still further, he walked towards the waiting man who, distracted by his own mission, had yet to notice Jake. Reaching into his jacket he pulled out the P30. He was only six feet from his target when he was spotted. The waiting man turned in surprise to see the approaching caretaker. For a moment, the pair of them stared at each other when they were distracted by a noise from inside. His opponent's attention was drawn back to the building, the panic of not fulfilling his role overcoming him. It gave Jake the opening and he took two steps forward, smashing the butt of the pistol against the man's head. The unconscious body fell to the ground, face first into the snow.

Stepping over the body, Jake tried the door handle. It was locked. Moving back to give himself space, he raised the P30 and fired two shots before following up with a hard kick to drive the wooden door open. Looking inside, he saw the other three men from the street, a body beneath them. The one in the grey coat noticed him first, shouted and pointed Jake out to his companions, who wasted no time in firing their weapons. Jake stepped back and sheltered round the side of the door, the bullets flying past him. He hoped the body did not belong to his brother. A pause in the shooting allowed him to lean round and fire a few rounds in return.

Within the store, a shout had followed his last shot. The return fire lessened for a moment before resuming again. Jake waited, debating how to proceed. Fear for his brother was growing. He heard more shouting and then what he thought was a door opening then shutting. The shooting had stopped, a calm stillness seeming to have crept over the store. Above him, he could hear a voice. Looking up he could just see the shapes of two people on the rooftop. It was Sam and a young woman. He had hold of her and was speaking urgently. Jake watched on as his brother then turned and dragged the woman away. The fear of finding Sam dead now dissolved to be replaced with excitement. He looked back into the store, but found the studio space empty. Steps could be heard running up what Jake guessed were stairs to the first floor. Moving carefully, he stepped inside and crept forward. The sound of another door came from upstairs. At least one of the attackers was pursuing Sam.

Jake decided he would be quicker running down the street. Still running as he left the store, he felt himself slip on the snow on the pavement outside, having to grab hold of a lamppost to steady himself. Pausing for a moment, he looked around. Above him, he could just see Sam helping the woman up onto a ledge. On the street below them a car came to a screeching stop. Looking over his shoulder Jake saw one of the attackers helping the man in the grey coat inside. Blood was dripping down one of his arms. So that left just the one on the rooftop.

Ignoring the now escaping vehicle, he ran after his brother's pursuer. Somewhere above him, he guessed the other attacker was chasing Sam. A car engine came alive in the car park ahead and Jake increased his pace. Stepping into view, he was just in time to see Sam climbing into the passenger seat of a grey Seat. The woman noticed him first and shouted for Sam.

Jake's attention was broken as the pursuer appeared on the rooftop. An easy shot. Jake fired twice, watching with satisfaction as the figure fell crashing to land on a car below. Turning back to the car, Jake was pleased to see the shock on his brothers' face. He gave him a mock salute before stepping back and allowing their vehicle to pass. Now was not the time for a reunion, the bragging rights of being his saviour could wait. Driving past, the two occupants stared out at him in bewilderment and confusion. Inside, Jake was bursting with glee. He would remind his brother of this one for years.

"See you later, big brother," he said as he waved goodbye.

FIFTEEN

NEITHER SAM nor Kate spoke as they drove away from the scene. Both were still trying to process the events they had just witnessed. What the hell was Jake doing in the middle of Berlin, Sam asked himself over and over again? How could he have known where to look for him? But then another sickening thought gripped him. Whose side was his brother working for? True, Sam had seen Jake shoot at least one of their attackers, but that did not prove he had arrived without his own agenda. Sam closed his eyes and ran his hand through his hair. What the hell was going on?

Kate had driven the car out of Charlottenburg and now rejoined the main Bismarckstrasse out of the city. Sam suddenly remembered Otto Schafer and turned to look at his driver. Tears were dropping down Kate's cheek as she stared fixedly at the traffic ahead. The knuckles on her thin hands were white as she gripped the steering wheel.

"Kate?" he asked softly. When she did not respond, he tried again. "Kate, are you all right?"

Kate did not respond to him. Sam had seen this type of reaction before, it would take most people a significant amount of time to process the vision of watching one of their friends being shot down in cold blood.

He reached out and gently placed his hand on hers, careful not to alter the car's steering.

Kate's attention was finally broken, her hands shaking slightly on the steering wheel.

"Sam, what just happened?"

Sam sighed. "I think our Russian friends found you." He was careful not to mention his worry that they had followed him to her hiding spot, or even worse, that his own brother had led them there.

"Otto. We need to go back for Otto."

Sam shook his head and rubbed his thumb across the back of her hand.

"Kate, I'm sorry, but it's too late for Otto. He's gone and he wouldn't want anything to happen to you."

Kate's brain seemed to be trying to catch up on everything that had just happened by throwing out even more questions.

"Where are we going?"

"Keep driving for now. We need to think."

"Who were they, Sam? Why did they kill Otto?"

Sam sat back in his chair. The truth was, they had killed Otto to get to her, but that truth would not be helpful for her to hear right now.

"The Russians are trying to silence anyone who knows the truth."

"Oh my God," she murmured. "What are we going to do?"

"Like I said… for now, keep driving."

She did as instructed and continued on the main road for a time.

"It does prove one thing," Sam told her.

"What?"

"That you were telling the truth! Any doubts I had about you are well and truly gone now."

She let out a strained smile, but said nothing.

"Are you hurt at all?"

"No, I'm okay, just a little shocked."

Kate then remembered the man who had come to their rescue.

"Sam, who was the man who saluted you?"

Sam folded his arms. "I'm not sure you will believe me, in fact I'm not sure I believe me."

"What do you mean?"

"It was my brother."

Kate nearly crashed into the car in front.

"Jesus! Careful," warned Sam, gripping the roof handle to steady himself.

Kate steadied herself and brought the car back under control. "Your brother? You said you hadn't spoken to him in ages. Did you bring him?"

"No! I haven't seen him in years. Look, I'm as surprised as you are to have seen him."

"Why is he working with them?"

"I don't know if he is, he killed at least one of them that we saw."

"Then why did he turn up at the exact same time?"

"I don't know Kate, but I don't believe he would be working with the people who killed your friend. It's more likely he was there for his own reasons."

Kate snorted. "Which were?"

"I have no idea."

The car fell silent again, both inhabitants alone with their own thoughts.

Sam eventually broke the silence. "I'm so sorry about Otto, he was a good guy. He did not deserve what happened to him."

Kate gave a weak nod of her head.

"No, he didn't. He was a good, kind man."

"We will find who did this to him Kate, I promise." Sam did not know if his companion believed him, but no doubt she appreciated the sentiment.

Something about the morning's events bugged him. The whole

attack on the art shop had been too brazen, almost desperate, all just to eliminate a woman already discredited. They could have simply waited for Kate to have resurfaced at a later date and then quietly disposed of her. It wasn't as if she had anything explosive on the perpetrators. In fact, it was quite the opposite. They had only suspicions and guesswork to go on. The only tangible evidence Kate had was the little silver USB stick.

"Kate, did you bring the USB stick you showed me yesterday?"

She turned to give him a brief look. "Yes, it's in my jeans. Why?"

"I was just thinking it might be our only physical proof."

"Not my dead friend, then?"

"Yes and Otto, but make sure you keep that USB safe for now. We need to think about how we can access it safely."

It had to be the silver flash drive that had driven them to such an extreme course of action this morning. He thought about how he could get access to its contents, but the risk was too high. A USB like this would be loaded with protection, any false attempts could lead to the deletion of the data within. With his limited technical knowledge, it was simply not worth the risk. The best they could do right now was to keep it in their possession while they tried to figure out what to do.

Sam's phone beeped. Jake had messaged him.

> Olympic Stadium, 9pm opposite Gate B. There's a bratwurst and bier stand – I'll get the drinks in. Come alone.

"What is he doing?" Kate asked after Sam had read her the message.

"I don't know, like I said earlier, I've not spoken to him for years. I don't even know him anymore."

That was true. The brother he had grown up with was long gone. He had known that truth in Afghanistan. But could Jake have been out to kill him this morning? No. Plus, Jake could have killed them in the car park but instead had shot their pursuers, saving their lives.

"What are you going to do?" she asked him.

Sam looked down at the message again. "I think I have to go and at least speak to him."

She shook her head. "No, you can't! Like you said, you don't know him anymore."

"I have to Kate, he's my brother, and what other choice do we have?"

She shook her head in disbelief. "For all you know he's trying to draw you out to have you killed."

Sam did not reply. Memories of his brother flooded his mind. The days spent playing football and cricket in the garden. Adventures with their sister, walking up the heather covered moors of the Pennines. Family holidays all together, happy times, good memories. But then there was Afghanistan, the final stare that had come Sam's way as they had parted. Had that godforsaken country been enough to drive them irretrievably apart?

Before Sam could answer, the phone vibrated again as another message appeared on the screen.

> Dispose of the phone. They will track you through it now they know you're with her.

Sam swore, turned his phone off, opened his window and launched the device out into the Berlin traffic.

"Jesus Sam, what are you doing?"

Sam swore again, this time with venom. "You stupid bastard."

Kate gave him another sideways glance.

"What?"

"My phone. The Russians followed me to Otto's place. I'm the reason they found you."

Kate shook her head. "Trust me, I don't think they did."

Sam was taken aback by the response. He had expected her to be angry with him for causing the death of her friend.

"But they could have been tracking me."

Kate sighed. "When did you arrive in Berlin? Yesterday? That customer who Otto was expecting and met at the gallery, he had been speaking to him the day before that. I heard Otto on the phone to him and he tried to visit the shop on the day of the gallery event, but Otto was too busy. He was obviously just using Otto to get to me. The Russians must have guessed I was with Otto for days. It had nothing to do with your phone."

"Oh right, well I'm still sorry."

"Forget it, but I'm telling you I recognise that man. I just don't know where from. Anyway, that still doesn't tell me what you're going to do about your brother."

"I'll have to meet him, he's picked a public place at least."

"Yes a football match, Germany is playing France tonight so it will be very busy. Lots of witnesses. He chose well."

"Sounds about right. Jake was always the football fan in the family."

"I guess you were more the bookish sort?" she teased.

Sam ignored her jibe. "Either way, I'll meet him. What other choice do we have? We have no leads, no plan and nowhere to go. Perhaps he will be able to tell us more about our Russian friends."

"Or perhaps he will blow your head off this time."

"I don't think so."

They were now on the autobahn, heading north away from the city. The traffic was heavy with Berliners. Sam was already thinking what he could possibly say to his brother later that evening.

"So what do we do now?" asked Kate, still concentrating on driving. "There's hours yet before you have to be outside the stadium."

Sam thought for a moment. "We stick to our original plan. Let's turn back and hunker down at the Ritz. We have to stay somewhere, so it might as well be someplace nice."

Kate eyed Sam, a glint of her humour returning. "What, dressed like that?"

He looked down and saw that underneath his open parka he was still dressed in his now crumpled suit. "Fair point, but I don't fancy going back to my hotel now, either."

"In all the confusion I also managed to leave my bag at Otto's," confessed Kate.

"Well then it's time for Uncle Ivan to fund our adventures again," said Sam, reaching down into his pocket and pulling out the stolen euros.

Kate took the next autobahn exit and they drove around until they came across a retail park where the two of them were able to purchase new clothes. Sam, now dressed in a solid pair of boots, charcoal cargo trousers, a polo neck and three quarter zip jumper, all underneath the original parka, stood waiting for Kate as she finished buying her own items. Standing outside, he leant back against the storefront and looked up at the clear sky. The previous day's snow had been shovelled into piles, creating pathways between the stores. The door behind him pinged open and Kate stepped out to join him in the bright sunshine.

"All set?"

She half nodded, her pale face showing less of the pain of earlier. "Not quite, we need to find somewhere that sells a laptop or tablet of some kind."

Sam frowned at her.

"Why?"

"I told you. I want to find out who the man with the blue scarf was. I know I've seen him before."

"Right, if you say so. There's a tech store just back there."

Sam drove back towards the city centre. He had kept quiet while Kate had purchased the iPad, doubting whether her search would provide anything of use. But it would at least give her something to think about. He kept looking over at her from the corner of his eye. She had gone quiet again since getting back into the car, spending most of the journey resting her head on the palm of her hand and looking out of the window. He wondered about her state of mind after everything that had happened to her over the past few days.

He followed the signs for the city centre. He remembered the hotel was just off the Potsdamer Platz and so followed the main Bismarckstrasse back through the Tiergarten. He followed the traffic right up to the Brandenburg Gate before turning right down the Ebertstrasse.

Reaching over, he nudged Kate. "What do you think? Shall we call in on the embassy and say hello to the Ambassador and Travers?"

She looked at him and gave him a look of disdain only a woman could give a man when he was trying to be funny. "Very amusing. Do you actually know where you're going?"

He did not and so allowed her to direct him until they arrived outside a white stone-clad building. Three flags stood limply in the windless air, next to where a glass roof stretched out from the hotel's doorway, giving new arrivals shelter from the city's elements. Sam pulled the car into a layby where a uniformed valet came striding out to meet them.

"Well here goes, time for some high living," Sam grinned at Kate.

Stepping out of the car, he gave the valet the keys and a tip. Then, taking Kate's arm in his and their newly bought bags in the other arm, he strode confidently into one of Berlin's most prestigious hotels.

A couple of hours later Sam was laid out on a bed and Kate was sitting on one of the suite's sofas. He smiled at the memory of paying upfront for three nights in cash for one of their best suites. But the receptionist had frowned when Sam had failed to produce any identification for their stay. It had taken Kate's perfect German to 'explain' that they were lovers trying to avoid suspicious spouses, coming for a romantic city getaway to break the deadlock. A look of disapproval had followed, but so had a room key, as the receptionist accepted the story. In fact, Kate's lie had been so convincing that a bottle of Champagne had been delivered up to their room.

Empty plates now surrounded them both. Lying back with his head resting in his hands, Sam looked up at the ceiling, listening as Kate went about setting up her new tablet. Occasionally, she would tell him where she thought she might have seen the man with the blue scarf, as she drank from her glass. He tried to sound interested, and occasionally gave an encouraging grunt or nod, but the room service had been too good and too filling. The large hotel suite they were now in was just slightly too warm and the large double bed was far more comfortable than Otto Schafer's armchair had been. So when his eyes did finally close, he did not try to open them again.

SIXTEEN

THE EARLY JANUARY night had fallen by the time Sam was woken up by Kate. Unlike Sam, Kate had spent her afternoon in a fruitless search for their unknown attacker.

"I know he has something to do with the embassy Sam, I've seen him before," Kate told him as he wiped the sleep from his eyes.

"I'm sure you're right," Sam lied. "But I've no idea how you're going to prove that unless you're actually inside the embassy."

She shook her head before coming to sit next to him on the bed. Passing him the iPad she said, "He doesn't work there. But I think I've seen him at events."

"Right, and how does that help you?"

"If it was a public event, either at the embassy or run by us, then there would have been a photographer taking photos. You've met Angela Cooper. Do you think she ever misses a chance to push her profile?"

"Fair point."

"And guess which dogsbody has to book all of the photographers?"

"You?"

She nodded. "Exactly. I know all of them. So I've been

searching all of their sites, trying to spot our friend with the scarf."

Sam gave his companion a sympathetic stare. He knew she was trying to find anything to cling to. It was becoming more and more of a personal crusade to try and find the person who had killed her friend.

"Okay, well you can keep trying while I go out and see my dear brother."

Now it was Kate's turn to give a sympathetic stare. "Are you still planning on going, then?" She bit her lip in thought. "I just don't like it, Sam. I know he's your brother, but you have to admit, him turning up like that was…"

He interrupted her. "Was bloody lucky, considering the circumstances. You keep forgetting the three gunmen who were also there."

Kate scowled at him. "I didn't think you would be the type of person who believed in luck."

"In my business you need all the luck you can get. How else do you think I found you?"

"I still don't like it."

Sam swung himself off the bed, stood up and stretched his back.

"Look, he was there for his own business, which unless I meet with him we will never understand."

He turned to look back at Kate, still sitting on the edge of the bed. He was struck again by how attractive she was. She had released her brown hair from its tight bun. While he had been sleeping she had changed her outfit and was wearing a tight white shirt and shorts.

Sam looked again at his watch. "I'll have to get going soon. What are you going to do?"

She shrugged and took his spot on the bed, stretching her toned, bare legs out across the covers. "I suppose I'll just have to get room service sent up and keep looking for our friend online."

"I won't be long," he told her, picking up his jumper. "There's no way Jake can convince me to stay and watch football." Sam picked up his new boots then looked at Kate sprawled across the bed covers. He couldn't help but notice her long legs, ankles gracefully crossed. "You know there's another bed in this room?" he said, pointing out the untouched bed in the suite.

"I like the warmth of this one," replied Kate, without looking up from her tablet screen. Sam stared at her for a while with his hands on his hips and an eyebrow raised.

Reluctantly, he pulled himself away and left the hotel not long later, following the instructions Kate had given him to reach the Olympic Stadium. She had told him to catch the U2 U-Bahn train, which would take him all the way to his destination. If that failed then he knew he could always follow the crowds. From the moment he left the hotel he had spotted the tricolour of France being paraded by fans excited for the game. There was no prize for guessing where they were heading that night.

Stepping out of the station, Sam stuffed his hands deep into the pockets of the thick parka. The winter cold had returned with the arrival of nightfall. Joining the now buoyant crowd, he followed the stream of people along the pathway leading under the main road. Walking briskly out of the tunnel, he found the pathway now surrounded by bare trees on either side. Still, the crowd carried him along, just another wanderer in the sea of humanity. A group of supporters had begun a chant somewhere ahead of them. Their drunk voices were in high spirits as they sung in unison.

The crowd now came upon the main Olympic Place concourse, a wide open space leading directly to the stadium, which Sam could now see in the distance. Bright floodlights shone up from the oval stadium to light the night sky. Around him, the crowd had grown as more travel routes converged in the open space. Somewhere, a group of outnumbered French fans had started up a chorus of the La Marseillaise, the national anthem of France. The historic rallying call to arms of the revolution was soon drowned out by a chorus of boos and whistles.

Sam sighed and walked on through the crowds. Along the sides of the concourse stood a variety of concession stands and food stalls. The smells of beer and food drifted over and Sam felt his stomach rumble. He wondered if Jake was already following him. He doubted it, but if he *had* managed to spot Sam in this crowd then he deserved to remain hidden. Nearing the stadium, he peered up at the two tall stone pillars towering over him, from which hung the five rings that guarded the eastern entrance to the park. Standing directly below the pillars, he looked up at the rest of the stadium. In a city steeped in history, the refurbished stadium had seen its fair share of world events, from Jesse Owen's four gold medals in front a of livid Führer to the more recent 2006 FIFA world cup finals. Now it was playing host to a different type of grudge match – a Taylor family reunion.

A roar came from within the stadium. Sam guessed the first of the players had come out onto the pitch to begin warming up, which meant he was early. He knew from Kate's briefing that his rendezvous location was on the western side of the stadium, so he slowed his pace. Following the edge of the giant stadium, he wandered through the queues of ticket holders waiting to get inside before kick-off. Sam could see the stadium's designers had taken more than a little inspiration from the world's original stadium, the Colosseum in Rome. The 74,000 seat stadium was ever so slowly coming to life as the atmosphere grew in intensity.

Sam's trepidation was at peak levels as he walked closer to where he was to meet Jake. A tension pumped through his veins as he wondered how the night's events would play out. He was certain his brother meant him no harm, but if he was honest with himself, he was not sure he could believe the same about Jake's intentions towards Kate.

The crowds around him seemed to be thinning as the spectators filtered into the stadium. Taking a deep breath, he set off walking again, counting down the gates until he was opposite Gate B. Turning, he gazed through the thinning crowds towards the lone food stand, which advertised the traditional German bratwurst.

Now walking against the current of the crowd, he slipped his way amongst the hurrying football fans eager to take their seats before kick-off, until he reached the counter. The wide circular grill was still full of pork sausages sizzling in their fat. A cheery woman wrapped in a thick coat and dirty apron asked him what he wanted in a thick German accent. Sam shook his head and looked around to see where his brother had got to. He spotted him easily enough, just to the side of the food stall, perched on a high stool next to a tall metal table. Jake raised an arm to wave him over. Sam took a deep breath to steady himself and walked over to join him.

Jake was the first to speak, motioning to the beers on the table. "I guessed you'd be happy with an Erdinger?"

Sam climbed onto the opposite stool and picked up the beer. "Dad's favourite when he's trying to look cultured."

The two of them went silent as they drank, watching the last of the crowd make its way into the stadium.

"This is for you as well," said Jake, passing him over a bratwurst hotdog.

Sam took it. "Do I need to worry about poisoning?"

Jake raised an eyebrow. "Mate, really? We are going to start with that?"

Sam shrugged and took a bite.

"If I wanted to kill either you or the girl then I'd have done it this morning."

"Well, for all I know you could have tried."

Jake put the beer down on the table and leant over. "I bloody saved your life this morning. You could at least show some gratitude."

"Okay, I agree. You saved us this morning, so... thank you. I don't suppose you got chance to speak to any of them?"

Jake shook his head. "No, I went back and had a look at one I found in the alleyway, but he was as clean as a whistle. Nothing on him of any use to anyone."

"Is it possible to speak to him?"

The younger Taylor brother took a deep swig of his beer.

"Alas, Ivan is no longer available for a conversation in this world."

The elder brother sighed. "Perfect, thanks for that. I'd have liked to have had a chat with one of them."

Another silence fell between the two of them. Sam took a deep breath. "Okay Jake, what the bloody hell are you doing here? We don't speak for years and then suddenly you appear out of nowhere and…"

"And save your life."

"And save my life. But that still doesn't explain why you're here, or why you decided to start shooting up some Russian thugs."

Jake looked up. "So they are definitely Russian?"

"We think so. I'm guessing you already know all about the North Sea Deal case?"

"I do."

"So what the hell are you doing here, Jake?"

"Sir Jeffrey bloody Doyle."

"Sir Jeffrey?" Sam asked in surprise, hearing his own mentor's name.

"Of course it's bloody Sir Jeffrey, he was friends with Grandad Gerry, remember. When I left the army, he recruited me into his merry band of Caretakers rather than the fancy repatriation office."

"So Sir Jeffrey knows you're here, and he didn't tell me?" asked Sam, a little hurt.

Jake chuckled. "No, I don't think he knows. He's in the Caribbean still. Christ, I didn't even know you were here until those idiots in the embassy told me."

"Bloody hell," Sam shook his head. "What the hell is a Caretaker? I've never even heard of them?"

"You wouldn't have done. It's a kind of black ops department within the Foreign Office."

Now Sam laughed out loud. "Why the hell would the Foreign Office need a black ops team? They are just a load of diplomats! The spying should be left to MI6."

"It's not about spying, not normally. Our job is purely to look after our people sent out into the world working in our embassies. Are you telling me you would trust a load of young people with access to confidential information, out there alone in capital cities across the world, not to get into trouble? Just yesterday I was in Dublin helping some silly bugger who'd got caught with his trousers down."

"Blackmail?"

"Yes, the simple thugs sent the threats to his work account. It took information security the grand total of three minutes to call us in."

Sam tried to imagine his younger brother as some kind of underworld enforcer. Even with Jake's size and build, he still saw him as the skinny teenager who he could put on his back in the garden.

"Right, so I'm guessing you're here to find Kate May?"

"Bingo."

"And our friends in the embassy, namely John Travers and Ambassador Cooper, have instructed you to what... clean up?"

"Let's just say the embassy would be quite grateful to see Miss May out of the picture right now. It's not the best look if one of its staff members is a proven spy at such a time of tension."

"She's not a spy, Jake."

"That's not my problem. I'm just paid to make sure she goes away."

"Jake, she's not a spy."

"Sam, I know."

Sam was surprised at the ease with which his brother had come round to his way of thinking. "*How* do you know?"

"Well, I'm guessing you're not a paid up FSB informant, and if you trust her then that's good enough for me."

Sam smiled at the compliment, but he was a little taken aback by the trust his brother had just shown in him.

"Right, well I'm glad we're on the same page."

Jake rolled his eyes.

"That and the fact that the FSB doesn't send three goons in the middle of the day to take out one of their own."

"Oh," said Sam.

"Ha, you thought just because you trusted her, I'd automatically follow suit?" Sam frowned and took another bite of the bratwurst.

SEVENTEEN

TAKING two newly filled cups of beer, the two brothers headed off walking around the stadium. Every so often they would stop their discussion to listen as a roar from the crowd echoed from the stadium. Sam had just finished filling Jake in on his time in the city.

"And then *you* turned up and decided to make your grand exit," Sam summarised, "which leaves me with one question." Jake waited. "Just how did you manage to find us?"

"Through your phone. As soon as I knew you were in the city, I had you tracked." Sam stopped walking.

"Bloody hell, I didn't think about being tracked. I never thought anyone would care about what I was doing. I was out of the case, remember." Sam swore and continued walking with his brother. "So, now you've heard our side of things, do you still believe Kate is not a spy?"

Jake shrugged.

"Sam, if she didn't bring in the USB then who did? It would have to be someone else, and by the sounds of it that can only be Travers or the actual Ambassador, which would take this whole mess to all new levels."

Sam didn't reply at first. "I believe her. Like you, I don't think the FSB guns down their own like that in broad daylight. They'd be far more discreet."

"Then who is it? Who's behind all this? Travers or Cooper?"

"I don't know… and to be honest, I've not got a plan yet, bar keeping Kate alive."

They had to move to one side as a line of stewards were led past them into the stadium. Two policemen brought up the rear, and the two brothers turned their backs as casually as possible, hoping to avoid any unwelcome attention. The night air was making Sam's lips dry. He thought of Kate alone in the warm hotel room. He steadied himself as he prepared to ask the question he had been fearing.

"Now you've heard all that, what are you going to do?"

Jake laughed. "I'll follow you back to wherever you're staying, kill the girl and then fly back home."

Sam punched the younger Taylor's arm. "I'm bloody serious, Jake. I need to know."

"I don't know, you don't normally get any grey areas in this job. It's not like I can ring a controller back in London and have my orders changed based on a relative's whims."

"What about Sir Jeffrey?"

"He's still in the Caribbean."

"Well, what have you told the embassy?"

"Just that I'll sort it."

Sam drained his cup and placed it in a nearby bin.

"You can't go back to them right now," he stated the somewhat obvious. "If we are right then one of them is working with the people you killed this morning. They won't be happy to see you."

Jake thought about that for a moment. "But surely they would have to accept that I was trying to stop a clear FSB led attack?"

"To your face, but you can bet they'd be after you the moment you left the building."

"Damn it. Can't argue with that."

"Looks like by saving us, you've screwed yourself over."

Jake scowled, a look which brought years of memories flooding back.

"Look, don't worry about it. You've just managed to get yourself onto the winning team."

"*Are* we winning?"

"Sure, they just don't know it yet."

They had arrived back at the main concourse, which led back to the train station.

"I want to meet the girl," Jake told him.

"I'll have to ask Kate about that, after today she may be a little shaken up."

Spotting a concrete bench, they sat together looking up at the stadium.

"It feels a long way from home," commented Jake. "When did you last see everyone?"

"I went up for Christmas," Said Sam, thinking of the family Christmas back home. The missing presence of Jake had been the elephant in the room. "What about you? When were *you* last home?"

Jake sighed and looked up at the sky. "I don't know, a year or maybe two ago. I saw Mum and Dad once in London."

"We've not been the best sons, have we?" said Sam, trying to make the younger man feel better.

A huge cheer shook the air and they both looked up.

"Germany beating France?" Sam asked.

"Probably."

"I'll speak to Kate tonight about you meeting her. I would certainly appreciate your help," said Sam, bringing the conversation back round to the problem at hand.

"You would?" Jake was surprised.

"Yeah, you're pretty useful in a fight – and a bigger target than me."

"Bastard."

Sam pointed at the scars on Jake's head. "That looks to have healed well."

Jake touched his face. "It's not stopped me winning any beauty contests yet."

Sam laughed and stood up, stretching. "Meet me tomorrow outside the Potsdammer Platz station, there's a monument to the Berlin Wall just outside. Be there for 8am and I'll take you to meet Kate. We can then decide what we do next."

The two brothers gave one another a brief nod goodbye, neither much used to big physical gestures. Sam was surprised to have found he had enjoyed the reunion. He took the train back to the hotel. Still, he thought about Jake and the stranger he had become over the years. He tried to imagine the carefree youngster he had once known as this cold blooded killer acting as the Foreign Office's faceless caretaker. It made him shiver at the thought. Why had Sir Jeffrey Doyle not even told him about it? In fact, why had such a close family friend ever thought that Jake would be a perfect fit for such a role? A flash of anger erupted within and Sam felt his hands clench. He would be having a stern word with the diplomat next time they met. It wasn't that he disagreed with the concept of the Caretakers, he had seen enough of the world to know there was a place for such people. He just wished his brother was not one of them.

Arriving back at the hotel, Sam called first at the hotel's bar to pick up two gin and tonics and leave instructions for another round to be delivered up to the room in thirty minutes. Carrying the two chilled glasses up to their room, he opened the door to find Kate dressed in a dressing grown and watching television. She jumped up expectantly as he pushed the door.

"I wondered when I'd be seeing you again!"

Sam shrugged and handed her one of the glasses. "Well, I didn't stay to watch the game."

"You missed a good one. The French came from behind to win."

Based on his past experience with football, Sam doubted he would lose any sleep over the disappointment. He took off his parka before pushing Kate's legs from the sofa so he could sit next to her.

She stared expectantly at him.

"So how was it?"

"Well, he didn't shoot me."

"That's good, but what did he say?"

Sam took a sip of the gin.

"Just that he's been sent here to kill you."

"Great – add another one to the list."

Sam chuckled and went about telling her about his meeting with Jake.

"I've never heard of the Caretakers before," wondered Kate.

"You wouldn't have. I bet only the security teams and the actual ambassadors are made aware of their services. You can't exactly advertise a bunch of hired thugs across the Foreign Office's websites, can you?"

"No I guess not, but still, how do they get away with it?"

"How does any government get away with things? Plausible deniability. Find the right type of people who are willing to get their hands dirty, pay them well, then keep them far enough away from you to be able to deny having even heard of them."

"It sounds horrible."

The moment he had finished speaking, he thought of Jake and the type of person Sir Jeffrey had seen him to be. He pushed the thoughts away.

"But Jake's not like that. I think we can trust him."

"You're sure about that?"

"He wants to help us. He asked if he could meet you tomorrow."

"And you said?"

"I said I'd ask you. I'm only here to help you, to keep you safe while things blow over. If you so choose, we could spend the next few days moving from hotel to hotel until the North Sea Deal is signed and things have calmed down a bit?"

"Or we can start hunting the people who are actually behind this," said Kate, a gleam in her eyes as she drank from her glass.

Sam studied her for a moment, trying to guess what lay behind her words. "I take it your evening was successful?"

"Very."

"You found the man in the grey coat and scarf?"

"Indeed."

Sam was impressed. "Who is it?"

She reached down over the arm of the sofa and retrieved her tablet. Switching the screen on, she handed it to Sam. "Miklós Rövid. He's a Hungarian antiques dealer in the city."

Sam took the tablet and looked at the screen. A small group of people were huddled together dressed in evening wear and holding Champagne flutes. All were smiling broadly up at the camera. In the middle of the group stood the podgy faced bespectacled man. Without his grey coat and blue scarf, Sam only recognised him from the round spectacles, which looked like they'd been pressed hard into the man's face so as to stick against the skin. Scrolling down the page he read the caption, placing the group at the British Ambassador's winter charity dinner the year before.

"I knew I'd seen him. It took me a while, but there we are. Miklós Rövid is a generous benefactor who made a significant donation to that night's auction. A painting, if I remember correctly."

Sam didn't reply. Instead, he was flicking through the rest of the images from that night. He spotted Rövid a few more times, in each photo surrounded by different individuals.

"Did you spot anyone else familiar in the first photo?" asked Kate.

Sam quickly scrolled back up to the original photo and zoomed in. He did not recognise anyone else within the small group. "No?"

"Top left. It's only the back of a head, but it's definitely him."

Moving the screen until he was looking at the back of a man's head, Sam knew in an instant the tall frame with its greying blond hair.

"Travers."

"Travers," confirmed Kate.

Sam handed the tablet back. "Doesn't necessarily mean anything."

"No, but it's a black mark against him."

Sam rubbed his eyes, the strain of the day's events beginning to take effect. He looked down at the green ringed watch and wished he was asleep in one of the two queen-sized beds behind him.

"Right, so what do you want to do?" he asked her.

"I found Rövid's shop online, it's in the east of the city. I think we should go and pay him a little visit."

"And what? Avenge Otto?"

She scowled. "Is that such a bad thing?"

Sam shrugged. "I've not got a problem with that, but bearing in mind right now that your, no *our* only goal is survival, walking into a known FSB agent's shop may not be the best idea."

"That's why we should take your brother."

Sam openly laughed. "You've changed your tune!"

She did not look amused. "This was before we knew who Rövid was and whose side Jake was on."

"So, now the hunted becomes the hunter? I like your spirit Kate, but you're forgetting we are still dealing with highly trained FSB killers. I can't promise to protect you."

"That's why we need a trained killer of our own."

Sam sighed and ran his hand through his hair. This conversation had not gone the way he'd planned it. He had not had a problem with Jake meeting Kate, but the thought of the two of them shooting their way across the city was disconcerting.

"I don't like it, Kate."

Kate now glared at him. "You just said you trust him."

"I do."

"Well, if you trust him then that's good enough for me."

"A minute ago, you didn't trust my judgement about visiting Rövid? Now you're back to being on my side?" He raised an eyebrow.

Kate May stood up, her pale, beautiful face staring down at him.

"Yes, because now you're helping me with my plans. Now Sam Taylor, tomorrow morning I am going to meet with your brother and then we are all going to pay a little visit to our FSB friend."

She stood there in the white hotel branded dressing gown, daring him to challenge her.

Sam sighed and downed the rest of his drink. "Then I'm going for a shower. If we are going to do this, I need a good night's sleep. Something you don't get on a sofa."

Later that night, as he lay there staring up at the ceiling processing the day's events, he heard the sheets of the bed next to him move and then felt his own lift slightly as the slim figure joined him. Tentatively, her palm rested on his bare chest. He lifted her palm and kissed it, then kissed each of the fingers. He felt her relax next to him, her body moving closer to his. Gently, he pulled her towards him and kissed her mouth.

Later, as she lay on him, his fingers running down her naked spine, he asked her the question that had been on his mind since the night before. "When we visited your apartment, Hendricks said he used to see you with someone… a man… a boyfriend?"

She stirred slightly, her thick dark brown hair splaying out softly on his chest. "Yes. He was."

"Was?"

She tilted slightly to look up at him, her pale face beautiful in the moonlight breaking through the gaps in the curtains. "You think I'd be lying here in your bed if he was still my boyfriend?"

"Fair point. What happened?"

"He left."

"Just left?"

"Just left."

They stared at each other, a stand-off in the moonlight. In the end she relented. "What do you want me to say? I met a guy, fell in love, quit my high paying consultancy job so that I could take an embassy secretarial post to stay in a foreign country just to be with him. Faked a whole resume, changed my entire life, only for him to go back to his wife in Hamburg. Which left me stuck in a soulless job that I just couldn't motivate myself to leave."

Sam stopped stroking her spine and instead brought his hand up to her cheek. The explanation made sense. He thought back to the desk and flat, devoid of any personal effects. It was almost as if Kate had been determined not make her stay in Berlin permanent.

"I'm sorry."

She grabbed his fingers in hers. "Why? It was his loss and its now just another scar."

Sam lifted her clasped hands to his lips. "Speaking from experience, I couldn't agree more. It's definitely his loss."

Kate May, once missing now found, raised an eyebrow. "I thought you were looking for a good night's sleep?"

EIGHTEEN

SAM WOKE EARLY the next morning. He lay still in the middle of the sheets and listened to the soft breathing of the remarkable woman next to him. Turning his head slowly, he looked over at Kate as she slept. He had grown to admire her in the short time they had spent together. The events of the last few days would have been enough to have crushed even the hardiest of people and yet here she was, still fighting, still believing. In the early hours of the morning, she had told him more about Otto Schafer, their close friendship and her guilt about his death. How he had been the one to pick her up after the failure of her relationship. Sam had gently wiped away her tears until she had fallen asleep.

Now, lying in the creeping rays of light emanating from around the curtains, he let his mind wander. His instinct told him this would be a crucial twenty-four hours. If they could survive until this time tomorrow, he was sure they would be past the moment of greatest peril. If the Russians were unable to stop the North Sea Deal today then, quite simply, they would never stop it. He just wished Kate would give up on the idea of hunting Rövid. Let the bastard waste his time searching for *them*, instead. There was no need for them to walk into the lion's den. But then another thought forced its way into his consciousness. Whatever else happened, there was still a spy to be found within the British Embassy, and they were no closer to finding them. Could he return home knowing that someone had betrayed them? Or worse, would the spy *allow* them to return to London safely? The question still eluded him. Was it Cooper or Travers, or the both of them?

"Bugger," sighed Sam, rubbing the sleep from his eyes.

They would have to go. If they were to fully exonerate Kate and ensure their own safety then they needed to find the spy. And it was a spy so established in the hierarchy of the British Embassy that they knew they could operate with absolute freedom.

Sam swore again and sat up, allowing the sheets to drop down around him.

Kate stirred sleepily. "What time is it?"

Sam looked at his Rolex.

"Seven. I'll order us some breakfast to the room before I go and fetch Jake."

She rolled over, wrapping her shoulders further into the sheets. She looked up, staring at him.

"Have you decided to accept I'm right about paying Rövid a visit?"

Sam ran his hand through his light brown hair.

"Yes, but I'm not happy about it. I'd suggest putting it to a vote, but I already know Jake will side with you."

"Because I'm right?"

"No, he'd do it to just piss me off. If I said these sheets were white," he bent down and grabbed the white bedsheets in both hands, pulling them off Kate and the bed, "he'd swear blind they were black."

Kate shrieked with laughter and rolled off the bed, covering her nakedness. "You bastard, I was comfy!"

Sam grinned back at her. "Time to get up, May."

Walking out of the glass doors of the hotel, Sam nodded at the waiting valets as he headed down to the Potsdamer Platz station. The snow from the day before was still settled on the ground all around him. Not cold enough to turn to ice, nor warm enough to become slush, the piled snow still had a crisp white freshness about it. The skies above were grey with low hanging clouds, the threat of additional wintery weather still looming over the city. Sam once again pushed his hands further into the parka's pockets and tried to ignore the elements.

The station lay just over the road from the hotel and Sam deftly made his way through the traffic to the central reservation. A square glass building covered the escalator which led down into the station. Sam walked to the left of the building, to where the five graffitied remnants of the Berlin Wall stood as a permanent reminder of what was thankfully a non-permanent time in the nation's history. There was no sign of Jake. Sam checked his watch, seeing he was a few minutes early. He knew that his brother would be close, probably watching him from somewhere, planning his entrance.

Sam decided to make things easier for Jake and went to lean against the corner of the station building. His back was now turned to the five standing monuments. Watching the Berlin traffic, he began to count in his head as the seconds went by. It took less than two minutes before he heard the familiar voice behind him.

"All right, mate? You know you stand out like a proper tourist?"

Sam turned to see the looming figure of Jake staring down at him. He was still wearing the blue beanie and a thick denim jacket.

"And what about you? Are you wearing Lederhosen underneath the cowboy jacket?"

Jake shrugged and pulled open the jacket to reveal a hidden holster, the butt of a pistol visible within.

"Easier to get this out from one of these."

"All right Clint Eastwood, let's not scare any of the locals."

Sam spotted a small bag hanging from his brother's shoulder. He pointed to it. "Are you planning on going shopping?"

Jake pulled a face. "Not everyone in this city accepts payment in cash."

Sam knew Jake was wanting him to ask who or what he was referring to, but he refused to be drawn in.

"Come on, you said you wanted to meet Kate."

The two of them retraced Sam's steps back to the hotel.

"What's the plan for today?" asked Jake.

"Kate found out the identity of one of the attackers from yesterday. She wants us to pay him a little visit."

Jake chuckled. "And I'm guessing you don't?"

"Not really, but I can't think of anything better to do."

"I think we should."

"Don't start."

They walked through the glass doors and into the lobby. Most of the other hotel guests were heading in the opposite direction on their own individual journeys into the city.

"Nice place, guessing you paid with the Russian funds?"

"You don't think I'd be paying for a place like this myself?"

A uniformed staff member gave a polite greeting as the two of them headed to the lifts.

"Good God, no. A bed and a room to sleep in is the same in a five star and a three star," Jake quoted their father.

Sam pressed the button for the top floor and the doors came together.

"But the most important question is, did you get two rooms?" Jake asked slyly.

Rolling his eyes, Sam answered, "No, it was safer to stay together."

"And you were a gentleman and slept on the floor?"

Sam ignored him, impatient for the lift doors to open. Following the corridor, he stopped outside their room and knocked three times. Kate was now fully dressed. She opened the door and let the two brothers inside.

Sam walked into the room to stand next to the window while Jake made himself comfortable on the sofa. Kate perched on the desk.

"Kate, this is my brother Jake," Sam introduced them.

Jake waved. "I know what you're thinking. I got the looks and believe me, our sister got the brains."

"Which left Sam with the?"

"Nothing, he is what we call the runt of the litter."

Kate laughed then went over and shook Jake's hand. "Nice to meet you, Jake – and thank you for coming to help us."

Jake sank back into the sofa and crossed his legs.

"Believe me, it is my pleasure. It's not every day I can come to the rescue of my brother and a beautiful woman."

Sam's patience was really being tested. "Okay Jake, reel it in, we have a job to do. Kate, do you want to tell him about Rövid?"

Kate nodded and, tablet in hand, came to sit next to Jake. Sam watched on as she took his brother through the plan for the morning. They would drive east of the city before entering Rövid's store. Kate held out the tablet and was showing Jake the same pictures as Sam had seen the night before. She had tied her hair back in a simple ponytail, which allowed her sharp facial features to stand out. There seemed to be a lightness within her today, which Sam had not seen before. It was as though some of the stress of the past week had somehow been washed away now that she had found a way of fighting back.

"And after we find him, is it a simple case of two shots to the head and job done?" asked Jake.

"No!" answered Sam, cutting off any response from Kate. "We are not walking in and shooting him in the head. We need to find a way to end this which exonerates Kate and protects the North Sea Deal. Shooting a Russian spymaster in the head does not help us achieve either of those objectives."

Jake pretended not to have heard him. "What we need is a

codeword. When you say it, I'll take Rövid out and then we grab anything of value before heading back here for cocktails. How about 'popcorn'?... Hold on a moment." He peered more closely at the image. "Actually, I think I may have already shot this one."

Sam frowned. "You did?"

Jake took the tablet from Kate and zoomed in. "Yes, he was definitely there yesterday, but the last time I saw him he was being helped into a car. I think I caught him in the arm."

Kate looked up at Sam. "I have to say I find your brother far more exciting than you."

"Then see how far following him gets you." Sam looked at his watch. "Come on, we need to get moving if we want to be there for opening time at ten."

The three of them left the hotel and waited for the valet to bring the car round. Kate got into the driver's seat, with Sam next to her in the front. Jake climbed into the rear. They drove quickly, making good time through the city centre before heading east towards the Lichtenberg district. It was a place Sam knew as once having been the location of the headquarters of the East German state security services, the Stasi. Not the best omen, he thought, as Kate drove through the traffic.

Pulling off the main road, she steered through a number of side streets, pulling up on a wide tree lined road filled with store fronts. The morning rush hour had begun to fade away as commuters reached their destinations, leaving only small numbers of shoppers slowly making their way between stores.

"That's the one, over there," Kate told them, pointing out a dull looking storefront nestled between a music shop and a café.

Sam followed her directions and read the purple signage overhanging the window. "Antiquitäten und Kunst?"

"Antiques and Art," Kate translated.

"Not the most creative is he, our Rövid?" dismissed Jake.

"It does the job," replied Sam, dryly.

"It's still locked down," commented Kate, indicating the heavy metal shutters over the window.

"Perhaps he's not fit to come to work after yesterday?" wondered Jake.

"No, I bet that store is the central location for everything he does. He will operate his network from there rather than his home. Which means that he will need to be here in case he's needed for something today," surmised Sam.

Jake nodded in agreement. "*Especially* today. I spoke with my people this morning and the North Sea Deal is very close to being signed. If the Russians are going to stop it, then they know they'd better do it soon."

The car fell silent as they watched on, waiting to see what would happen as the minutes ticked by. Sam's eyes kept darting from the street ahead of him to the wing mirror, to watch the people approaching from behind. His heart leapt at the sight of a figure in a grey coat walking towards them and the store, but he was disappointed to see the figure was too young to be Rövid. The time was now only one minute to ten and the tension in the car had grown unbearable.

"Perhaps he's already inside?" pondered Jake.

"Maybe, but I can't see any lights on. Give it another five minutes and we can check. But it would be easier to just walk in as customers than trying to break down the door," said Sam.

Kate's voice cut across him. "There, over there, getting out of the taxi on the other side of the street!"

All three of them turned to watch a familiar silver-haired figure climbing from the back of a parked taxi. He was no longer wearing the grey coat – instead, he was dressed in a dark jacket – but wrapped tightly around his neck was the distinctive blue scarf.

"That's him," confirmed Sam, thinking of the previous occasion their paths had crossed.

"Bastard," Jake grunted.

"You were right about the arm," observed Kate. "He's wearing a sling."

"That doesn't make a difference. I've killed people with one arm before."

Sam turned in his seat and stared at his companions in turn. "I'm telling you both for the last time, you do not shoot him. If you do, all you're doing is condemning Kate… and probably us, too."

Jake gave Kate a wink. "Remember 'popcorn'."

"No, we cannot shoot him until we know Kate is safe and exonerated."

"Yeah I know that, but *he* doesn't," replied Jake.

The three of them waited until Rövid was inside and had rolled up the shutters before exiting the car. None of them spoke as they crossed over to the antiques shop. Sam tensed his hands into fists inside his jacket pockets. A nervousness had crept in as he walked up to the door. Taking his hands back out into the cold air, he knocked twice on the window, pulled the door outwards and stepped into the Hungarian spymaster's den.

NINETEEN

SAM STEPPED INTO THE STORE, followed by Kate, with Jake close behind. The room had a distinct musty smell, which attacked his nostrils from the moment he walked inside. All around him were piled a variety of antiques, from furniture to ornaments, all covered in a thin layer of dust. Mixed in amongst the odd collection stood a selection of World War Two memorabilia. A mannequin stood dressed in a Russian helmet, with a German greatcoat over an American GI uniform.

The three of them made their way further inside, to a desk filled with papers next to an old fashioned till. The last payment price was still displayed on the small glass screen. A large leather sofa stood directly opposite the desk, the green material well worn.

A voice called out from the back in German just before the figure of Miklós Rövid came into view. He was dressed in a smart brown suit, the top two buttons of his shirt left open. His right arm, while still in its sleeve, was tied to his chest in a black strapped sling. The chubby face, with its rimless glasses seemingly squashed on, showed little surprise at seeing the three new arrivals. He paused for a brief moment and then continued to make his way into the middle of his store.

"... Or would you prefer me to say, 'Good morning my friends'?" He greeted them warmly in accented English. The three of them did not reply and Rövid continued. "I must say I'm surprised to find you here this morning. I would have thought you would have been in hiding, or even attempting to leave the country, after what happened yesterday."

"Sorry to disappoint," said Sam.

"Quite, come let us talk. Please take a seat." He gestured at the leather sofa while taking a high-backed chair behind his cluttered desk. "I would have offered to shake your hands, but I'm sure you understand." He gestured at the strapped arm. "Your handiwork, Mr Caretaker. Thankfully only a flesh wound, but a painful one, I can tell you."

Jake smiled. "To be totally honest I was aiming for your head."

Sam took the offered seat and sat directly opposite their host. Kate, her face full of unconcealed contempt, simply sat on the arm of the sofa. Jake continued to wander around the store.

"I guess I'm speaking to Miklós Rövid?" asked Sam.

"Indeed, and in return I take it I'm speaking to Sam Taylor of the Repatriation Office, his brother Caretaker Jake Taylor and the delectable fugitive Kate May?"

Score one to the Hungarian, thought Sam, impressed he knew of the family connection.

"Yes on all fronts," replied Sam.

Rövid smirked and rubbed his chin. When he spoke again it was at a slow, steady pace. A heavy accent made the words sound clumsy. "Interesting. I've never met a Repatriation Officer before, or a Caretaker. It's like I have Sir Jeffrey Doyle's entire world right in front of me. How *is* the old trickster?"

"Enjoying his retirement."

Rövid laughed. "He's about as retired as I am. Don't be a fool, boy. And don't try to treat *me* like one."

Sam, irked by the condescending comment, forced himself to let it slide.

Kate, however, did not. "How dare you? How *dare* you sit here and lecture us after what you did?"

Rövik turned his eyes to Kate. "Pardon?"

"You sit there acting all pious, when you're nothing more than a petty murderer."

Jake had stopped browsing and turned to listen as Kate accused their host. But the Hungarian did not seem to be upset by Kate's words.

"I take it you are referring to what happened yesterday at Herr Schafer's studio? That was unfortunate, but really I'm not sure you can blame me, Miss May. It was not me who dragged the young man into all this, was it? Perhaps a mirror for your purchase today?"

"You piece of shit!" Kate jumped from the chair arm towards Rövik.

A loud clang interrupted her, and she stopped mid-flight, then froze, as they all looked back to see Jake had dropped a metal tray. The noise had jilted Kate from her anger.

"Sorry about that. It slipped," lied Jake.

Sam reached forward and pulled Kate back to sit down next to him.

"Right, enough of this Rövik, let's not waste each other's time."

"Agreed, Mr Taylor. I think it's fair to say you are the brains of this little outfit."

"You are doing Kate a disservice. It wasn't me who found you."

Rövid gave Kate a slight bow. "My congratulations."

Sam was losing his temper. He did not like the man's arrogance.

"What are you playing at? You seem pretty confident for a spy who's been discovered. How do you know I'm not going to let my brother over there shoot you again?"

Again, Rövid laughed, he was enjoying himself. "For a start, you are not here to kill me. If you were, you would have done it already. In addition, you *cannot* kill me, because doing so would only condemn you all to a life on the run. Either my people or your own people would eventually catch up with you."

Sam did not disagree. It was exactly as he had told Kate himself. "And for the finish?"

Rövid sat back and waved his uninjured arm. "You call me a spy? I am many things, but I am not a spy."

This time Sam laughed aloud. "You're not? You could have fooled me."

"Mr Taylor, there are no spies left in this city. Years ago, you could not move for them. Our people, your people, all spying on each other, desperate to know what the other person was thinking. Now? Espionage is dead. A noble art gone, extinct from the world."

"Really? After everything that's gone on this last week, you sit here claiming espionage is dead? What does that make you then, a simple businessman?" challenged Sam.

"It makes me an influencer."

"What, like an Instagram model?" Jake called out from behind a shelf. "You don't look like the ones I've seen."

Rövid nodded. "Indeed, an influencer. A spy was someone who would be tasked with finding out the other side's secrets. But in this age of technology, what is there left to find out? We all know each other's secrets, our ambitions, our strengths and weaknesses. Why spend our taxpayers' money on something as simple as espionage?"

Sam looked on, unsure what Rövid was getting at – and more importantly, how it all fitted in with their own situation.

The older man seemed to be enjoying himself, having all three of his visitors listening to his lecture. "My friends, people like me are influencers. Our job is to help direct others to achieve our mutual goals. To reach out and tap into the minds of millions, to shape their outlook on life until they don't even recognise their own interests anymore. It is mind control without the science fiction."

"You're talking about information warfare? The social media disinformation campaigns, the fake accounts, bot factories, fake news, AI, all of that? How else does an old man in an antiques shop influence the minds of millions?"

"Like you said, I'm just an old man, but I have my uses. One thing we allies of Russia are very good at is playing the long game. It's all good having the technology, but every so often you just need that human touch to make it personal. A little win here, a little nudge there and before you know it, we have something very special in our hands."

Now, Sam was confused. This was not what he had been expecting. All this talk had thrown him. What did it have to do with Kate, or the North Sea Deal?

It was Kate who asked the question. "Then why have you dragged me into this sordid world?"

"My dear Kate, I did not drag you anywhere. It was you who picked up that USB, not me. No one asked you to."

"So I should have let your agent finish the job?"

Rövid looked at her in confusion. "That's exactly what I would have done. Self preservation young lady, is paramount. Always remember that."

Sam ran his hand through his hair, scratching his head.

"I don't get it. You sit here claiming not to be a spy, rather this modern day influencer, but then you essentially admit to being involved in trying to steal industrial secrets? I don't see how your influencing machine will be able to stop the North Sea Deal. None of the governments involved are going to stop it just to please an online climate campaign."

"Maybe, maybe not. We still have to keep *some* secrets, don't we, Mr Taylor?"

"Like the identity of your embassy insider?" asked Kate.

For the first time that morning, Rövid looked confused. "You mean you don't know? After all this, you don't even have an inkling who placed that USB in the Ambassador's computer?" He chuckled. "Well now, this is a turn up, I was convinced you would have at least known that. I have to say I'm genuinely disappointed."

Sam did not like this man, his arrogance irked him. The temptation to let Jake finish the job he had started yesterday was steadily growing.

"So what now?" he asked. "What do you want from us? What will it take for you to let Kate go back to living her normal life?"

"What makes you think I can do that?"

Sam now stood to his full height. Towering over the seated Rövid, he slammed his hands down on the counter in front of him. "Because, you bastard, it was you or one of your men who framed her with that bag of shit hidden under her bathtub. You may claim not to be a spy, but I'm betting you know how to be one. So, take all this sanctimonious shit down a level and start talking, or I might let butter fingers back there take the lead." He pointed at Jake, who on cue dropped a photo frame to the ground, smashing it.

Rövid seemed unmoved by the show of force. "You want to talk business, Mr Taylor? Then please sit down. Sir Jeffrey would not like this side of you."

Sam took a deep breath, then did as he was asked.

"That's better, so that's what you want, yes? To just let Miss May go back to her normal everyday life?"

Kate was about to speak, but Sam stopped her. "Yes."

Rövid thought for a moment. "She won't be able to return to her old job. Agreed?"

Again, Kate was about to answer, but Sam got in there first. "Agreed."

The antiques dealer shifted in his chair. The light glinted off his rimless glasses as he considered the proposition.

Eventually, Rövid spoke. "I think we can arrange for Miss May to go back to England, but in return you must hand over that flash drive you took from the embassy. I trust that you still have it?"

Next to him, Sam felt Kate place her hand on her jeans pocket.

Rövid noticed it too and Sam quickly spoke to cover her movements. "We don't have it here," he lied and Rövid knew it.

Rövid gave him a knowing look. "I understand, but that is my one and final offer, Mr Taylor. If you simply return to me what is mine, I will return you all back to the life that was yours."

Sam and Kate looked at each other. Somewhere in the store Jake could be heard fingering another of Rövid's products.

"And that's it? You will just let her and us go?"

Rövid nodded. "Indeed. What else can you do to me? You said yourself you don't know anything else. Who would believe you if you did?"

Sam knew he was lying. Even if they did give up the USB stick, he knew the FSB would still want to silence them in case of any loose ends. But the question kept coming back to him. Why did they want the USB? The files weren't on it. Surely they could just give whoever their inside man was another stick to get what they needed?

He decided to ask the question. "Why do you want the USB? Can't you just replace it?"

Rövid now stood and moved to motion them out of his shop. "I have my reasons Mr Taylor, I think the terms are more than reasonable."

"We would have to go and retrieve it."

"I understand," Rövid replied, knowing full well his prize was in Kate's pocket. He looked past Sam to where Jake stood admiring himself in a Soviet era helmet.

"I'm not sure the Red Army would accept you."

Jake grimaced then took off the helmet and dropped it next to a porcelain vase.

Rövid flinched. "Careful you fool, that vase is worth three thousand euros."

Jake raised an eyebrow, but moved away.

Their host returned his attention to Sam and Kate. "I will give you until noon. If you return the flash drive to me here, I will ensure that you are able to return home tomorrow as a free woman. I give you my word."

Sam neither wanted nor needed this man's word. There was no chance he would be handing over the small silver device in Kate's pocket until he at least knew why he wanted it so badly.

Standing again, Sam reached down and offered Kate his hand to help her from the sofa. He gave Jake a brief nod and switched back to Rövid. "Thank you for your hospitality. We'll be in touch."

Kate pulled herself free from his grip and walked towards Rövid. "You may think that you are something special Mr Rövid, but my friend was worth ten of you. I swear whatever happens, you will pay for his death."

Sam tensed as the pair of them stared at each other. He was pleased that Kate was unarmed.

Without another word she walked out of the store. Jake followed her.

Miklós Rövid looked at Sam.

"I recognised you at young Schafer's exhibition. I can see what Sir Jeffrey sees in you."

Sam scoffed. "You speak as if you know him."

"The circles people like us hang around in are pretty narrow." Sam did not reply. "Perhaps you should ask yourself what it is he sees in you, and perhaps your brother. Is it not strange to have the two of you in such different roles? I wonder why?"

"Until next time, Herr Rövid," said Sam, walking towards the door.

But just as he reached the glass door, Jake walked back into the store. Gently pushing past him, he walked back to the expensive vase on its shelf. He picked it up, looked at Rövid and dropped it to smash into a hundred pieces.

"Influence that, you bastard," he grunted at the shocked Rövid as he walked outside with Sam.

Outside, Sam elbowed his brother. "That was a bit gratuitous, wasn't it?"

"I'll be honest, don't know what that means mate, but I can tell you that the bastard had it coming."

TWENTY

BACK INSIDE THE ANTIQUES STORE, Miklós Rövid shuffled over to the wide glass window that looked out. He leant against the thick glass to watch as his three guests walked the short distance back to their vehicle. Groping inside his pocket with his uninjured arm, he pulled out his phone and with some difficulty, typed in the number. A voice answered almost immediately. "Hello? What are you doing phoning me directly?"

"Guess who I just had the pleasure of meeting?" he answered.

"The Pope? How the hell am I supposed to know?"

Rövid watched on as the vehicle pulled away from the curb and into the Berlin traffic. Squinting through his glasses he made a mental note of the registration plate before it disappeared from view.

"I just met the two Taylor brothers and your missing Miss May."

The voice at the end of the line paused before asking, "And?"

Rövid chuckled. "Don't worry, you're safe for the time being. We were wrong – they don't have any idea as to your identity. It seems I gave the Taylor brothers too much credit. Sir Jeffrey Doyle must be losing his touch."

The relief at the end of the line was palpable even over the phone. "And what does this mean for us? The North Sea Deal will be signed any day now and we are no closer to getting what we need. What I need, Miklós."

"Relax, it will all be fine. I found out they still have the Griffin. I have offered to swap it for their freedom."

"How kind of you. I take it you only mean freedom from life?"

"Of course."

"We are playing with fire, Miklós. I've strived too long for this opportunity. Do you think it has been easy, waiting all this time to only see some stupid girl and two fools blow it for me?"

Miklós Rövid rolled his eyes and moved away from the window to retake his seat behind the wooden desk. He had run many agents over the years from this desk, but he had rarely met any as impatient as the one on the end of the phone right now.

"I know my friend, we both have. Let us wait and see if Taylor gives up the Griffin without a fuss. If he does, I'll have it delivered to you straight away. If he doesn't? Well, I have the registration of the car they are using. I can use some of my old contacts to locate them within an hour."

"Very well, I'll leave you to it Miklós, but beware there is a major diplomatic dinner tonight and I'll be on duty. It may not be that easy for me to get to a computer."

The old spymaster rubbed his eyes. "That is not my problem. I will leave that conundrum to you."

A loud sigh could be heard from the other end of the call. "Miklós..."

"Yes?"

"I don't want to see any of them alive again."

The line went dead and Rövid placed it on his desk. The wound in his arm hurt like hell and he had forgotten to take his painkillers in all the excitement of the morning. He had genuinely been disappointed, if not a little surprised, by the two Taylor brothers. Everything he knew of the great Sir Jeffrey Doyle had told him to expect great things from someone considered to be his protégé. Yet both of the Taylor brothers had seemed rather dull, bereft of any type of ingenuity he had seen over the years from their mentor. He rubbed his chin and pulled out a bottle of brandy, pouring himself a glass. The old days were fading, the new dawn was coming... and he would ensure it was a red sunrise.

Kate was struggling to keep control of her temper having walked away from the man who had killed her friend. Only by concentrating on the road ahead was she able to keep her hands on the wheel. Jake, meanwhile, was more concerned for his fellow passengers than himself. He had seen men like Rövid before and they only knew one code. Either they killed Rövid, or he would kill them. Looking at the back of his brother's head he wondered how long it would take for Sam to reach the same conclusion. For all his intelligence he could still miss the obvious. It was now a case of who would win this game of nerves, his brother or Miklós Rövid.

"What's the plan then?" Jake asked no one in particular.

"Well, we are not giving him the USB," replied Kate.

"Tell me something I didn't know."

Sam did not respond. Instead, he directed Kate to pull into a retailer's car park so they could talk. Kate did as she was instructed and parked the car in a far corner. Turning the engine off she turned to stare at the two brothers.

"Come on then you two, what just happened?"

Jake looked to Sam who answered. "I don't really know. I didn't think we'd solve all our problems by visiting Rövid, but I did not expect to leave with more."

"What do you mean?" asked Kate.

"Where do I start? The USB? The mole in the embassy? His offer? Or the fact that he seems to be the only one who knows what's going on?"

Kate frowned and looked at Jake, who shrugged. "Don't look at me! If you'd followed my advice, we'd have shot him by now."

Kate turned her gaze back to Sam. "Start with the USB. Why does he want it back so badly? Surely it's just a replaceable storage device?"

"I'm as confused as you are. Do you still have it?"

She pulled it from her jeans pocket and passed it to Sam, who passed it straight to Jake.

"Any ideas?" he asked him.

Jake took the device but shook his head.

"We can't give it to him Sam," warned Kate.

"Agreed," said Sam.

"Rövid wouldn't have kept his word anyway," commented Jake. "You've seen and learnt too much to be kept alive. He would have had you killed the moment you had handed over the device. Even if it was to just protect his agent in the embassy."

"Agreed," said Sam again.

"Which then leads us to the next question – who exactly is the person working for Rövid in the embassy?" Kate mused.

Sam squeezed his forehead between forefinger and thumb. "Again, I don't know, but we have to presume it's someone high up. All that crap about being an influencer, there's something we are missing. A bigger picture we have barely begun to understand."

Jake sat back, rubbing his chin. "I think you're right. You don't influence someone immediately. You need time and patience. Something the Russians are pretty good at. With that in mind, who's the more likely to be *influenced?*"

Sam mused for a moment before answering. "I think we have to stick with the original suspects of Cooper or Travers."

"What about any of their underlings? Their assistants or security teams?"

Sam shook his head. "Based on everything I've seen so far it has to be one of those two. Something doesn't sit right with me about Rövid, either. It was like he was taunting us."

"He's a bastard," said Jake, venomously.

"Agreed," added Kate, with even more bite.

"Whatever he is we need to be careful, he knows all of the pieces on the board and we don't. Right now, we don't even know the rules, let alone how to win."

The car fell quiet. Each carried their own thoughts about the morning's events, but no one had any idea what to do next.

"We at least have until twelve?" Kate said to no one in particular.

Sam shook his head. "No, we don't. Rövid knows that while we are alive he's not getting that USB. He will have put in calls to his people the moment we left his store. Whatever else we do next, we need to go back into hiding, find somewhere safe."

"The hotel?" asked Kate.

"If we can get rid of this car then yes."

"I don't feel right just going back into hiding," Kate said resentfully. "It feels like giving up again."

"It won't be for long," lied Sam, knowing full well their list of options was painfully thin.

Jake held up the USB and turned it in his fingers. "We still have the thing they are looking for. That's a positive."

"It would be if we knew what it was," said Sam.

Undeterred, Jake pressed on. "Whatever it is, they obviously want it – need it – badly. That makes it valuable to us, too. What about if we could find out what it actually is and why the Russians want it so badly?" He threw the device at Sam, who caught it. "Right big brother, out you get, we are swapping places."

Sam raised an eyebrow. "What are you talking about? How do you expect to find out what this thing is in the middle of a city that has everyone looking for us?"

"Remember, it's my job to find out things." Jake lifted up the small bag he had been carrying since the morning. "Sometimes in life it's not what you know, but who you know… and I know someone who will be very keen to have a look at that."

"Who?"

"An old friend of mine. Now come on, get out and I'll message him to say we are coming. I thought we might be seeing him, so brought along payment just in case."

Intrigued, Sam did as he was told and switched places with Jake before Kate drove them out of the car park. Rejoining the main road under Jake's instruction, they headed southward, out of the city. Sam sat back in his seat and listened as Kate questioned Jake about their childhood.

"He was always the golden boy was Sam, could not do anything wrong in our mum's eyes," Jake told her. "There was this one time he poured a glass of water over our sister at the dinner table and then told our mum that she had done it herself just to get her into trouble."

"And your mum believed him?"

"Of course she did! Saint Sam couldn't do anything wrong, could you?" he called back to his brother.

Kate laughed. "What about the rest of your family?"

"Not much to tell really, pretty ordinary."

"How would you know? You never see them," scoffed Sam.

Jake blushed. "Yeah, well, can't be helped. The rest are pretty regular, a couple of uncles and aunts, two grandparents, one of whom is Spanish. Did Sam tell you he's fluent?"

"No!" exclaimed Kate. "Really?"

Sam nodded. "And in French. Don't ask Jake though, he barely speaks English."

Kate brought the car onto the motorway before asking her next question. "Who's this Sir Jeffrey everyone keeps talking about?"

"He's our Granddad Gerry's old friend. Been part of the family ever since Granddad died. He was a big figure in the Foreign Office back in the old days. Did all sorts of things," Jake told her.

But what type of things? wondered Sam, thinking back to the conversation in the antiques shop. Their next dinner conversation was going to be interesting. It was time that old bugger started talking a bit more.

Jake was still speaking about the retired diplomat. "He's had his fingers in pies from here to New Zealand, but he's always kept an eye on us. Been there to help out."

"You're forgetting Uncle Robert," Sam contradicted him.

Kate gave Jake a sideways glance. "Who's Uncle Robert?"

"Uncle Knobhead," said Jake. "There's one in every family."

"My mum's brother. He used to work with Sir Jeffrey many years back, but they fell out. Sir Jeffrey says Robert made some nasty decisions and went rogue," said Sam.

"What do you mean went rogue?" Kate asked, intrigued.

"No idea," the two brothers answered together.

Sam continued. "We don't know, only that no one's seen him since. I think he's still alive, but no one talks about him. I think they are embarrassed."

"Hoping he's dead, more like," muttered Jake.

"I doubt he is. I suspect we will run into him one of these days," said Sam.

They headed further south, into the countryside, where thick trees could be seen in the distance. Sam saw a sign for the Dahme-Heideseen Nature Park just as Jake directed Kate to take the next exit. The younger brother then continued to direct Kate along a few main roads until they were completely surrounded by a thick forest of pine trees, their green branches still covered in white snow.

"In a minute there's a righthand turn down a narrow road," Jake warned Kate. "Take it slowly, as it may still be covered in snow. I doubt he gets many visitors these days."

Sam leant forward and rested his arm on the shoulder of Jake's seat. "Are you going to tell us who you're actually taking us to see yet?"

"In a minute," replied Jake, distracted looking for the turning. "Down there now, but take it slowly. I want his cameras to spot us. It's best not to spook him."

The trees seemed even thicker now. Staring out of his window, Sam could see nothing but more woodland to either side of him. Without his phone he felt completely lost in this unknown forest.

"There we go – just a little further," Jake told them. "Just round this bend… there it is."

Sam and Kate both looked through the windscreen as the car exited the trees into a wide open space. Ahead of them lay a shimmering blue lake whose waters rippled gently in the wintery wind. A jetty ran out from the shoreline leading up to a large building clad in stone and wood. Its dark slanting roof ran steeply from its summit to half cover the top floor windows, which ran the whole length of the building. A green wooden door had been built into the centre of the building, in front of which stood a man dressed in a thick fur coat. Sam stared at him as Kate drove nearer before parking up opposite where he stood. They could now clearly see the short sturdy man wearing an old Russian *ushanka* hat. Underneath that, a thick bristling beard could be seen protruding from a square face. Two dark eyes stared back at them. They did not look friendly.

"Who the hell is that?" asked Sam, nervously.

"That, my friends, is the last spy in Berlin."

TWENTY-ONE

AFGHANISTAN

The armoured vehicle bounced unsteadily as it drove across the rocky road that led from the camp. Gripping onto the handles on the side of the roof, Lieutenant Sam Taylor felt his stomach twisting into knots. A mixture of fear and travel sickness was tearing at his insides. He could feel the stares from the soldiers around him. All were fully dressed for combat. Each carried the standard SA80 A2 assault rifle across their chests. The squat looking rifle could unleash 770 rounds a minute on an unfortunate enemy. Next to these heavily armed servicemen, Sam felt naked. Raising his hand, he adjusted the old red beret on his head and wondered what the hell he was doing here.

Behind them, a line of armoured vehicles were motoring over the rough road, their thick tyres throwing up a cloud of dust which swirled in the light wind. Sam could see the small market town drawing ever closer with its thick plume of black smoke drifting into the sky. Somewhere in there was Jake, but whether he was alive was anyone's guess. He gripped the sides of the vehicle tighter as they drove over a particularly large pothole. One of his companions saw the movement and grinned at him.

"Regretting your decision yet, sir?" he shouted over the noise of the engine.

"Only in the choice of companions, private!" Sam called back.

The men around him gave each other sideways glances. Let the crazy military police do what they liked. If they wanted to run into a warzone wearing nothing but a T-shirt and a red beret, let them.

They were in the town now and the road had become smoother as the vehicle slowed slightly. All around them, the civilian population seemed to be in a hurry to get off the streets and return to their homes. The peace of the past weeks had been shattered by this new explosion. Sam looked at their faces and saw only fear. Very few looked up at them as they drove past. The struggle of fighting the invisible enemy had made these innocent people victims in a war not of their choosing.

One of the soldiers raised a hand to his ear, listening to his radio.

"What's happening? Is there any news about the explosion? Any casualties?"

"I don't know sir, it was just the rest of the patrol confirming the area was clear."

Sam called back to the soldier with the radio. "Who was it that called in? Sergeant Taylor?"

The soldier shook his head. "No sir, it was the lieutenant."

The convoy was close now and Sam watched as his companions readied their weapons and received the final instructions. Sam, an intruder in this operation, kept quiet as they drove through the marketplace with all its stalls now empty as their owners decided trade for the day had finished. Leaving the open marketplace they followed the main road which led out of the town and, turning a corner, could now see the cause of the billowing black smoke.

Ahead of them was a scene of destruction. Two explosions had detonated on either side of the road, sending a blast wave through the street. Glass and debris was everywhere, the buildings on either side burned as flames licked from their windows. Bodies were strewn across the floor as the surviving troops tended to the wounded. Civilians were amongst the casualties and Sam watched as some of the marines tried to help a wounded woman to sit up against the remains of her damaged house. There was no sign of Jake.

The armoured vehicle drove forward slightly before coming to a stop at the edge of the impact zone. Sam's companions all jumped down and headed off to complete their assignments. Behind them, the remaining vehicles from the response convoy also came to a stop and a mix of reinforcements and medical teams ran forwards. Sam followed behind, careful not to draw attention to himself. He followed a marine sergeant towards the centre of the blast where the response team's commanding officer was now directing the operation.

"Sergeant Jones, take your squad and push forward, I want a perimeter formed just by that building over there." He waited until his orders were being followed before calling out. "And I want some eyes on that building over to your right, Marcus."

The officer spotted the approaching Sam and, confused at his attire, called out to him. "What the bloody hell are you doing here dressed like that?"

Sam brushed off the challenge and instead asked, "Casualties?"

"I don't know the exact number, it seems the locals got it worse than our chaps, but the ones that did get hit got hit pretty bad. I've three dead and five pretty badly injured. I'll be amazed if they all make it through."

"Christ, I'm sorry."

The officer waved his hand. "Don't be, what can you do? We are just sitting ducks. But what the hell are you doing here? You should not be here."

Sam stopped, unsure what to say. "I'm just here to support. I'll help assess the scene. I've already radioed for my team to follow up with my equipment. Until then I'll just stay out of your way."

The other officer looked like he was about to answer, but his attention was taken by the sound of a wall collapsing in one of the damaged buildings. Taking his chance, Sam moved away and tried to find one of Jake's squad. Spotting a dust covered soldier searching a pile of debris, he walked up behind him.

The soldier jumped up, spooked by Sam's approach. Sam raised his arms. "Don't worry, I'm just looking for Sergeant Taylor, have you seen him?"

The dust covered soldier looked back at him in confusion, trying to take in Sam's informal attire in the middle of the bombsite.

"Ignore the outfit, please answer the question. Have you seen Sergeant Taylor?"

The soldier blinked, then pointed down the street towards the centre of the explosion. Sam guessed he was still suffering from shock. "He was leading the front squad, I was in the back. I'm sorry, I've not seen him."

Sam gave the man a pat on the arm, told him to stop what he was doing and to see a medic. Following the directions, he walked further into the blast zone until he was at the centre of the detonation. Around him there was only destruction and the charred remains of what was once a busy street. The injured lay spread across the area with different groups of emergency responders hovering over them. It was a mixture of uniformed marines and locals all caught up together in the violent explosion. Blood, shining bright in the sunlight, was spread across the roadway. Swallowing down bile, Sam walked onwards and began to check the faces of the injured marines. Looking over the shoulders of the medics he saw young men hurting from their wounds. Some he saw had suffered life changing injuries, which the medical teams desperately tried to lessen.

The dead lay temporarily forgotten as the living focused on attempting to save those that they could. Sam stepped backwards to allow a stretcher bearer to go past. After checking on all of the living, Sam moved his search onwards to the already deceased.

He knelt down next to the nearest body and felt relief at not recognising the face. Repeating this process twice more, the relief – and confusion as to his brother's whereabouts – increased. There was no sign of him.

Sam saw a marine he recognised from his earlier encounter with Jake and walked up to him.

"I've not seen him," the marine answered. "He wasn't one of the dead or injured that I've seen."

"But he must be somewhere?"

"I'm sorry sir, I've not seen him since just before the explosion. He was in the front group and so must have been caught up in it."

Sam swore. Again, he gazed around at the scene. He had checked every one of the injured or deceased on the ground around him. None of the standing marines matched his brother's profile. Where the hell was he? He would have to speak again to the officer in charge and report Jake missing.

Giving the area a final sweep, his eye was caught by a trail of blood which led away from the roadside. Small puddles had formed on the curb leading towards a doorway. Following the trail, Sam stepped onto the curb and saw a bloody handprint on the door frame. The thin wooden door had been broken down, whether from the blast or due to someone breaking in, he did not know.

Sam pulled out his Glock 17 pistol and switched off the safety. Moving forward, he gripped the gun in two hands and climbed over the broken threshold. Peering inside, it took a moment for his eyes to adjust to the darkness within. A staircase ran upwards to an unseen landing. The bloody trail continued up the wooden steps. There were further bloodstains on the lefthand wall of the staircase. Cocking the weapon, Sam walked forward and began to climb the creaking stairs. There was no sound coming from above.

Steadying his nerves, Sam continued upwards. Whatever was awaiting him up these stairs, there was no point in delaying it further. He was about halfway up when he first noticed the odd shape. He looked upwards, trying to process what it was that he was seeing. A booted foot was hanging over the lip of the top stair. Any trepidations he may have had disappeared within an instant and he leapt forward, taking the final steps two at a time. Reaching the top, he found the booted foot still connected to the rest of the body, which was on the floor slumped against the wall. It was Jake.

"Jake, Jake, can you hear me?" Sam knelt next to his brother, searching for a pulse.

Jake, his eyes closed, groaned slightly as Sam spoke. The left hand side of his face was a mask of crimson as blood spilled from a wound at the side of his head. An open gash was gushing blood where his ear had been.

"Medic, man down inside. Medic!" Sam shouted back down the stairs.

Running his hands over Jake's tactical vest he pulled out the first aid kit before pressing a dressing to try and halt the bleeding from his brother's head.

Sam shouted again for a medic. The sound of his voice caused his brother's eyes to flicker.

"Hey it's okay, you're going to be okay," Sam told him.

Jake muttered something, but Sam was unable to catch it. Jake tried again and this time tried raising his right arm.

"Don't move Jake, help's coming," Sam looked down the stairs again and shouted once more.

"Sam," Jake muttered. "Over there." He again raised his arm, this time pointing with his fingers.

Sam's attention was taken by the sound of heavy boots on the stairs. He twisted round to see a marine and a medic climbing to meet them. Stepping to one side to allow them to get to Jake, Sam watched as the two soldiers assessed the injury.

"He's going to be okay sir," the medic told him. "Looks like he's got a thick head there. We will get him back and sort him out."

Sam felt a swell of relief flow through him on hearing the news. He stood up and moved away as they prepared to move him. A pair of stretcher bearers appeared, and once Jake's wound had been dressed, the small group carried the wounded marine back outside. Sam followed. Blinking, he stepped out into the bright sunshine. Already, the majority of the injured had been carried away to continue their medical treatment. Those that remained were either sitting up or walking wounded. He watched as Jake was carried away back to the waiting transport back to the camp. Above him, he heard the beating roar of two Chinook transport helicopters flying over the town towards the camp, ready to carry the remaining wounded to the main hospitals back at Camp Bastion.

All around him, people were moving, going about their business as they tried to bring normality to chaos. Standing there on the pavement, Sam realised he was still holding the Glock. Coming to his senses, he quickly switched the safety back on before holstering it in his belt. The shock of seeing his brother lying there covered in blood was a vision which would not be leaving him for some time. But then another thought came back to him. What had Jake been trying to show him?

It was probably nothing, a confused act by an injured mind. But Jake had seemed pretty adamant about something. He looked up to see two open windows looking down into the street. Their wooden shutters had been blown off in the blast and Sam could see a fan still swirling on the ceiling. It wouldn't hurt to be certain, decided Sam, and he turned back towards the broken doorway. Climbing the creaking stairs, he drew out the Glock again and released the safety. Whatever Jake had seen, it had been enough to pull him away from his injured comrades.

Reaching the landing, Sam spotted Jake's discarded rifle. He saw that he had walked into a family's sitting room. A pair of threadbare sofas were facing an old fashioned television set. A coffee table was laid out ready for what Sam guessed would have been a lunchtime meal, with empty plates and cups. A cabinet stood to one side with photos of a smiling family looking out at him. Another door led to a kitchen and another to what Sam guessed was the bedroom. But it all became overshadowed by what lay underneath the open window.

"Oh Jake, what have you done?" Sam groaned as he walked round the threadbare sofa.

Kneeling, Sam turned over the two bodies and checked for a pulse. They were both dead, each with numerous bullet wounds across their torsos, fired from what Sam was certain to have been a SA80 A2 rifle. To his left, the wrinkled face of a grey-haired man stared lifelessly up at him. A look of shock was still etched across his face. Sam gently closed the man's eyelids. To his right lay a smaller body, the skinny arms and legs not quite big enough for the clothes that were now drenched in his blood. Moving the still warm body towards him, Sam saw the face of a teenager staring back up at him.

"Oh Jake, what have you done?" Sam repeated as his stomach lurched.

Standing, he moved away from the bodies and walked back over to Jake's discarded rifle. Picking it up, he quickly sniffed the barrel, the smell of nitroglycerin enough to tell him it had recently been fired.

"Bloody hell," he swore.

Outside, the investigation had begun into the explosion that had killed and maimed the people on the street. Soon, experts would be attempting to piece together the explosive device that had killed both British marines and civilians. But inside this small flat, only Sam knew what had killed an innocent grandfather and grandson. His own brother.

TWENTY-TWO

"WHERE THE HELL have you brought us, Jake?" Sam asked his brother from the back of the car.

Jake did not bother to turn around. "You wanted answers so I've brought you to a place where you can get them."

"Yeah, the location of every horror film ever written," retorted Sam.

"I'm getting out to see my friend and if you want to know what's on that little stick of yours I suggest you come with me." Jake unbuckled his seatbelt and opened his door.

Kate turned to Sam and raised her eyebrows. "What have we got to lose?"

"I'd say he will start with our livers."

She laughed, but left the car to follow Jake. Sam sighed, again thinking of the joys of having a sibling, before also exiting the car.

A cold wind blew from across the open water and Sam shivered. Their host had not moved from the doorstep. A pair of narrowed dark eyes followed their every move towards him. The rest of the face looked old, weary from years gone by. The driveway around them was covered in virgin snow, so clearly no one had been to the house since the previous day's snowfall. They caught up with Jake as he approached the mysterious figure.

The taller Taylor brother opened his arms in greeting. "Klaus Bartel, it's been far too long, my friend."

Klaus Bartel did not return the warm greeting. Unlike Jake, he kept his hands deep within his coat and glared back at the new arrivals. "Jake Taylor, you bastard, you dare to show your cheating face here after what you did to me?"

Undeterred, Jake continued. "Bartel, now don't be like that, you can't blame me for what happened."

"You still took my money, you English bastard. A man like you has no honour."

"Let's hope he just shoots Jake and takes pity on us," whispered Sam to Kate.

Jake shook his head and pointed at their host. "Don't you dare, Bartel. It was your idea… In fact if I remember, you insisted that I agree to it."

Bartel glared daggers at the Englishman and then burst into a wide, welcoming smile. "You cannot tell me that was a penalty and I'm telling you only a blind man would have given that second goal."

Jake laughed and embraced Bartel in a giant bear hug. "I told you not to bet, Bartel. It's not my fault the German football team is inferior to the mighty England."

"I have learnt my lesson my dear Jake, until the next time." He stepped back and patted Jake's chest. "It is good to see you, my friend. It has been too long since you passed my way."

"I don't choose the journey, Bartel. You know that better than anyone."

Klaus Bartel smiled before turning his attention to Sam and Kate. "And this time you bring friends. How unlike you."

Jake waved towards his companions, beckoning them forward. "I wouldn't go as far as to call them friends. The girl, yes, but…"

"But your brother not so much?" interjected Bartel. "The resemblance is a giveaway. He has your handsome looks, and your British demeanour of carrying the weight of the world upon his shoulders."

"*You* try growing up with him," said Sam, nodding towards Jake. Reaching out to shake Klaus Bartel's hand, he tried to guess the man's age. He must have been well over sixty, if not seventy. "Sam Taylor, nice to meet you."

Bartel beamed. "Pleasure. I'm going to make an educated guess and say you must be Kate May?"

Kate took the proffered hand. "How do you–"

"Know? Hasn't Jake told you anything? I know *everything* that happens in our city."

"He's not told us anything," replied Kate. "Just that you may be able to help us."

Bartel nodded before looking past them to stare round the grounds. "Indeed, although perhaps one for when we are inside."

Bartel led them in through the thick green painted door, into an open entrance hall. Doors led off in different directions from wood panelled walls. A large wooden staircase took centre stage, leading up to unseen floors. Bartel unfastened his thick fur coat and threw it onto the bannister. The hat was thrown frisbee style to hang off the antler of a mounted deer head.

"Welcome to the former hunting lodge of one of my long deceased family members, who may or may not have been both a Nazi Party member and part of the Socialist Unity Party at varying points in their life. To be honest, I don't really care. You see, I come from the long line of Bartels, a very ancient and noble line."

"Until you came along," Jake jibed.

"Indeed… I have somewhat ruined that reputation."

Bartel led them into a large sitting room. Brown leather chairs were placed around an open fireplace, bright with flickering flames. The floor was polished wood, and Sam felt his feet slip slightly as he walked. He paused for a moment to look round at the walls, surprised not to see them decorated with more hunting trophies or traditional paintings of some sort. Instead, every available inch was covered in football memorabilia. Framed shirts were hung all along the sides of the room, the majority of which were the white, black, red and yellow of the German national team. All were adorned with the black scribbles of signatures from past players. Glass cases stood proudly on top of polished furniture containing a mix of old leather boots, worn out balls and in one, a pair of football gloves.

"I take it you like your football?" mused Sam, looking around.

"Like football? You do not like football, you love it like a woman. You fall in love with the game as if you were being seduced by the most beautiful of muses. It is a drug – a glorious, heartbreaking addiction greater than any substance known to man."

"Or woman," said Kate. "Don't forget it's no longer just a man's sport."

Bartel beamed at her, his joy evident to all. "My lady, your beauty seems to grow with every word you utter. To have such a fair football fan in my presence is an absolute honour."

"But you're wasting your time on him," said Jake, thumbing towards Sam. "I'd be surprised if he could tell you who the England captain was these days."

Bartel's face went from joyful happiness to one of complete shock and confusion. He stared at Sam.

"You don't like football?"

"I don't *dis*like it."

Their German host threw his arms into the air. "Jake Taylor, you dare to bring a non believer into my home? How can you even refer to this man as your brother?"

"I don't," answered Jake, flatly.

Bartel shook his head in disappointment as he went and threw a log onto the fire. The sparks from the wood flew up the wide arching chimney. "A heathen in my home. Whatever next."

"Mr Bartel," began Kate, speaking to the crouching man.

"Just Bartel," he replied, still tending the fire.

"Bartel, we need your help. I need your help."

The German turned from the fireplace, one hand stroking his thick beard. "I know you need my help my dear, in fact I know all about you. But before I can listen to your tale I need a coffee to help me over this insult." He gave Sam an exaggerated rueful stare.

Sam replied, "Love one. Americano, no sugar."

Klaus Bartel gave him a wolfish grin before standing up and striding from the room.

"Glad to see you're good at making friends," said Kate as she took a seat by the fireplace.

Sam joined her. "Don't blame me! I still have no idea what's going on. Who is this guy?"

Jake took the opposite chair. "Klaus Bartel inherited an ancient family fortune, which has allowed him to indulge in a football addiction."

"That still doesn't explain why you brought us here. What was that about being the last spy in Berlin?"

"I am." A voice called out from behind them and Bartel came back into the room carrying a tray. Setting it down on the coffee table he handed mugs to each of them. "Freshly prepared after I saw you arriving on my cameras back near the main road. A special blend from a nice family in Columbia who, when not exporting a banned white powder, make one of the best coffees in the world."

"Are you sure they don't mix the two?" asked Jake.

"I wish. That would give it a kick."

Sam sipped at the hot liquid, finding himself pleasantly surprised.

"Where was I?" pondered Bartel, standing above them having handed Kate the last cup. "Ah yes, behold the last spy in Berlin." He held out his arms and waited for a response. When none came he continued. "I had hoped for a better reception, but you're English, which means you're always going to be a little reserved."

"And those two are from the north of England, so you can add grumpy as well as reserved," said Kate.

Bartel winked at her before taking a seat by Jake.

"What do you mean you're the last spy in Berlin?" Sam asked their host once he'd settled down in his seat.

"Exactly that! I am the last true spy remaining. All of the others have either died, left or given up. Once upon a time there were more spies in this city than bars. But then the Soviet Union collapsed, the British went bankrupt, the Americans found new interests in the Middle East and we Germans all became the best of friends. Each of the great agencies began to reduce their numbers until there was only little old me left."

Jake placed his mug on the table. "Bartel was one of the ultimate spies in the city towards the end of the Cold War. He knew everything that happened on both sides of the wall. What's more, he worked with the Americans, the British, plus the Germans and the Russians."

"The Russians?" Sam was suspicious.

"Yes, the Russians as well. You see, everyone knew Bartel, and everyone knew that Bartel did not pick sides. He was wealthy enough not to need money and was not stupid enough to align himself to idealistic political causes."

Bartel sat back in the chair and rested the back of his head in the palms of his hands.

"My dear Sam, only a fool wastes his life in the name of king and country. I instead dedicated my life to information. I traded my wares to both sides. Both sides respected that. In fact, this very house was the centrepiece of it all. Local agents from both sides would come here and discuss terms together. The moment they entered my estate the Cold War paused. It was neutral ground."

"What… the CIA and MI6 came here to trade with KGB and Stasi?" Sam couldn't quite believe it.

"Indeed, right in these very chairs. The room where you are now sitting has seen more than you could possibly imagine," confirmed Bartel. "Until the wall came down and the liberal West won. Then everyone left and gave it all up. Now it's just little old me."

"I'm not sure Miklós Rövid would agree with you there. From what we've seen I'd say you are not *quite* the last spy in Berlin," warned Sam, still unsure about the strange figure in front of him. The bearded Bartel seemed friendly enough, but he had admitted to working for the Russians.

Bartel scoffed. "Rövid's not a spy. The little fool thinks he's something special, but believe me, the old KGB regime would have had him in a Siberian gulag long ago for being inept."

"I wouldn't write him off just yet, he's got someone working for him in the British Embassy," cautioned Kate.

Now Bartel openly scorned them. "He's got someone in the British Embassy? My dear, everyone has someone in the British Embassy. I have someone in the British Embassy. How do you think I knew who you were? You British think you are a nation of great spies, but believe me your best agent was a fictional character with a license to kill!"

"We think it's someone senior though, like the Head of Security John Travers or even Ambassador Cooper herself," said Sam.

Bartel waved his hand. "Please, Travers is no spy… and from what I know about Ambassador Cooper she's not got the intelligence to even know how to spell espionage."

"Klaus," said Jake, firmly. "You should listen to what Kate has to say before you dismiss it."

The older man rolled his eyes before gesturing for Kate to begin. He sat there in silence, not once interrupting as Kate told her story. A single eyebrow was raised at the retelling of how she had found the device in the Ambassador's laptop, but no word was spoken. He stroked his beard as he heard about Rövid's attack on Otto Schafer's studio. Only when Kate described the offer for the USB did he let out any type of noise, a small grunt, but Sam could only guess what it meant.

Kate finished speaking and Jake took up the story. "… And so

I suggested we come to you. If this USB stick is so important to Rövid, we'd at least like to know why."

Klaus Bartel did not speak at first, instead he dropped his chin to his chest and tapped his fingers together. Sam watched as the dark eyes focused on his moving fingertips, lost in thought.

Eventually, he came back to the present and spoke slowly. "I think I need to ask for your forgiveness my friends, it seems I spoke too quickly earlier in my appraisal of Rövid. He is indeed playing a strange game. One which I would say with the imminent signing of the North Sea Deal has very high stakes indeed. To raid an innocent man's store in broad daylight and leave him for dead is no longer in the FSB's playbook. I would say you have them very spooked indeed."

"That's what we thought," mused Sam. "But the question surely has to be, why? We know absolutely nothing concrete. At the very worst, we have suspicions, which could be squashed at a later date."

Bartel shook his head. "But that is *not* all you have, is it? No, you have the USB stick that holds the key to all of this. Well, that's the answer to why they are chasing you so hard." Bartel held out his hand. "Do you have it with you? Can I see it?"

Sam looked at Jake, who nodded his encouragement. He pulled out the silver USB then handed it over. Bartel took it and twirled it in his fingers, muttering something as he did so. Spotting the engraved 'G', he let out a sly smile and once more spoke in his native tongue.

"What do you see? What is the beautiful little thing you talk about?" Kate translated.

Bartel smiled and held the device up. "Your German is good, Fräulein. But you were wrong to think there are millions of USB sticks like this. You see, this little device is not one of millions, but one in a million. What you have here comes straight out of the CIA's most secret file. It's a piece of equipment so classified, that if our American friends knew you had it, there would be heads rolling in Washington tonight. This is a device which in my circle of colleagues many consider to be a myth, something which only exists in fiction. Even I doubted its existence until now."

Sam leant forward. "Right, so what is it?"

Bartel looked at each of his guests, his excitement evident. "This, my friends, is a Griffin."

TWENTY-THREE

KLAUS BARTEL CONTINUED HOLDING the silver USB aloft for them all to see. The tiny engraved 'G' glinted in the firelight. Silence fell around the room as Bartel waited for a response from his guests to his great reveal. Receiving none, he lowered his hand and looked at all three of them.

"None of you know what a Griffin is, do you?" he asked, disheartened.

Jake shook his head. "Nope."

"It can't be something to do with the mythical creature? You know, half lion, half eagle?" suggested Kate.

Bartel laughed. "No. Christ, you are an uncultured bunch."

"So what is it, then? Enlighten us," said Sam.

"Like all good stories this one began on the Internet," Bartel went on, clearly enjoying his lecture. "A message began to appear on chat rooms across the dark web, claiming to have created code that could bypass any computer security in the world. You have to understand that IT security is a trillion-dollar business. Without it, everything that we take for granted in today's world would crumble. From your online banking transactions, right through to a person's private social media account, all of it is protected by varying levels of information security."

"The type of stuff that blocks viruses or hackers," nodded Kate.

"Yes exactly, but now imagine that on a huge scale, protecting a global organisation or even a country's national defences. A bit more than your run of the mill social media password," Bartel continued. All three nodded. They were familiar with this, in their lines of work. "So, back to these mysterious messages that kept appearing across the web. Someone out there was taunting the security world by claiming to have the magic key that could open any door. Of course, like nearly all outlandish claims, most sane people just ignored it as another lone loser in his mother's basement trying to get the attention he fails to receive. But like any outlandish claim, no one takes them seriously – until..."

"They are proved not so outlandish," finished Sam, his attention now fully engaged.

"And hacking into the private servers of the Director of the CIA would probably be enough to get treated seriously."

Sam nodded. "Yes, that would do it. What happened next?"

Bartel waved his arms. "I don't know, no one does. But I have a good idea."

"I'm sure you do," Sam said, wearily. "But you're not going to tell us?"

"I may do, but there will be a price. So far I've welcomed you here out of the kindness of my heart and my admiration of your brother." Bartel nodded at Jake, who watched on, bemused.

"We can pay you," Kate answered. "We have money."

Bartel waved her away. "I don't need money, look at me." He turned to Jake. "*He* knows what I want. Go on, ask him."

Kate and Sam stared at Jake, who scratched his chin and looked at his brother. "I told you this morning mate, not everyone can be paid off with cash."

Sam watched as Jake pulled out the small bag he had been carrying over his shoulder since the morning, now intrigued to know what could be inside.

"I've got you one Klaus, but I want my money's worth first.

Finish telling us your story. We can all see you're enjoying it, you old bastard. Then I'll give it to you. I'll also be wanting some merchandise as well as whatever tale you're going to give us now."

Bartel's eyes flashed excitedly as he looked down at the small bag currently in Jake's hand. Licking his lips, he continued. "The Americans, slightly put out by this little intrusion, managed to track down the mystery developer to a dorm room in Harvard University. They discovered a very frightened postgraduate, who they gave a very simple choice: work for them, or go behind bars for the rest of his life. Which would have been very short, believe you me, as our American friends would not have been happy to allow someone with that kind of knowledge out of their sights. So, there would have been some sort of accident."

"That developer must have shat himself," commented Jake.

Sam shook his head. "That developer just lost himself a shitload of cash. If he'd have waited, he could have sold that kind of thing for millions in the private sector."

"Quite right," toasted Bartel. "That fool got too cocky for his own good. But anyway, he was put to good use and in turn he created this little trinket. A Griffin. By refining his code and implementing it with a bit of traditional CIA technology, this little bastard can be plugged into any computer in the world undetected and then send a copy of all of its contents to another pre-programmed computer anywhere else in the world within minutes."

"It can't even be detected when inserted into the actual laptop?" questioned Kate. "The embassy computers automatically lock down if you even put an iPhone charger into their USB ports."

"I guess that's why whoever is working for the Russians was given one of these."

Sam sat back in his chair and crossed his legs, pondering the old German's words. He still had a few questions.

"How does it send off the information?" he asked.

"There's a 5G card hidden within this casing," Bartel waved the Griffin.

"Is there a way to find out where it's sending the information to?"

"You would need the original computer that loaded the programme. At the moment this device is coded to copy any computer it's connected to."

"And you say these are extremely rare?" Sam continued his questioning.

Bartel raised his eyebrows and nodded. "Extremely. To be honest, I can't quite believe our Russian friends could have actually got their hands on one, but here we are. Someone in the CIA will be getting fired very shortly. This piece of tech is so far ahead of the game that I can't even begin to tell you how pissed the Americans will be to hear the Russians have it."

Sam tapped Kate's leg. "Well, that explains why Rövid is so eager to get it back. If it's the only one they have then he's not going to be in their good books when Moscow finds out it's missing."

"It also means that whatever game they are playing, there are some serious stakes," added Jake.

"Perhaps even more than the North Sea Deal?" suggested Sam, concerned about what that could possibly mean.

"What do we do now?" Kate asked. "Now we know what it actually is, does that change anything for us?"

"Nothing," the younger Taylor brother said. "But we know we definitely cannot let Rövid get it back."

"That still doesn't really help us, does it?" Kate sighed. "We are back at square one: we can't go to *our* people as we don't know who we can trust, and there's not much *we* can do to hurt Rövid and his plans."

"We could destroy the Griffin?" suggested Jake.

Bartel brought the USB up to his chest. "After all I just told you? I would offer you 300,000 euros for this."

"No deal," said Sam. "Although the problem for us still remains, what the hell are we supposed to do?"

The room fell silent. Only the crackling of the wood burning amongst the flames could be heard.

"I suppose I had better earn my reward," Bartel said, scratching his beard. He gave the Griffin a final longing look before throwing it for Sam to catch, which he did. "I think you have a third option. That device you have there is one of the most secretive pieces of equipment the CIA has in its arsenal and somehow it has ended up in the grip of a Russian agent. My suggestion would be to walk right into the American Embassy and swap this for their protection while *they* do all the investigating. It will scare Rövid back into the gutter, where he belongs, and you can leave your mole to the Americans."

Sam thought for a while. In principle, it would offer Kate protection – at least until the investigation had been completed. But her fate would not be in her own hands. Instead, she would be reliant on the CIA clearing her name as part of their attempts to discover how they had lost this particular Griffin. He twisted round to study her, waiting for a response.

She looked at him. "What do you think?"

"It's not my call, it's not me everyone is after."

She frowned and bit her lip. "Then what if you were me? With everything that is going on?"

He answered honestly. "You would at least be protected."

"But what if they are unable to clear my name? Perhaps they'll come to the conclusion I was the original owner of the Griffin and they'll keep me locked up."

"We'd have to hope that they would rather catch the real culprits," said Sam, not quite convinced by his own words.

"Hey, you managed to convince us," added Jake, "and now you have some pretty good evidence to back up your claims. The attack on Schafer only helps your case, in my eyes."

Kate looked at the two brothers and then at Bartel. "What would *you* do?" she asked him.

The old spymaster took a deep breath and thought for a moment. He looked at the three of them as his mind ticked over the proposition. Sam could see he was weighing the odds.

"Right now you have two big enemies against you. The Russians and, to be quite frank, your own side. Do not forget they brought Jake here to kill you rather than bring you in. Officially, you are a marked woman. And while these two brothers are extremely resourceful, I think you need a bigger ally on your side."

Sam found himself agreeing with the German's logic. He knew his strengths were no match for the FSB, while it was only a matter of time before their own side increased the hunt for Kate.

"You would go to the Americans?" she asked him.

"I would. In my experience they tend to be the good guys. Yes, there's always the chance of a bad apple, but given a choice between Uncle Sam and Uncle Ivan we Germans prefer the stars and stripes."

Kate slouched in the sofa, her face full of worry.

Sam placed his hand on her knee again. "I think he's right, and for what it's worth, I will come with you." He was not sure what Emma Read would say about that back in the Foreign Office, but that would have to be a problem for another day.

She stared into the fireplace as she settled on the conclusion that would define her future.

"Okay, I'll go."

Bartel slapped his legs and jumped up. "Very well, decision made, no point worrying about it now." He looked at his watch. "Can I convince you to stay for lunch?"

"Only if your kitchen is as good as last time," said Jake. "But first…" He waved the small bag at Bartel. Jake handed it over to their host. "You will find all of the authenticity documents inside as well. I got it from the football museum in Manchester."

They all watched as Klaus Bartel, his eyes alight with childlike excitement, tore open the bag and pulled out the bright red clothing. He held it up in front of him and let out a contented sigh of delight."It is wonderful! As always Jake, you know how to please me."

Sam had to stifle a laugh as Bartel turned the football shirt round to face the room. Little black signatures adorned the front.

"It's the twenty thirteen squad," Jake told him. "The last time Sir Alex Ferguson won the league."

"And probably the last time Manchester United will, as well!" chuckled Kate, causing Jake to glare at her in warning.

But the now openly emotional Bartel ignored her comment. He gently folded the shirt over the back of the sofa before looking lovingly at it. "Gentlemen, and of course lady, you have my complete and utter attention."

Bartel motioned for them all to follow him out of the room. Sam whispered to his brother as they followed. "Sometimes you impress me."

"Only sometimes?" Jake whispered back.

The three of them followed Bartel back into the hallway and through another door, which led to a long, open kitchen area. Like the rest of the building it was decorated with a mix of wooden beams and stone brickwork. Where the rest of the house had been covered in wooden floorboards, here a stone flagged floor ran throughout. At one end a large open fire was smouldering, its flames dying. In the middle was a long wooden island with a polished wooden surface. A wide window let in sunlight, at the end of which a door opened outwards. They walked round the edges of the room, where a stout iron stove was embedded in the wall.

Bartel pointed to it as he walked. "I have never been able to use that contraption, this kitchen should belong in a museum."

Sam chuckled and nodded at the shining copper pans hanging on the wall. "Either you have a good cleaner, or they've not been used either?"

"Not since the fifties," Bartel called back as he exited through a far door at the opposite end of the room.

Still following, the three of them stepped out of the kitchen and into a garage area where two vehicles were stored. The first of which was a big black Audi SUV, which gleamed from a recent polish.

"Have you seen my pride and joy?" Bartel asked Sam, watching him admire the car.

"It's a nice car," admitted Sam.

"No, not that – this!" Bartel indicated behind him, to a deep blue Volkswagen campervan.

Sam, amused again by the man's eccentricities, followed as Bartel guided him round the van's exterior.

"Two-litre turbo engine, four wheel drive, tinted windows, heated seats, pop-up roof and all top of the range inside," Bartel boasted proudly.

"It's very nice," Sam said approvingly, as Bartel opened the sliding side door, allowing them to peer in.

"Look at this," their host said excitedly, pressing a range of buttons which made the leather interior flash in a rainbow of colours from tiny lights embedded within the roof.

"If you were a bit younger Bartel, I'd have been worried about you with this, it looks like the inside of a swingers' club."

Bartel flashed a wide smile. "What do you mean if I was a bit younger? I'm going to be touring the world and its ladies in this beauty."

Kate peered past them and looked inside. "Where's the toilet?"

"Wherever you put the bucket," Bartel teased.

"There you go, being a millionaire still can't buy you class," laughed Jake.

Bartel scowled. "I was going to let you have a ride in it, the keys are only over there," he indicated a locked metal case. "But now you can get lost."

The campervan tour over, Bartel continued through the garage until he reached a door at the far end. Unlike the rest of the house, this door was made from metal and fixed in place with thick steel hinges. The modern aesthetics looked alien compared to the old-style house.

"What is this?" asked Sam.

"My link to modernity," answered Bartel, placing his finger on a scanner before looking into the camera. "Jake's seen it before. He's one of the few people I'd trust to show it to."

"You see what buying a football shirt can get you?" Jake elbowed Sam.

Bartel let out a laugh. "I wish I'd had a brother growing up, it all looks so much fun."

"Debatable," the two brothers answered simultaneously.

"You do make me laugh," said Bartel as he opened up a hatch to reveal a keypad before keying in a number. "I bet you like winding each other up. Allow me to show you a quick way to get under your brother's skin, Sam."

Jake groaned. "Here we go."

Bartel continued. "What are the greatest ever years in football?"

Sam didn't have a clue and Jake refused to answer. Instead, it was left to Kate.

"1966."

"Try 1954, 1974, 1990 and 2014. All are glorious years for world football." The locks on the door thudded open and Bartel was able to pull the heavy door outwards. "Welcome to my little cave."

TWENTY-FOUR

IF THE REST of Klaus Bartel's home had become a monument to classical Germanic country house building then the room they entered belonged in a different universe. Stepping through the unlocked metal door, the small group walked into a windowless corridor lit by bright fluorescent lighting, which ran down to the end of the room. The corridor itself was barely two metres wide, with open cabinets lining the walls. Within each cabinet, stacked on rows of racking, was stored a range of weaponry and equipment. From small arms to assault rifles, Bartel's collection had it all.

"Jesus Bartel, where's the army?" asked a shocked Sam.

Bartel shrugged. "We all have to make a living. Although things have got harder for me since you shut down the Nile."

"How do you know about that?!" asked an even more surprised Sam. The Nile was the illegal black market organisation Sam had closed down the year before in Amsterdam.

"I was one of their customers," Bartel grumbled. "You put a hole in my operation with that little escapade. But I don't hold it against you, they had become a bit too dangerous in recent years."

Continuing down the corridor Kate stopped by an open cabinet.

"What are they?" She pointed at a small metal object, which looked like a miniature exercise dumbbell. A pin protruded from the top of a handle that ran down the length of the device.

"It's an M84 stun grenade," Sam answered for Bartel. "It's an American made device that they use when they don't quite want to blow something up."

"Well put," Bartel said. "It's still a nasty little bastard. When fired, those things will make a loud bang and emit a blinding flash. For those unfortunate enough to be close by, it will leave them temporarily deaf, dumb and blind."

"We used them in Afghanistan," explained Jake.

Kate pulled a look of disdain and continued walking.

Reaching the end of the corridor they came to a small computer centre with six screens surrounding a desk. Bartel took the lone chair and swivelled it to face his guests.

"Over to you Jake, fill your boots."

Jake smiled and rubbed his hands together before heading back down the corridor. Sam followed and placed his hand upon the taller man.

"Slow down, we don't need anything if we are just going to the American Embassy, do we?"

Jake looked over his shoulder. "I'm not going to the embassy. I'll drive back to the city, but I can't go in. I'm not exactly an innocent civilian, am I?"

"Right, but that doesn't mean you need a full arsenal to take with you."

"It's a long way between here and the Brandenburg Gate, so if you don't mind, I need some spare ammunition."

Leaving Jake to his work, Sam returned to where Bartel sat waiting. He was in the process of answering more questions from an intrigued Kate.

"Why did they call it a Griffin?"

Sam had already guessed the answer. "H.G Wells."

"What?"

"In H.G Wells' *The Invisible Man,* the main character is a

mysterious stranger called Griffin. I guess it's someone's idea of an homage," surmised Sam.

"Top marks," confirmed Bartel. "Like the invisible man, the Griffin device is invisible as it enters any computer."

Sam looked over Bartel's shoulder at all the technical equipment set up on the wall and desk behind him. "You don't fancy giving us a demonstration with one of your computers?"

"Absolutely not! I don't want some FSB agent poring over my files."

Jake returned, carrying four extra ammunition clips and a spare pistol, which he held aloft. "The new SIG Sauer?"

"P365," Bartel confirmed.

"Nice, right, that's me done. Lunch?"

A short time later the four of them were perched on stools around the long wooden table, having helped their host prepare a lunch of freshly baked bread, cheese and cured meats.

After they had all eaten, Sam asked Bartel if he could use one of his phones as he brought the kitchen fire back to life.

"Sure, they are all secure. Go use the one back in the living room."

He found the promised phone on a stand in one of the corners and dialled the memorised number.

A curt Irish accent answered at the other end. "Emma Read."

"Hey boss, how's it hanging?"

The Irish accent became very sharp, very quickly. "Sam, is that you? Where the hell have you been? I've had the Foreign Secretary all over me."

Sam moved the receiver away from his ear as his manager's voice increased in volume and speed. He looked at the nearest framed shirt and wondered who the scribbles belonged to. After a few minutes the voice faded away and he returned the receiver to his ear.

"I'm okay thanks, sorry for not calling earlier."

"Not calling earlier? Are you taking the piss?"

"Yeah look, I'm sorry, but things took a bit of a turn over here."

"You don't say? I've had my ear chewed off non-stop. You were sent home, job done, two days ago and you're still over there? From what I've managed to get out of the Foreign Secretary, Kate May is not the innocent victim we thought she was, but some kind of Russian spy!"

"She's not a Russian spy," he told her calmly.

"How the hell do you know that?"

"I found her. In fact, I'm still with her."

There was a pause at the other end of the line. "I should have guessed. It's my fault really, isn't it? I send you off to find a beautiful girl, so you're not going to stop just because of something as trivial as orders."

"It was more by accident than anything."

"Don't give me that shit, Taylor," she snapped down the line. "How do *you* know she's not a spy when it seems the entire British government, including the Prime Minister, thinks otherwise?"

"Someone at the embassy wants us to think that." He began to describe the events of the past few days. How he had doubted the authenticity of the planted bag in Kate's flat, but his concerns were ignored. How he had followed Schafer to his studio and then the attack by the FSB. Emma listened in silence even as he told her about the interview with Rövid and his offer for the Griffin. He neglected to mention Jake or Bartel. That could wait.

"Jesus Sam, you don't half get yourself in some shit. What are you going to do? You can't return here with the girl. I've had enough of a job trying to cover for you these past two days."

"We are still thinking on that," he lied, not wanting to tell her about their plan to go to the embassy, "but I need your advice on something."

"Go on."

"If I wanted to prove who the actual spy was in the embassy, what would I need?"

"I'd say... at least two separate pieces of evidence. At the level you're talking about I think two would be enough to snare them. Why, what are you thinking?"

What *was* he thinking? It was true there was an idea beginning to form in the back of his mind. Everything that Bartel had said since their arrival had been leading to thoughts formulating inside his mind. The Griffin, its potential for causing trouble in the wrong hands, the Americans and their desire to find the people responsible for stealing their prized asset.

"Nothing for now. Just musing. Have you spoken to Sir Jeffrey?"

"I've left him a few messages, but he's not replied, must still be drinking rum punches." She swore violently down the phone. "Christ Sam, we are supposed to be signing the North Sea Deal any day now. What am I supposed to do?"

"Nothing," Sam answered honestly. "What can you do?"

"I suppose you're right… and you're certain that without this Griffin device there's no alternative threat to the signing of the deal?"

"As far as I'm aware. If there was, I don't see why they would be so desperate to get hold of it."

Emma casually swore again. "You're not going to tell me what you're going to do, are you?"

"Probably not," Sam admitted, "but I'll let you know when it's happened."

"No you won't, you lying bastard."

The two of them went quiet at either end of the line.

Emma broke the silence. "Be careful, Sam."

Sam smiled at the gesture of concern from his colleague. "You know me," he said, before hanging up the phone.

Returning to the kitchen he found his companions still seated along the great wooden island that filled up most of the space. Bartel was in the middle of telling them a story from years gone by when Sam interrupted them.

Their German host stopped his tale, swivelling on the stool to look at Sam. "Everything okay?"

"Just about, but I think we should be getting going soon. If we are going to the Americans I'd rather do it and get it over with."

Kate placed a half empty glass on the table and stood up. "Are you sure about this, Sam?"

He nodded, showing more confidence than he felt.

Jake stood up and stretched. "Well, I'll drive you there, but after that you're on your own."

Sam gave his brother a reassuring smile. "I understand… and if I'm honest, I don't think it's a bad thing to have someone on the outside still. If the Americans don't play fair then at least you're still at large with the truth."

Bartel nodded. "When you get there ask for Andrew Hall, he's the local CIA man for Berlin. You can tell him I sent you if you have any problems, but I doubt you will. The moment you show them your little package he will be very eager to meet with you."

A beep echoed around the kitchen and all four heads turned to look at a small monitor nestled in a corner on one side. Looking at the bright screen, they saw the video of a car being driven down the private drive that led from the main road.

"Expecting visitors?" asked Sam.

Bartel shook his head and scratched his beard. "No, I'm not expecting anyone."

Jake walked over to the monitor, which had changed to another camera angle. "At least three males by the looks of it."

"In a car like that you'd expect at least four," advised Bartel, watching on as the vehicle made its way down the long road to the house.

"What do we do?" asked Kate, nervously. "It could be the Russians."

Bartel let out a brief laugh and put his arm around her shoulders. "My dear, it is not *could* be the Russians, it is *almost certainly* the Russians."

Jake swore and pulled out his gun. "Between us we can take them, the more the merrier."

"Absolutely not, this house has been a neutral location for

decades. I'm not having you break that tradition," Bartel warned, his face flushing red.

Jake pointed the gun at the screen. "I don't want to upset you old man, but I don't think they are coming to swap football stories."

Bartel turned on Jake. "Listen, spies of every country have been meeting here in peace for decades, long before you were even born. Even that rat Rövid knows to respect tradition."

"Then what are we supposed to do, just sit here and wait?" snapped Kate.

"No, of course not, you need to leave. There's another exit behind the house. It takes you into the trees back there." He indicated out of the kitchen window, to the forest beyond the snow-covered garden. "Follow the track and it will take you round to the other side of the lake."

Jake glared at their host and then looked to his brother for direction.

"We go. There's no point starting a firefight here. All that matters is getting Kate and the Griffin to the Americans," Sam decided.

Jake swore again, but did not argue. Instead, he began to move to the kitchen door. Stopping on the way out, he grasped Bartel by the shoulder. "Klaus, as always, it's been a pleasure."

Bartel placed his hand on Jake's. "Take care of yourself, you fool."

Jake gave a brief smile then continued out into the hallway.

Kate gave Bartel a quick kiss on the cheek. "Thank you for everything. I really hope we meet again."

"Go lovely lady, get away from this place and get your life back." He pushed her out of the kitchen, leaving him alone with Sam.

The Yorkshireman gave a curt nod. "Thank you for your help."

Bartel reached out an arm, and gripped Sam's wrist in a firm grip, stopping him in his tracks. "You know who the mole in the embassy is, don't you?"

Sam gave the old German a surprised look. Bartel suddenly looked old.

"I do. Well, I *think* I do."

Bartel gripped his wrist tighter. "Then you know how dangerous they are?"

"Yes."

"And they call *me* the last spy! Do not underestimate them Sam, they've made it this far and survived this long."

Sam gave a curt nod. "I won't."

"They are desperate Sam, and desperate people do stupid things," warned Bartel. "I'm sure a pupil of Jeffrey Doyle will understand what that means."

A call came out from the hallway as Kate shouted out after him, but Sam's wrist was still caught tightly in the old man's grip.

"I do. Trust me, I've already been thinking about it."

Klaus Bartel finally released his grip on Sam. Stepping back, his face lit up once again, becoming that of their friendly host. "Then stay safe, my friend."

"Come with us," Sam told him. "You are right that they are desperate – desperate enough to ignore the old ways. Who's to say they won't kill you?"

A smile cracked from underneath the thick beard. Klaus Bartel put his arm around Sam's shoulder, guided him into the hallway and patted his chest.

"There's a reason they call me the last spy. I am the last connection to a better age. Rövid could have killed me many years ago."

"Rövid doesn't believe in the old ways of spies anymore. He's given up on those traditions."

They had reached the main entrance and Sam could see his companions waiting for him in the car. The engine was running, ready to depart.

"Then he's a fool. There will always be a place for people like me."

Sam left Bartel in the same location as they had found him,

standing on his porch looking out across the snow. Taking his place in the back of the car, Sam peered through the rear window to watch as Kate sped across the driveway. The old man stood still, watching them go round the corner of the house. Sam ran his hand through his hair. Klaus Bartel was wrong, he was *not* the last spy. There was one more in the British Embassy and Sam Taylor thought he knew exactly who it was.

TWENTY-FIVE

KATE DROVE QUICKLY across the rough track and the car bounced violently as they entered the forest. The thick trees blocked them from view of the house, but Sam still fully expected to see the flash of headlights streaming up behind them. It would not take long for the Russians to work out where they had gone.

"What did Bartel say to you?" Jake asked him.

"Only to be careful," dismissed Sam, not wanting to get into a debate with his companions just yet on the identity of their foe.

"You should have said the same to him," said Jake.

"I did."

Kate shook her head. "I don't like leaving him alone like that. Will they really just let him off?"

"They have done for years. He's right – if they wanted to kill him they could have done so many times." Jake's words sounded hollow to everyone in the car.

"Do you think he will he be okay, Sam?" Kate asked him.

"I honestly don't know. The fact that no one has followed us is making me uneasy." He looked out of the windscreen. "Pull over here, there's a gap in the trees. Let's see if we can see anything back at the house."

Kate did as instructed and brought the car to a stop. Sam, still concerned they were being followed, told Kate to stay in the car and keep the engine running. "Deadlock it. And if you see any headlights behind you, just drive."

Leaving Kate in the driver's seat, the two brothers clambered out of the car and pushed through the foliage until they were able to see unhindered across to the hunting lodge. Even at this distance Sam could see the outline of a car.

"Looks like they decided to stay," murmured Jake.

"Why do I feel uneasy about it?" wondered Sam, aloud.

"Because you know that for them not to be following us, they will have to be still questioning Bartel, and they don't ask nicely."

Jake was right and Sam knew it. They should be still driving down the track out onto the main road back to Berlin. Sam had presumed that the Russians would have seen the tyre tracks and sped straight off in pursuit. But it seemed that whoever had driven up in the car had decided to stay. Crouching there in the trees, Sam thought of Bartel's final warning and his confidence of his own safety. Yet in the cold hard light of day, neither brother had felt comfortable leaving the aged Bartel to face their pursuers alone.

Sam peered across the shimmering surface of the lake and thought he could see a lone figure leaning against the car. A sentry, he guessed.

"Why do you think they stayed?" asked Jake.

"They must want to get as much out of Bartel as they can before they continue the pursuit. Perhaps they think he's hiding us, or that he has the Griffin."

"Jesus."

"We can't leave him."

Jake had a glint in his eye. "Are you thinking of returning to danger, Mr Cautious?"

Sam turned from the gap in the trees and made his way back to the stationary car. He rapped on the driver's door until Kate opened it, and spoke quickly.

"We are going to go back."

Kate's face brightened at the news. "Thank God. I'll turn the car round."

Sam shook his head. "No, you're going to stay here, it will be too dangerous."

"You can't leave me all on my own. What do you expect me to do?"

"You will be fine. If we are not back in twenty minutes, just go. Get back to the city and head straight to the American Embassy. They will look after you."

Kate began to argue, but Sam shut the car door. Turning, he zipped up his parka and began to walk back the way they had come.

Jake followed. "I'm not sure Mother Taylor would be happy knowing what we are about to do."

"I'm not happy about what we are going to do either."

"Well, for a start you need to get rid of that," Jake pointed at the coat. "It's not very practical for this type of work."

Sam looked down at his nice warm coat. As much as he did not want to admit it, Jake was probably right. Unzipping it, he took it off and placed it on top of a pile of snow to one side of the track. Standing there in nothing but a jumper, he felt the icy wind stabbing at him.

"Jesus it's cold," he stuttered, rubbing his arms.

Jake grinned. "My cowboy jacket isn't looking so bad now, is it? Take one of these." He reached behind him and handed Sam the P365. "German made. Just remember the safety catch is placed..."

"I was also in the army Jake, I've held a bloody gun before," snapped Sam. The cold was beginning to make him shiver. "Come on, I'm jogging the rest of the way to stay warm."

The pair of them continued down the track, their breath misting in the air as they ran. The sun was beginning to set in the late afternoon, making the tree covered track even darker. Reaching the end of the tree line they both dropped to their knees and crawled to the edge. The remaining foliage provided cover from any onlookers who might have been staring from the house's windows. Watching from their hiding spot, the two of them looked for any telltale signs from within the building. Nothing moved inside the house. From where they knelt they had a clear view to the rear of the house from across the snow-covered rear garden. Ahead of them, the light from the wide kitchen window spilled out over the ground.

"Through the kitchen door?" breathed Jake.

"Maybe. I don't like leaving that sentry at the front, but I don't think we have the time to go round without being seen."

"We can deal with him later," whispered Jake, checking his weapon. "You cover my six, yes?"

"Piss off, I'll go first and you follow."

"Don't start, mate. Who's the trained marine here?"

Sam rolled his eyes. "And who's the military police officer trained in dealing with marines? We don't have time for this."

"Rock paper scissors for it?"

Moments later, Sam led a disgruntled Jake across the open garden towards the kitchen. Keeping low, their weapons cocked, the two men expected to see movement at any minute. Sam could feel his heart beating hard against his chest as he made his way closer to the stone brick building. Somewhere inside, he guessed there were at least two highly trained FSB agents and the unfortunate Bartel. Not the for the first time in their short excursion, the thought of returning to Kate and driving back to Berlin crept into his mind. He sprinted the final steps to the door before resting against the wall to the side of it. Jake followed and took his position on the other side.

"Ready?" Sam mouthed to Jake. "Remember, it opens outwards and there's only seven or eight feet between this door and the main door into the hallway. Keep quiet."

Jake raised his middle finger in acknowledgement.

Sam took a deep breath, turned the handle and pulled the door outwards, expecting to find the kitchen still empty, how they had left it. Instead, moving into the brightly lit room, he stepped onto the stone flagged floor at the exact same time as an unsuspecting FSB agent entered from the opposite door. For a brief second the two men looked at each other in mute surprise before instinct kicked in. Sam raised his pistol and fired, but the enemy agent had already dived headlong behind the long island table that divided the room. Another agent had followed the first. Hearing the gunshots, he came in firing his weapon blindly, forcing Sam to also duck on his side of the island. The shots from the new arrival flew over him, shattering the window above and showering him in shards of glass. Where the hell was Jake?

The answer came swiftly moments later as the looming figure of the Caretaker flung himself through the open door and, firing at almost point-blank range, sent the second agent falling to the ground. Sam got to his feet and moved to follow his brother when he saw the original Russian springing from his hiding place behind the table to dive onto Jake. The force of the dive drove the younger Taylor against the wall, causing him to drop his weapon as he grappled with his assailant. Sam raised his own firearm, but Jake's body was facing towards him, blocking any shot. Instead, Sam jumped onto the wooden surface of the table and slid over to get a better angle. Landing firmly on the ground, he aimed at the Russian's back. Just as he was about to fire, a roar came from the unseen hallway and a third FSB agent charged him. Sam desperately tried to turn the muzzle round, but he was too slow – a pair of rough hands grabbed his own and pushed them upwards.

This new attacker drove Sam backwards into the kitchen. His gun, now held aloft by two pairs of hands, fired three times into the ceiling. Sam stared into the face of his attacker, only seeing two narrowed eyes in a red cheeked face. The man was screaming in his native language, almost spitting the words as he drove him backwards. Sam, having no momentum of his own, had to keep stepping backwards to avoid falling over. He felt himself being thrown against the brickwork of the open fireplace, knocking the air from him. The roaring fire to Sam's left had been stacked before they had left and now flames licked high into the chimney. The heat of the roaring fire stung his bare face as the pair grappled against the brickwork.

Sam's attacker tried again to tear the pistol from his grip, this time by savagely twisting Sam's arm downwards to his left then using the muzzle to force his wrist backwards. His fingers began to lose their grip. Freeing his right hand, Sam pulled it back and punched the attacker in the kidneys. The force released the pistol from both of their hands to land across the floor and rest on the other side of the fireplace. He swung again, this time aiming for the man's face, but missed as his attacker stepped back to throw his own punch, which landed square in Sam's stomach. This blow sent whatever air he had left out of him and he doubled over.

Somewhere in the kitchen Jake's struggle was still ongoing and Sam knew he was alone at the opposite end of the long room. He tried to grab onto the man's clothes to try and pull himself upright, but the FSB agent just pushed him away. Next, the rough hands grabbed him and went to headbutt him. The move was slow, and Sam was able to step back from it, but in doing so he felt his ankle bash against the fireplace's lower lip. Losing his balance, he fell to the ground and as he did so he felt his fingers brush past the butt of the fallen pistol, pushing it just out of his reach. The FSB agent, seeing the proximity of Sam's hand to the fallen firearm, panicked and dived forwards in an attempt to land on his fallen opponent.

Looking up and seeing the leaping figure of the FSB agent coming towards him, Sam brought up his legs, caught the man in mid-air and kicked him into the open fire. The FSB agent landed square amongst the burning logs and shouted as the flames licked him. Dressed in what looked like a cheap linen suit, the man's clothes quickly caught fire. He tried to roll out of the flames, but Sam kept him firmly in place with his boots pressed against the torso, trapping him against the brickwork. A wretched scream poured from the man's mouth as he tried to claw at Sam in an attempt to free himself from the burning pain. Now the trousers had caught alight, causing the Russian to jerk ever more violently in his attempts to escape.

Sam used this moment. He kicked away from the burning agent to reach for the fallen weapon. In one swift movement, Sam was able to grab his weapon, bringing it round to fire a single shot into the middle of the FSB agent's forehead. The body fell back into the fireplace and went still as the flames continued to grow around it. Sam struggled to his feet and looked for his brother. Jake was still fighting with his attacker. The ex-marine had somehow got the unfortunate Russian pinned down on top of the large iron oven, where he was currently slamming one of the thick copper frying pans over his head. A final huge blow landed on the Russian's skull as Sam called out. "I think you've got him!"

Jake stopped and turned. "Have you finished with your barbecue?"

Sam let out a sarcastic laugh and took a deep breath to refill his lungs. He bent down and pulled the deceased FSB agent from the fire. Using his boots, he kicked the remains of the fire from the dead man.

Jake had walked over to have a look. "You made hard work of that."

"Speak for yourself. What were you doing with that frying pan?"

"Bastard unclipped the gun," Jake scorned.

"He was nearly half your size," Sam chided him. "Bloody marines."

He looked around the room and at the three dead bodies. "What have they done with Bartel?" The fact that he had not come in at the sound of the fight filled Sam with renewed dread.

Jake rubbed his face. "Come on."

They hurried along the kitchen, stepping over the bodies. As they reached the doorway, Jake turned to Sam.

"Shit, the sentry."

Sam looked down at the bodies on the floor. "Could he be one of them?"

Jake shook his head and crept into the hallway. The thick wooden door remained closed. Sam guessed the sound of the fight might not have reached the lone sentry outside.

"I've got this," said Jake, confidently.

Sam watched, intrigued, as his brother walked to the door, opened it and called out "Comrade!" before simply raising his gun and firing two shots. He closed the door and gave Sam a broad grin. "That was easy."

Sam shook his head slightly, disconcerted by his brother's nonchalance at killing a person. But any sympathy he might have had for their Russian attackers evaporated the moment they entered the sitting room. The room had been completely ransacked since their last visit. Every glass frame, cabinet or box had been smashed. Their contents had been thrown across the room or torn to shreds.

"Bastards," Sam muttered.

A faint cough sounded from behind the leather sofas and the pair of them hurried to find Klaus Bartel slumped on the floor. His face had turned ashen, the lined cheeks barely moving. Two bullet holes bubbled in his chest as the air from his lungs seeped out.

"Klaus," called Jake, desperately kneeling next to the old man. Taking his hand he called again. "Klaus."

Sam could see it was already a pointless cause. The now frail face moved slightly as the eyes flickered. The elderly German spy tried to speak, but nothing came out. Instead, he raised his hand from Jake's and pointed.

Looking on, Sam saw where the finger was pointing and went to retrieve the desired item. Kneeling next to Jake he gently placed the white material in the fingers of the hand and closed them round it. The eyes closed a final time as the hand brought the German football shirt up to the bloodied chest. Klaus Bartel, the last remaining spy from the golden age of espionage in Berlin, was dead.

TWENTY-SIX

SAM PLACED his hand on his brother's shoulder, giving it a little squeeze.

"We should go and get Kate."

Jake, still kneeling over Bartel's body, did not respond.

"Jake, we still need to get to the Americans."

The broad-shouldered caretaker seemed not to have heard, so Sam tried again.

"Snap out of it and get your fucking head in gear!" he snapped, giving his brother a gentle knock over the head.

The blow seemed to bring Jake round and he slowly stood up. "Whatever."

Sam stared at his brother. A stern look had appeared, which seemed unnatural on the generally friendly face. For the first time since they had reunited in the German capital, Sam could see the caretaker within.

"We can't do anything for him Jake," Sam said firmly. "But we can still shaft his killers by helping Kate."

Jake's voice was cold as he spoke. "Then we best be going," he told Sam blankly, before leading the way from the living room.

Sam gave the body of Klaus Bartel a final forlorn stare before following his brother out of the ransacked room. They left the way they had come, exiting back through the kitchen with its trio of corpses still spread across the floor. The stench of burnt clothing filled the air as the two left to exit back into the frigid dusk. The sun, which had been setting as they had entered the building, had now disappeared behind the tall trees that surrounded the estate. There seemed to a peaceful air to the place, a sharp contrast to the violence that had occurred within the walls of the hunting lodge.

The Taylors retraced their steps over the snow-covered ground, neither one in the mood for much conversation. Sam's mind was already working on how he would convince the Americans of Kate's innocence and the real mole's identity. Now, in the gloom that had fallen since they were last outside, it felt like this task had become even more pressing.

They pushed through the foliage and stepped back onto the rough track that they had driven on in their attempt to escape earlier. Sam checked his watch and was surprised to see it had been less than an hour since they had been sitting in the warm kitchen all together. It was strange to think that since that moment, five lives including that of their host, had been violently brought to an end. The thought sickened him.

Walking steadily along the track they could see the outline of the car up ahead and Sam gave a wave to reassure the waiting Kate that everything was all right. He was not looking forward to telling her about the death of Bartel.

A thought occurred to him as he walked. "Why did Bartel give you access to his secret equipment room?"

"He didn't?" replied a confused Jake.

"Yes he did, he basically told you the pin code to get in. All that crap about the years Germany won the World Cup. The end numbers of each of the dates were the same four digits he put into the keypad. Did you not watch him?"

Jake shrugged. "Not really, but even if he did there was all that biosecurity to get past."

"I'm willing to bet that wily old bastard has your details stored in there. Why else would he tell you the pin code? Be a waste of time otherwise."

"I hope you're right. I'd love to get my hands on some of that weaponry and give Rövid a little visit," said Jake, eagerly.

The snow on the ground was still thick around their boots as they walked. It had been years since Sam had seen snow like this back home.

"Don't forget your coat," warned Jake, pointing to the folded parka still perched where Sam had left it.

"Yeah, cheers," said Sam, picking it up and putting it back on. The heavy material felt comforting, a reassuring presence.

"Have you still got the Griffin, or did you leave it with Kate?" asked Jake as they began walking again.

Sam reached down and checked his trouser pocket. "Yeah it's still with me, I never even thought about leaving it with her. I guess we were bloody lucky nothing happened to us, could you imagine what she would have said if we lost it?"

Up ahead, the car was a dark shape awaiting them through the trees. Sam was surprised that Kate had not turned on the lights or the engine at their approach. He guessed she was frightened, unable to see who was approaching in the dusk. They walked unsteadily along the woodland track, unsure of their footing in the low light. Suddenly, Jake stopped and threw his arm across Sam's chest. A moment later he had brought out the dull metal pistol from within his jacket.

"What is it?"

"The car, there's no one in it."

Sam peered forward, peering towards the shadowy vehicle.

"Are you sure?"

"Positive."

"It's facing away from us though."

Jake shook his head and cocked the pistol. "Exactly. She would have been twisting in her seat looking for us, and trust me, nothing has moved in there. I doubt she's fallen asleep."

Sam swore, knowing his brother was probably right. He felt

the sudden kick of adrenaline beginning to pump through his veins. His senses instantly flicked into life. The simple gloomy forest track now seemed to be alive with tension. Reaching into the parka he groped clumsily for the SIG Sauer pistol.

They were close now to the vehicle and Sam realised Jake had been right – it was empty. A feeling of dread sunk into his stomach as they approached. He indicated for Jake to take the passenger side while he carefully made for the driver's side window. They peered in. It was completely empty. Please God, thought Sam, don't let anything have happened to her.

"Where the hell is she?"

Sam shrugged his shoulders. "I don't know."

Jake swore and began to call out. "Kate!"

"Jake, stop it, she's not here."

He stopped calling out and glared at his brother. "She may have been watching the house from the trees?"

"Then she would have seen us coming back. Trust me, she's gone."

"But where?"

That was a question that Sam did not want to answer. In his heart he knew that there was only one likely explanation. The car had been deadlocked, after all. But before he could bring himself to admit it, he had to be certain.

"The snow," he said, carefully stepping away from the car and looking about his feet. The white powder immediately around the car had been trampled over by what Sam guessed had been multiple sets of feet. All around the car most of the remaining snow had been squashed to muddy slush, but here and there he could still make out extra footprints that were not his own.

He pointed to a set, clearly imprinted. "Look there, at least one person came from the other direction."

"Shit," Jake cursed. "There's at least three sets coming towards the car."

"And look here." Sam walked forward a little away from the car to where two distinct lines could be seen amongst the broken surface of the white ground. "That's the imprint of a pair of feet being dragged away."

They both looked up the track, which led further into the trees.

"I'm betting we will quickly find some tyre tracks up there as well."

Jake began to pace forward. "They may still be there."

Sam shook his head looking at the footprints around him. "No, they've gone. I'm sure of it."

"What happened, then? How did they get hold of her?" the younger brother asked.

Sam rubbed his chin, looking at the scene around him. "I think they knew about the track and guessed this would be our escape route. That first car was only there to drive us up here to the real ambush, then when we didn't appear I bet they scouted ahead to see where we were."

"Surely Kate would have seen them coming? She was facing up the track."

Still looking at the ground around his feet, Sam shook his head and headed towards the back of the car. "No, I think the moment we left she got out and waited standing against the rear of the car. She was trying to listen to what was happening. Probably planned on following us." He crouched and pointed. "Look, you can see a smaller set of footprints in the snow between the two tyre marks. It will have been where she was standing."

Jake came and looked. "So her attackers were able to just creep up and take her?"

"The snow will have muffled their approach. I bet they were even watching as we left her."

"Why didn't they go for us, then?"

Sam shrugged. "Could be many reasons… An unsuspecting woman alone would have been easier than us two. Plus, she was the last person Rövid knew of who had the Griffin," he told Jake, thinking about their interview earlier in the day. "He saw her put her hand in her pocket when we were talking about it…"

"I bet their orders were to get the girl at all costs and we were just to be seen as collateral," surmised Jake.

Sam slammed his hand on the roof of the car. "For God's sake how stupid were we? We left her alone in the middle of a bloody forest. We might as well have just given her over to them ourselves."

Jake did not reply. Instead, he walked over to stand next to his brother and rested his arms on the car roof. "What will they do with her when they find out she no longer has the Griffin?"

"I don't know, this is beyond me now," admitted Sam. "I've been behind the curve at every stage."

"Surely they will try and ransom her? Kate for the Griffin."

"Probably," sighed Sam. He thought back to the last conversation he'd had with the now dead Bartel. How he had warned him his enemies were getting desperate. But now it was he who had become desperate.

"Bloody hell, Jake, we've fucked up and now Kate is in the hands of the very people who have been trying to destroy her."

Jake looked him up and down, giving him a withering look. "Nah, it's just half time isn't it? Seriously, it's just a setback, we will be alright by the end. You've spent too long in the city, you've forgotten all of the scraps we used to get into. Bartel was telling us you already know who the real mole is, so why don't we start hitting back?"

"Wait, what did Bartel say?"

"That you'd already worked out who the mole in the embassy is and you'd be thinking of a way of bringing them down."

Sam stared at his brother in bewilderment. "What the hell are you talking about? Bartel never said that?"

"He did, when you were on the phone in the other room. Told us both that you were simply putting the final pieces together in your head."

"What a sneaky old bastard," laughed Sam. "I've got a pretty strong suspicion who's pulling the strings, but that doesn't mean anything."

"*Make* it mean something. You're supposed to be the clever one of the pair of us."

"Any other day I'd have been very happy to hear you say that," said Sam.

Finding the car unlocked, they drove it back to Bartel's house. Darkness had now fallen as the pair of them walked back into the warmth of the kitchen. Jake began to search through the cupboards to find something to drink, carefully stepping over the bodies from earlier. Sam meanwhile picked up a fallen stool and pulled out the Griffin. The silver device seemed to shine in the kitchen lights. Somewhere, Kate was being held for this and the thought of her fear made him feel sick.

"Well, the old man did not like gin, so I'm sorry but you're going to have a proper drink." Jake slid a beer over to him.

He took a swig from his own bottle. "I'm going to move Bartel, I don't think I can have a drink while he's just left there."

"I'll come help," said Sam, standing up, but Jake stopped him.

"No, you stay here. By the time I get back you'd better have a plan."

"Do you still have your phone?"

A suspicious Jake reached into his pocket and threw the mobile over. Catching it, Sam placed it down in front of him and took a long mouthful of beer. He now had two choices left to him. He could continue with the original plan, heading off to the Americans and swapping the Griffin for their help retrieving Kate. Or he could admit defeat to his enemies. Pick up the phone, ring up the embassy and agree to trade the Griffin for Kate's life. The very thought of sucking up to those bastards was too much for him to bear. But what could he do? Every minute they sat there was another that Kate was left in danger. There was nothing else left to do, he had to make the call.

Jake re-entered the kitchen just as Sam finished on the phone. Taking the empty seat next to his brother, he drank from the open beer bottle. He eyed his brother before asking the next question.

"Are you sure you've done the right thing?"

"I think so."

"You're relying on a lot going your way."

Sam stood up, finished his drink and slid the phone back over to his brother. "You don't have to come with me, I can do it alone."

"Mum's already not going to be happy with me. Imagine what she would say if she found out I'd let you do this on your own?"

Sam, reassured by his brother's belief in him, suddenly felt tired as the events of the past few days caught up with him. To save Kate they had to surrender the Griffin. They had lost.

TWENTY-SEVEN

THE HISTORIC REICHSTAG building had been at the heart of German politics since the end of the nineteenth century. Its colossal four towered neo-renaissance form, originally designed by the architect Paul Wallot, was built on the south bank of the River Spree. The iconic building had only re-opened at the end of twentieth century as the country reunified after decades of division. A new feature had been added to transform the building as it broke into the new millennia. A huge glass dome had been built atop of the historic monument, its publicly accessible walkways providing 360-degree views of the city. It was the city's crown upon its most treasured building.

This evening, however, the whole building had been closed off to allow the great and good of the German diplomatic community to attend a charity ball hosted by the Chancellor himself. The front of the building was illuminated by bright spotlights, which cast shadows across the imposing pillars embedded within the walls. A bright red carpet led up from the roadway, up the stone stairs, which led into the main entrance of the building. Lightbulbs flashed as the press corps jostled to take photos of the arrivals as they exited their limousines to take the stairway. Most of the guests were more than happy to walk slowly or to stand for a moment to ensure that they were caught by the cameras being pointed in their direction.

Standing away from the scene was Sam Taylor. He watched on as the evening's guests continued to make their way into the building. One of those cars would be carrying the British contingent, the guests of honour that evening as the signing of the North Sea energy deal moved ever closer. One of those guests would be waiting for him inside and the thought of seeing them again made his skin crawl. Ever since the phone call in Bartel's house, Sam's mind had been on Kate. Where was she now? What had they done to her? Would they agree to the exchange – and more importantly, honour it? The person he was about to meet would be able to tell him. Until then he would have to wait in the cold night air, his hands firmly shoved into the deep pockets.

It began to snow again, forcing Sam to pull the fur lined hood over his head. He had grown tired of being cold. It seemed that everywhere he went in this damn city all he found himself doing was waiting in the cold with his hands in his pockets. He made a mental note to ask Emma to assign him somewhere warm next time. Stamping his feet, he wondered who would come to greet him. The message had been to wait here to be collected and then escorted inside the building opposite. He guessed that did not mean walking up the red carpet.

Twenty minutes passed. He took out his hand from the warm pocket to check the time on his Rolex. Whoever it was they were late by a good ten minutes. The night before, spent back in the high hotel between the soft warm sheets with Kate, now seemed a long time ago.

"Sam?"

He turned, surprised by the familiar voice. Wrapped up against the cold was Hendricks. The young security officer looked visibly confused.

"Hendricks," replied Sam, cautiously.

"Well I wasn't expecting to see you again," said Hendricks,

breaking out into a welcoming smile. "What the hell are you doing here? I thought you had gone home?"

"I'm sorry to have dragged you out from the party."

The younger man shook his head. "I'm not invited, I'm just here on driving duty."

"And delivery detail, it seems."

The two of them set off, Hendricks leading Sam towards the Reichstag. They crossed the road, dodging the still arriving vehicles, before heading right to follow the side of the building.

"I don't know what it is you've done to get this treatment, but I think it's fair to say you've upset a few people," Hendricks told him.

"I don't take it personally, it's kind of what I do."

Hendricks laughed. "There's a staff entrance just round here. I've had to pay the security guard fifty euros to keep it open for us."

Hendricks flashed his pass at the bored-looking security guard, who simply waved them in and returned to looking at his phone. Thankful to be inside and away from the snow, Sam unzipped his coat and followed Hendricks along the different corridors which crisscrossed through the building.

"Where are you taking me?"

"Right to the top, there's only one place quiet enough for whatever it is you're doing here tonight. We had to pull a few strings, but we are heading to the glass dome. It's going through some renovations so it's closed off from the public at the moment."

"Well at least I'll get a nice view."

They reached the end of the corridor and arrived at a pair of metal elevator doors. Hendricks pressed the button then stood still as the doors opened.

"Sorry Sam, I've been ordered to go no further. This will take you right to the top."

Sam stepped into the small box and waved merrily to his guide as the metal doors closed. There was a slight judder as the mechanical system came to life and began the slow climb up through the floors. Sam watched as the digital display showed the numbers of each floor until once more, the elevator gave a little judder as it came to a stop. A loud ping sounded as the doors in front of him gradually pulled apart to reveal the waiting figure of John Travers standing feet apart in the middle of the deserted room.

Keeping his voice steady, Sam greeted the waiting Scotsman. "Glad to see you've sacrificed your evening of champagne and canapés to be here."

The weathered face narrowed as he glared at the new arrival.

"You have some nerve, Taylor. Why you are not back in London, I'll never know."

Sam shrugged as he stepped out of the elevator to join the Head of Security in the hallway. Ahead of him stood a set of glass doors that led into the main part of the dome.

"I prefer the climate here."

The Scotsman's eyes furrowed. "Let's get this over with. I do have better things to do with my time than to stand talking to you."

He indicated for Sam to follow him and they walked on past the line of elevators which would lead visitors downwards into the main part of the Reichstag. Pushing the glass doors outwards, they stepped onto the open floor of the glass dome. Looking upwards, Sam could see swirls of snow pattering on the thick panes of glass above him.

Travers turned to Sam. "Let's get this done then. Spread your arms."

Sam stretched both his arms and legs outwards, allowing the swift hands of the Head of Security to pat him down. There was no warmth in the man's face as he scowled down at Sam. In response, Sam gave a simple smile and tried to feel more confident than he felt.

Travers took another step back. His job completed, he called out, "He's clean."

Another voice answered, this time a woman's crisp tone. "Thank you John, you can leave us now. Wait for our friend back in the room over there."

Sam looked over his shoulder to see the slim frame of the British Ambassador to the German Republic, Angela Cooper. She was dressed that night in a long evening coat. It covered a shimmering silver dress, which glittered as she moved. John Travers gave a curt nod to his manager before leaving Sam alone with the Ambassador. Cooper waited until the Scotsman had closed the door behind him before turning to look at Sam.

"Well Mr Taylor, you *have* been causing a lot of trouble, haven't you?" The voice seemed different than before, more confident, as if with all of the subterfuge removed she could be her true self around him.

Sam kept his voice level. "I think we have a different opinion of who's been causing the trouble, Ambassador."

Cooper smiled. "Indeed. Shall we?" She waved her hand at the spiralling walkway that led to the summit of the dome. Not waiting for Sam, she set off. "Shall we start with the pleasantries, Mr Taylor? You will be glad to know Miss May is alive and well."

"And you have proof of that?"

Cooper stopped walking and turned back to Sam, who had yet to move. "Do you think I carry photos of captive young women on my phone Mr Taylor? No, you will have to just take my word for it. Now do come along." She waved her arm to indicate that he should follow her.

Sam took a breath to steady himself before following. It was going to take a good deal of self-control not to throw the Ambassador through one of these glass windows. "Fine, I'll take your word for it. Does that mean you've decided to accept my offer? The Griffin for Kate?"

She waved her hand nonchalantly, not even looking at him. "Later, let us at least reach the top first."

They continued to follow the spiralling walkway, which

wound around the edges of the glass dome. Every few feet provided a new vantage point of the city.

"I have to say I have been very impressed with your tenacity, Mr Taylor. Ever since you arrived in this city it has been non-stop. From finding the girl to now, I do feel we've had to play our best cards just to keep up with you."

Sam ignored the compliment. "It hasn't felt like it, from where I've been sitting."

"No? Then perhaps you will be as pleased as we are that this little show must soon come to an end."

Sam grunted. "Don't worry, the Griffin will soon be back in your hands so you can let your friends stop the signing."

"Stop the signing?" she asked in surprise. "Why would we do that?"

Now Sam stopped, caught off guard. "Surely that's what you're after? To release whatever incriminating documents you have to stop Britain and EU signing the North Sea energy deal?"

She laughed, a high-pitched noise that seemed to emanate from her nostrils. "No, you silly fool, it's quite the opposite. We want the deal to be signed. In fact, we are counting on it."

Sam frowned. "But why? I can't imagine your friends at the Kremlin being happy about that?"

Cooper flicked at her black hair before once again indicating for Sam to continue following her. "Now Sam, I have no problem telling you everything, as at the end of our conversation I will make you a personal proposition, which I do hope you will honour me by accepting."

Sam highly doubted he would accept anything from this woman, but kept silent.

"You see, you forget the one key rule when it comes to dealing with the Russians. They are only interested in the long game. It is one of the beauties of a dictatorship that you don't need to worry about the next election because the electorate already knows who to vote for."

"That's how I knew you were the mole – after Rövid's little

speech about influencing and playing the long game. He was trying to make me think he was referring to Travers and his years of service, but I knew it was you. So did Bartel; he guessed straight away. He knew you would be the only person Rövid had eyes on. Travers is a grumpy bastard, he didn't like me cross checking his work, but he's no spy."

Cooper gave one of her sly smiles, then asked in sickly voice: "Anything else the great detective spotted?"

"You accepted the false spy story too easily."

"I did?"

"Yes, as soon as I met Kate, I knew she couldn't be a spy. You worked with her more than anyone, so surely you would have at least questioned it. I could have understood Travers suspecting her, he hardly knew her, but you should have known better."

"Well done. For all the good it's done you. You are still in the exact same position as you were in Rövid's store. The girl for the Griffin."

She had a point, thought Sam, but he would be damned if he admitted it. "Tell me then, how does using a Griffin to steal official documents help you 'influence' the world in this case, if it's not to stop the deal?"

They had reached the top of the dome. Cooper had led them to a bench, which overlooked the east of the city. Sam could see the outline of the mighty Fernsehturm in the distance. The tower was a monument to the eastern half of the capital's history.

"The media."

"The media?" queried Sam.

"The media is the most powerful tool that any state has at its disposal. Just think about any authoritarian state in the world and how they prioritise controlling the media. Even more than the police or military, those in command of the media have access to the hearts and minds of a population. If you can make your audience love you then the need for force becomes irrelevant."

The conversation was not going the way Sam was expecting it

to. But the way in which Angela Cooper now spoke intrigued him. He could not help wanting to know more.

"This is what Rövid was getting at when he talked about influencing?" said Sam, thinking again of his speech earlier that day.

"Exactly! Now think of social media: its potential, its lack of controls. The West has managed to create something that allows countries like Russia, who have spent decades honing influencing skills on its own people, to reach into the homes of their native populations. Now, people like us are able to decide what information is read by civilians of all countries. We can influence people in ways Western governments can only dream of."

"You mean such as influencing elections?"

"Elections, referendums, Christ even local council elections can now be fixed to our advantage. We can destroy a politician in a single post, which is then reposted by thousands of fake accounts across all platforms. Soon, with the promises of AI, the possibilities will be endless."

Sam was beginning to see where this was going. These state-run misinformation campaigns were becoming the bane of the Western world as governments tried to combat them. But here in front of him, one of the most prominent representatives for Britain was openly touting the power of those who wanted to damage the country.

"Let me guess, you want to leak parts of the North Sea Deal to… what… make you look better? Help you sell more books?"

Ambassador Angela Cooper laughed once more and gently punched Sam's arm. She was clearly enjoying being able to share her grand schemes.

"Well that would also be nice, but no, I want to leak parts of the North Sea Deal to help me become Prime Minister."

TWENTY-EIGHT

FOR A MOMENT, Sam thought that he had misheard the Ambassador. He needed to take a moment to process what it was she had said.

"To help you become Prime Minister?"

"Yes, that's right."

Sam shook his head. "You're joking."

"Do I look like someone who jokes?"

"How does all this help you become Prime Minister?

"It is really very simple, Mr Taylor. First we allow the signing of the North Sea Deal. Next, we leak documents showing how I played a key role in achieving the country's great new commercial deal and how the PM was a constant thorn in my side. For example, he's been very concerned about the global warming impacts. Imagine how his voters will feel about something as trivial as that when there's money to be made? From there, I return to parliament to take a place in the cabinet to help prop up an unpopular Prime Minister. Finally, after a short period of time when the PM has to step down due to the unpopularity of the party, I am elected by the members to save the day."

Sam shook his head. "You're mad, everything you've just said is a fantasy."

Sam moved away from the woman who had her eyes on the highest position in the land. Angela Cooper would not only be Prime Minister, but she'd be in the pocket of the Russians, and the Griffin was the tool that would enable her to take the first step. A tool which Sam was going to hand over in return for Kate's life.

"What about after you become Prime Minister? What will you be doing for your Russian masters? I guess they will be wanting something in return for helping you?"

Cooper crossed her legs. "You know, the usual. I'll be able to share confidential documents, policies, intelligence. Let's say our Russian friends would like to know the latest NATO compositions, or when we next trade information with our CIA allies. It would be a real shame if someone spilled their secrets. Or perhaps I can damage the UK economy with some extreme policy or budget? Come out with an ill thought-out referendum which splits us from our closest allies. The possibilities are limitless."

Sam felt a shudder of disgust. "You said you had a proposition for me?" he asked her, coldly.

"I've just told you that within twelve months I'll be Prime Minister. At which time I will be in need of resourceful men like yourself. I've already said how impressed I've been with everything you've done these past few days. Perhaps we can come to some arrangement beyond the exchange of the Griffin for Miss May? Perhaps a career in the Foreign Office – fast tracked by sponsorship from above?"

Sam raised an eyebrow.

"I think together we could make some great changes in our country. But if you decide otherwise…"

Sam held up his hand. "Don't. Just… stop. I'm not interested in what you have to say. Whatever you have to offer only comes gift wrapped by the FSB and I will not be getting into bed with those bastards. If you want to sell whatever is left of your soul, be my guest. Just give me the girl and then I can piss off."

Her good humour disappeared in an instant, to be replaced by a look of pure venom and scorn. "You self-righteous bastard standing there and judging me? You, with a cold-blooded murderer for a brother? Yes, I know all about Caretaker Jake. You would know all about getting into bed with the wrong type of people."

"Get on with it, Ambassador. I'm here for the girl and you're here for the Griffin. Tell me where she is, and we can get this over with.

Angela Cooper sidled over to join Sam standing by the rail. The sound of her heels echoed in the empty dome. She looked up at him with a mixture of disappointment and anger. "Rövid will meet you with the girl at 64 Gartenstrasse. It's a building site, so an open space like you asked for. Bring the device at midnight this evening."

"Thank you. I don't think there's anything else left to say." He turned to leave and head back down the ramp when the sound of her heels echoed again. He turned.

"Taylor, there is *one* last thing to say."

Sam sighed and steeled himself for a final jibe. "I don't think there is."

"Oh, there is. You know how this type of thing ends. Even when you hand over the Griffin, you know it does not end there. Do you know what happens to people like you? What our British government will do when it gets hold of you all? Remember, to them you are still wanted double agents working for the Russians."

Sam just stared back directly into the fiery eyes. "I'm sure you're going to tell me."

"It would be my pleasure. There's a small airfield just outside of London and within one of the hangars is a soundproof container. In this container are two doors. One leads to a comfortable office, the other to a… less comfortable room. In between is a one-way mirror. I'm sure your imagination can do the rest."

"If you say so."

"I do – and believe me when I say those that enter one door do not come out. Instead, they arrange for you to have a little accident. Generally, a crash of some sort. It helps to hide any remaining injuries."

Sam gave the Ambassador a final fleeting smile before turning and walking away. It took every sinew of his self-control not to lash out at her. Instead, he focused on staring in front of him as he walked quickly back down the walkway. Above him, the Ambassador watched on. As he reached the bottom, she called out to him.

"Remember Taylor, this will never be over. You and the girl will always be running. You had your chance."

Walking across the floor of the dome he saw John Travers push open the glass doors and come towards him. Sam stopped and looked up at the still watching Ambassador, then raised his middle finger.

"What the hell are you playing at?" asked a visibly angry Travers.

"I should ask you the same question. How long have you been Head of Security?"

"Over thirty years. Why?"

"Then in over thirty years, you've failed to learn anything, you useless bastard."

John Travers grabbed Sam by the coat and held him upright. "Say that again."

"You need to open your eyes and do your fucking job."

"Let him go, John," Cooper called out from the top of the dome. "You will soon be able to hunt down Mr Taylor yourself."

Travers reluctantly let go of Sam's coat. "You're a lucky bastard Taylor, I hope you know what you're doing."

Sam stepped back from the Scotsman and gave the peering figure of the Ambassador a final glance before turning to head back the way he had come. Stepping into the corridor he leant against the wall and swore. He closed his eyes and tried to comprehend everything that had just happened. The sneering face of Angela Cooper swam into view and he rubbed his face trying to force it away. The thought of her getting her bloodstained hands on the keys of Number Ten scared him. Images of the damage she could cause flashed through his mind. She could ruin the country, she could hand over state secrets, their own and those of their allies. There would be a Russian plant at the top table of every major western establishment from NATO to the UN. But what else could he do? He had to save Kate. Whatever came afterwards would have to be dealt with by others.

The doors to the elevator pinged open and Sam stepped in to see Hendricks.

"That was quick?"

Sam shrugged. "They didn't invite me in for canapés."

Nor was there any alcohol on offer, he thought sourly. After that experience he felt he could do with one. They made their way back through the corridors which made up the inner workings of the Reichstag. Hendricks tried to make conversation as they wandered back to the exit. Sam kept his replies minimal, dodging the building's staff who were busily walking past them. His mind tried to run through the conversation to see if he had missed something of use from the Ambassador's speech, but it was already becoming a blur. The way that Cooper and Rövid saw the world was beyond anything he had expected when he had arrived. Then there was the comment about Jake. He felt the barb still sticking into him. She was right, his own brother was nothing more than a hired killer, so what did that make him?

They reached the exit and the bored security guard barely acknowledged them as Hendricks pushed the door open. Stepping out into the fresh night air the two men turned to face each other.

"I'm guessing whatever you're up to, it isn't good?" Hendricks asked him.

Sam fiddled with his zip and fastened the coat against the snow, which was now falling heavily over them. "Something like that, Hendricks."

"Well just be careful, Sam." He stuck out his hand, which Sam took. "This city may be safer than in the past, but it still has its fair share of bad eggs."

Sam grinned. "You have no idea."

Now alone in the Berlin night, Sam stuffed his hands back in his pockets against the cold and began to make his way away from the Reichstag. Behind him the photographers waited for their targets to reappear at the end of the night. He was certain Angela Cooper would ensure she was in the centre of plenty photos when it became her turn to leave. Trudging along the pathway which bordered the Platz der Republik he paused for a moment to take a final look at the illuminated Reichstag with its crowning glass dome. Taking in the sight, he wondered what the rest of the evening would bring, when he noticed a pair of walkers had also stopped. Both were dressed in black jackets, their heads covered in woollen hats. For a moment, both stood still, unsure of what to do. A tail, thought Sam, watching the indecision play out between the men in front of him. FSB, he guessed, they had probably expected Sam to have kept walking as quickly as possible to escape the area. By suddenly stopping to take in the view he had inadvertently stitched them up.

He continued to follow the street, but increased his speed. Perhaps Rövid wasn't keen on waiting for his prize. Well, if that was his game then so be it, thought Sam as he walked onwards. Reaching a crossroads, he had to wait for a moment for the traffic to stop and used the interruption to see where his followers were. The pair had paused and were pretending to unlock a public hire bike. Internally, Sam laughed at their incompetence. Whoever this pair were, they were not the FSB's finest. The traffic came to a pause and Sam strode confidently across the road. He heard his pursuers as they ran to beat the resumption of flowing traffic.

Sam was now walking down the Scheidemannstrasssse, which then joined the John Foster Dulles Street, named after the famous American Secretary of State. John Foster Dulles had been a major opponent of the communist Soviet Union in his day. Sam guessed the old politician would have approved of what he planned on doing next. Around him, lit only by the odd streetlamp, were rows of trees as the street circled the Tiergarten. A perfect place for an ambush, thought Sam, as he continued on. With only the bare branches of the trees and the swirling snow for cover, the now empty street would give the FSB agents everything they needed.

A line of cars was parked alongside the path. Sam slowed his pace to a leisurely stroll, then ran his hands over the tops of the vehicles to drive off the settled snow. He whistled an old Beatles song as he made his way along, only breaking his movement at one vehicle where he gave the briefest double knock on the rooftop before continuing on his way. Behind him he could still hear his pursuers and wondered when the moment would occur. He risked a quick look over his shoulder to see the two agents had closed the gap between himself and them.

Still whistling, Sam continued onwards and looked to the dark sky as flurries of snow still fell all around him. Then he heard the muffled sound of a scuffle behind him. Spinning around, he saw the outline of one body already prone on the ground and another one falling as it joined its companion on the pathway. Standing over them, holding a large iron wrench, was Jake.

The taller Taylor brother looked down at his handiwork. "I take it they didn't like what you had to say to the Ambassador?"

Sam shrugged. "Probably more than they liked that wrench."

Jake hefted the large tool that had once belonged to Klaus Bartel, and threw it up before catching it again in his other hand. "Told you it would come in handy."

Sam shook his head. "Come on, let's move them before anyone sees us."

Moments later, with the two unconscious Russians hidden in the surrounding trees, the brothers returned to the waiting blue Volkswagen campervan. Sliding into the driver's seat, Jake turned on the engine, allowing the heat to flow.

"Bartel sure did have good taste in vehicles," said Jake, rubbing his hands in front of the heater. "I bet he's got all sorts packed up back there." He thumbed behind him into the rear of the Volkswagen.

"We can look later."

It had been Sam's idea to take Bartel's campervan. Its sliding doors gave enough room for a quick entrance or exit and would be useful for what they knew was to come.

"What did Cooper have to say?" Jake asked his brother.

Sam told him everything. The whole episode seemed even worse in the retelling. Everything about the Ambassador now caused Sam to burn with a simmering anger.

Jake shook his head and looked out of the windscreen. "I don't use this word lightly, but what a bitch."

"She did give us the location for Kate's exchange, though." He relayed it to Jake, who passed Sam his phone. He flicked onto Maps to study the meeting site. "She said it was a building site at the moment so we should be able to drive right in."

"Driving in won't be the problem, it will be the driving out," muttered Jake. He looked down at the steering wheel and gave it a gentle pat. "Although Bartel did say it was a four-wheel drive."

"But not bulletproof."

"Aye, fair point."

The two brothers sat still in the front of the campervan as the bonnet continued to be covered by the falling snow.

Sam elbowed his brother. "Well, remember you said I was the clever one."

The caretaker shook his head and turned on the engine, bringing the vehicle to life. "I'm beginning to regret that."

The repatriation officer laughed and stretched out his legs, making himself comfortable. "Also, before I forget, thank you."

"For what?"

"For saving me again back there. Without you, who knows what those bastards would have done to me."

Jake gave a huge, satisfied grin and put the van into drive. "About bloody time I got some gratitude."

TWENTY-NINE

AFGHANISTAN

Lieutenant Sam Taylor stood in the middle of the living room with the two bodies lying at his feet. Outside, he could hear the clear-up operation ramping up as voices giving orders drifted through the open windows. Somewhere down there, Jake was being prepared for transport back to the base and probably evacuation back to the main medical facilities back in Camp Bastion. What fate awaited him afterwards was now a decision for Sam to make. Reluctantly, he looked back down at the two bodies as they lay in their death poses. The older man had thick wavy hair that had turned a light shade of grey. He looked shocked at the vicious act of violence that had brought his life to a premature end within his own home. The second body was that of a boy, barely in his teens. He looked peaceful, as if he had fallen asleep in this unnatural position.

Sam stepped back, took off the red beret of his regiment and ran his hand through his hair. What the hell was he supposed to do? So far, no one down below even knew of the two bodies. He could simply walk away and leave them, let events take their own course. If Jake was implicated, so be it. There were mitigating circumstances, it was a warzone, these things happened. In Jake's defence, he was clearly concussed from his injuries. There was no chance that he would have committed such an act if he had been in control of his senses. The levers of military discipline would take all that into account, and whatever happened, he was sure Jake would be treated fairly. But then there was another factor. Jake would have to carry this with him for the rest of his life. The brother he had once known would be haunted by this every day he woke up on this planet. In Sam's mind two lives had already been ruined, so he had to protect a third.

Still unsure of what he could actually do to help, he left the two deceased Afghans and walked downstairs to the street below. All around him teams of people were attempting to bring normality to the scene of carnage. Further down the street a line of marines could be seen guarding the far end from the curious onlookers who were venturing back outside now that the danger had passed.

"Christ, you look terrible," a familiar voice called out.

Looking round, Sam saw Corporal Bell walking towards him.

"All right Tim, what the hell are you doing here?"

Tim Bell gave his commanding officer a shrug and held up Sam's helmet and tactical vest which held his body armour, along with all the kit expected of a soldier in the middle of a warzone.

"I saw you driving off dressed only in your underwear and thought you might like to feel a bit more dressed for the occasion."

Sam gratefully took the offered equipment. The heavy weight of the vest and helmet gave him a comforting sense of familiarity.

Bell was looking at the scene around him. "Bloody hell, this is shit, isn't it?"

Sam nodded. "It really is. I suppose we should be grateful for the calm we've had over the past few weeks."

"Did you find your brother?"

"Yes, he was caught up in the blast. Last time I saw him, he was being carried back."

"Is it serious?" Bell asked, concerned for his officer.

"A head wound, but he will live. We Taylors have thick heads."

Bell laughed. "Stubbornness must run in the family. Did you want a lift back?"

Sam sighed, the temptation was to return to the forward operations base. But his indecision around Jake kept him rooted to the damaged street. Suddenly, a thought struck him.

"How did you get here, Tim?"

"I came in the truck." He saw the look on his officer's face. "I'm sorry, but there was nothing else going out."

Sam raised his hands to calm his subordinate. "No that's fine, in fact I'm glad you did. Is it parked up there?" He pointed back up the road.

"Yes, sir."

"Grand. Right, what I'd like you to do is go and find whoever's in charge and ask them if they need any extra military police personnel down here. He will likely say no, but less politely. After which, return back to the truck and I'll meet you there."

Bell gave a brief nod to his officer and left to start his search. Sam waited a moment to watch him go. Then, still unsure of his chosen course of action, he walked briskly back up the street. Bypassing a couple of armoured vehicles and groups of marines, he soon found the truck. Wandering around to the rear as casually as possible, he opened the back door and pulled over the nearest crate. Opening the lid, he looked down at the collection of recovered AK-47 assault rifles he and Bell had been reviewing earlier. They looked very worn, their casings scratched and dented. All were well used from campaigns dating back to fighting off Russian invaders in the eighties.

Could he actually do this? It would be seen as planting evidence. It would be committing a crime, implicating an innocent man. Sam's mouth was dry as he tried to think straight. Now that he was actually here, the choice did not seem quite so simple. But then he remembered his brother. The poor civilians were dead, yes they were innocent, yet nothing he did could bring them back. Biting his lip he made his choice, grabbed the top rifle and a couple of ammunition clips from another case before shutting the truck door. Looking around, he saw no one was watching him. He was just another uniformed soldier in a street full of them. No one was paying any attention to the type of weapon he was carrying.

Now walking a little quicker, he headed back to the centre of the explosion. There was no sign of Bell or any other officers who may have stopped to question his reappearance. The thought of what he would actually say if challenged about carrying a Soviet era rifle, flashed unwelcome into his mind. He reached the entrance, which led back up to the flat, and he saw the bloody handprint was still bright on the doorway. Reaching the top of the stairs he re-entered the room and rushed to the waiting bodies. Placing an ammunition clip into one of the rifles he turned back to the top of the stairs where he had found Jake. He aimed just ahead of the entrance to the stairs and fired a quick burst.

Shouts erupted from the street below and Sam called out through the open window. "All clear, it was just a misfire. Silly buggers had some old Russian made rifles up here."

Gently, he knelt and placed the rifle just in range of the deceased man. A wave of nausea flooded his senses and he was overwhelmed with guilt over what he had just done. It was the opposite of everything he believed in. He felt like he had thrown all his honour away for his brother. Stepping back, he gave the room a final look and left. Outside, he looked up at the clear sky and closed his eyes. It took all his self-control not to run back in and retrieve the weapon he had just planted.

He was brought back to earth by the sound of the same commanding officer from earlier calling out to him. "You there, MP?"

Sam opened his eyes and turned to face the approaching officer. "Yes, sir?"

The marine officer studied Sam.

He indicated the entrance to the flat. "That's where they found Sergeant Taylor, yes?"

"I believe so, yes. I've just been inside and it looks like he found two insurgents in there."

"Did he indeed? Good man, that Taylor." The officer beamed and pushed past Sam to head inside, then stopped in the doorway.

"Your corporal said you were heading back, yes?"

"That was the plan."

The officer thought for a moment and nodded. "Very good, I'll see you back at the base."

Sam was glad to be released from the scene of his crime and wasted no further time in leaving the bombsite. Finding Bell waiting for him by the truck, he opened the passenger door and told the younger man to get them back as quickly as possible. Bell was trying to make conversation as they drove back through the market town, but Sam was in no mood to listen. Instead, his mind drifted back to Jake. He wondered how bad the injuries were. Head wounds were always messy, the blood would flow freely even from the smallest of injuries. Whatever happened, Jake was going to be left with a nasty scar for the rest of his life.

Another thought popped into his mind. Should he contact their parents? He could ring and at least prepare them for the news, which would soon be arriving. No, he decided it would be best to leave it to the usual army channels. An ill-informed call from him would only create more questions than answers.

"There go the Chinooks," said Bell, looking out of the windscreen.

Sam opened his eyes and followed Bell's gaze to see the silhouettes of two large helicopters flying overhead, back to their base and the medical facilities at Camp Bastion. Even inside the bouncing truck, the engine of the helicopter pounded in Sam's ears. Jake would be in one of those aircraft, hopefully drugged up against the pain.

"Least those poor sods will be sleeping in a proper bed tonight," commented Bell.

Sam chuckled. "I've told you before, if you want a ride in one of those birdies just lie down in front of the truck and I'll drive over you."

"I can't do that sir, it would mean leaving you here all by yourself."

"I'll survive."

"With respect, you can't even dress yourself properly. Who runs into a warzone with just a T-shirt and his red beret? You know they will be talking about this in the mess for years."

"Goddamn you, Corporal."

Bell gave a rueful smile. "By the time I've finished telling everyone the story, you will be running out of the camp in nothing but your boxers."

The sun was setting when the last of the clean-up teams returned back to base. Sam perched on a chair outside the main operations cabin with a mug of tea. He watched as the weary troops clambered off their vehicles and began to unload what remained of their gear. They looked worn out from the day's efforts, their faces covered in a mixture of sweat and dust. Sam had forgotten most of them were newly arrived at the base and this day of death had been their first on the site. Welcome to the war gentlemen, he mused to himself.

Stretching out his legs he held tightly to the warmth of the tea as he watched on. All afternoon, he had been wrestling with his conscience. The rational voice in his head kept repeating that what had happened had happened and no amount of worrying could change that. All that was left was to face whatever the future held.

Across the assembly yard he recognised the officer in command from earlier walking over to the operations cabin.

"Everything go okay?" Sam asked the approaching marines officer.

The officer paused his stride for a moment and stared down at

Sam before a look of recognition grew on his tired face. "Yes, we got there in the end, thank you."

"Good stuff. I'm sorry you've had a rough start to the posting."

He gave a polite nod of thanks and began to walk past, but stopped before entering the cabin.

"You didn't tell me you were Sergeant Taylor's brother?" He made the accusation a question.

"No, I'm sorry. I did not want to complicate matters. It's why I followed the response teams."

The marine nodded and rubbed a layer of dust from his eyes. "He never told us he had an a military police brother. Well I'm glad you tagged along, if only to help us find Taylor. The man's a bloody hero."

Sam shifted slightly in his seat, uncomfortable at having to face his actions. "He is?"

"Yes, I had my men do a full search of the flat after you found the rifles. Turns out the whole place was full of hidden supplies and weaponry. Whoever the man was that was living there, he was knee deep in shit."

Sam looked up at the officer, confused by what he was hearing. "What else was there?"

The officer took off his helmet. "In the bedroom we found more of those bloody Russian rifles. You will have to get your man to collect them tomorrow to go with the rest. The kitchen was worst, it was a bloody bomb making lab. Our chaps were over the moon with what they recovered. It will help them learn about what the current trend in detonators are."

Sam shook his head in shock. "Bloody hell, what about the two he killed?"

The marine officer gave a dismissive wave. "They were definitely the ones that lived there, we even think the younger one might have placed the explosive. One of the neighbours saw him earlier. Probably stole it without his father's knowledge otherwise why use it so close to home? Bloody idiot."

"Christ, I did not expect you to tell me that."

"Looks like Taylor will be getting rewarded for having his ear blown off. Although between you and me, those who were with him reckon he had no idea what he was doing. Concussed, probably, he got lucky. It will no doubt look good back at HQ."

With that the marine officer went inside the cabin to give his report, leaving Sam to process what he had just heard. Taking a deep sip of the still warm tea he looked out across the rest of the operations base. He was off the hook, the two rifles would be scooped up with the rest of the cache. The two deceased civilians were in fact insurgents and no one would hold that against Jake. Yet after all that, it still left a sour taste in his own mouth. No matter what else, Jake had shot two people in cold blood and Sam had tried to cover it up.

THIRTY

SAM WATCHED as the clock on the van's screen continued to count the seconds down towards midnight. He was sitting on the leather bench at the back of the campervan, his legs once again stretched out in front of him. But unlike that evening in Afghanistan there was no warm mug of tea to keep his hands occupied. Instead, his arms were folded against the cold as he continued his constant monitoring of the electronic clock as it slowly progressed through the night. Sitting there, he thought about that day in the dusty market town. It had been the last time he had seen Jake, ever since the two of them had managed to contrive excuses not to be in each other's company. For many years, Sam had laid the blame on his brother, suspecting it was Jake's way of dealing with his shame. But now he wondered if it had not been him who had kept the distance between the two of them.

"Klaus could have at least kept a few beers in his swingers' van," complained Jake from the front seat. "He always was a tight bastard."

Sam looked out of the window onto the side street where Jake had pulled up. The snow was still falling, heavier now than at any other time since he had arrived in the city. The scene outside seemed to make Sam's mood worse.

He kicked the back of the chair, causing Jake to look round in surprise.

"All right mate, calm it down. What was that for?"

"Don't give me mate. It's you. I've been feeling it ever since you showed up yesterday. We've not spoken for years and now you walk back in as if nothing's changed? Last time I saw you, half your face was missing and now not a single word? I find you here in Berlin as a glorified contract killer and you expect us to just be mates?"

Jake's face paled at the unexpected onslaught. A hurt look crept across his usually cheerful features. "I don't really know what you're talking about."

"Yeah you do, you absolutely know," snarled Sam, angry at his brother's pretence of innocence.

Jake reached down and pulled the lever that allowed the driver's chair to turn to face into the campervan's interior.

"You really want me to say it, don't you? Why? Will it make you feel even better about yourself? Allow you to look even further down on your little brother?"

"Perhaps it will help with that chip you have on your shoulder."

Jake's face flushed. "You should try always living in your shadow. It was never easy having to be second to the great and mighty Sam."

"Why did you bother turning up here, Jake? You could have just gone back home once you realised it was me."

Jake stiffened and looked uncomfortable. "Because I wanted to prove to you I was better than the marine you found at the top of those stairs."

Sam went to reply, but paused as he realised what Jake had just said. "What do you mean?"

Jake looked down at his feet. "You alone know what I did that day. Everyone else thinks I'm some kind of hero who, while injured, hunted down the two insurgents who had blown his squad to pieces." He looked up, his eyes slightly watery. "But you know the truth, you know that all I did was murder two innocent civilians. I had no idea they were insurgents, I just saw them and gunned them down." The pain was obvious in his words. Jake continued. "I can just about remember their faces as I fell back, but I know they were not carrying any weapons. I know that I killed them in cold blood. No, worse, in anger. But when I woke up the next day I had everyone telling me how great I was. How I had uncovered this great stash of weaponry and unmasked a local terrorist."

Sam rubbed his chin, picturing the scene. He remembered the words of the marine officer, praising the sergeant as a hero.

"Yet even then, lying there with my head strapped up, I knew what must have happened. How my great and noble brother must have found the hidden weaponry then made it look as if it had been heroic. So while everyone else was congratulating me, I knew that you would be looking down on me. Judging me as the killer I am."

"Listen, Jake–"

"Don't *listen* me," Jake whispered. "You try to imagine just for a moment how it would have felt to have seen you, to have been around our family knowing that you were mocking me. Having this secret to hold onto, to use at a moment's notice."

Shaking his head, Sam said, "It wasn't like that, Jake."

"Do not lie to me, big brother. I may be a murderer, but I'm not a fool."

"I never said you were. If anyone is a fool, it's me."

Jake calmed his voice. "What do you mean?"

"You were right, the old man you killed did not have a rifle. But I had no idea there were actually weapons in the house. For all I knew you had just gunned down two civilians and yet I still placed that rifle there. A rifle from the base camp not the house. I planted that weapon to protect you. I lied and I was willing to frame an old man and his son as terrorists."

The younger Taylor looked at Sam, his shock evident. "You did what?"

"I planted the rifle. I wanted to protect you. You were right that I knew what you did, but I never judged you for it. I knew you couldn't have been in your right mind. I had no idea what else was in that house at the time. All I wanted to do was to protect you, to save you from yourself."

"It still doesn't make it right. Two wrongs and all that."

Sam leant forward and gave his brother's leg a gentle tap. "No, but you now know that you're not alone. That I never judged you for what you did, that no one including me would ever have blamed you. None of us have been in that situation. Surely the fact I was willing to risk my own career and freedom to help you proves it? Christ man, only one of us actually committed a crime. You did kill an insurgent, so no blame there. Whilst I did plant evidence."

"Perhaps we can share a cell?"

Sam laughed and sat back, putting his arm along the back of the bench. "That would be torture. Is this why you've stayed and helped me and Kate? To prove... what? That you're not a bad person?"

Jake shrugged. "Kind of. I thought if I helped you then that would at least give me some self-respect."

"Mum's going to go nuts when she finds out she's not had a full house at Christmas for a few years because of this."

Sam rubbed his eyes. The awkwardness that had existed between them seemed to have lessened slightly. He looked past Jake to the digital clock. It was nearly time to leave.

Pointing to the clock he asked, "Do you remember the plan?"

Jake winked. "Yes sir, captain."

"Ha, about time you showed the rank some respect. But seriously, are you good to go?"

"I mean I could do with a piss, and perhaps a cup of coffee," Jake replied. "I jest. I'm ready, although you're not."

"What do you mean? I am."

Jake shook his head and moved forward to kneel on the floor of the campervan. He struggled to remove the denim jacket in the confined space. Finally, he was able to fold up the heavy material and hand it over to Sam. "You should wear this, it will help."

Sam gave his brother a wry smile and took the jacket with a nod.

The two brothers took their respective positions in the campervan. Sam slipped into the denim jacket. He passed Jake a duffel bag with the remaining items they had removed from Bartel's house. Next, he picked up the pistol from the countertop next to him and checked the clip before carefully placing it inside his trouser waistband. He fiddled with the position, checking that the denim jacket covered the butt of the weapon. Up front, Jake started the engine, bringing the vehicle to life.

"So let me get this right, we are going to drive into a trap set by highly trained FSB agents to retrieve a woman?"

"Yes."

"Outstanding. I can't wait to tell this one at the next family dinner party."

Jake steered the campervan out of the side street and rejoined the main roads of the German capital. They had parked up not far from their destination, just to the north-east of the city centre. Having checked the site on Jake's phone they had seen that the destination was far enough away from the main roads of the city to avoid drawing any attention. By now, the roads were quiet. Pulling into the side street, with its entrance to the building site, Sam placed his hand on Jake's shoulder.

"Keep going and drive past first, they don't know what vehicle to expect and I'd like to have a look before we pull in."

Doing as instructed Jake drove steadily along the road. Keeping his speed low he released the pressure off the accelerator, ensuring the heavy camper van decelerated even more.

Sam looked through the van's tinted windows and stared out at the FSB's choice of location for the handover. A metal fence surrounded the building site with a gate already open in its centre. Whatever was to be built had yet to be started and all Sam could see was an open stretch of land lit by a set of spotlights in the centre. Building supplies were stacked high to one side: a mixture of fenders, pipes, bricks and other equipment all grouped together ready to begin construction. In the centre, a pair of portable cabins were bright under the spotlights. All that could be seen of human life was a trio of vehicles parked next to the cabins.

"What are you thinking?" asked Jake.

"They will want us to drive in and park facing away from the exit. I suspect they will have people on the outskirts of the site, hiding at the edge."

"I didn't see any sign of Kate?"

"Me neither, I suspect she will be in the cabins with Rövid. They will come out as we arrive to insinuate there's not that many of them."

Reaching the end of the street, Jake brought the van to a stop. "So it's a go then?"

"Any better ideas?"

"No."

"When we get in make sure you turn the car away from the cabins. Keep the sliding door facing towards the centre."

"Yes, driver's side. I got you."

Sam paused a moment. "What about the gates? If they shut them do you think this thing will be able to bulldoze its way through?"

Jake tapped the steering wheel. "This Volkswagen must be nearly three tons, and Klaus paid for every extra possible. It would be like a knife through butter."

They drove round the block and re-entered the quiet street. This time, as they reached their destination, Jake turned the wheel and pulled in through the metal gates. The silence in the campervan was deafening as both Taylors watched for any sign of movement. As they passed through the gate and drove onto the main building site, Jake turned the wheel, driving in a wide arch before bringing the vehicle to a stop ten metres from the nearest cabin. They waited, neither moving nor opening their doors.

"Where are they?" Jake wondered aloud.

Sam shook his head. "Inside, but what they are waiting for, I don't know."

Twisting round to look the other way, Sam saw the gates were still open. He thought about abandoning the operation all together and driving away.

"There's someone in that cabin," said Jake. "I definitely saw movement."

"Perhaps it's like those gangster films and we need to flash the headlights or something," said Sam, sarcastically.

"You mean they don't teach you things like this in police school?" chuckled Jake. "There's no 'How to deal with FSB thugs level one'?"

"Not when I was there, we never had time for useful things like that."

It was no use – they were going to have to make the first move.

"Turn the engine off," he instructed.

Jake eyed him. "Are you sure?"

"Just turn it off and get ready."

The camper's big engine fell silent, leaving the building site eerily quiet. Now, Sam saw movement from within the cabins, but no one stepped out of the temporary building.

"In for a penny, in for a pound," sighed Sam and pulled open the thick sliding door to let in a blast of cold air, which flooded the campervan.

"Here's when all the fun starts," whispered Jake.

Sam clambered out of the van's interior to stand in the rising snow. Adjusting the denim jacket over the SIG Sauer pistol in his waistbelt, he stepped towards the cabin. He was careful to count each step until after eight paces, he came to a halt. A face looked out at him from one of the windows, but he failed to recognise it.

"You thinking they've gone to sleep?" Jake called out unhelpfully.

The repatriation officer stood still, a tall lone shape in the swirling snow. Behind him the blue campervan stood open as a doorway to safety. Ahead of him and probably all around him, unfriendly eyes were watching, waiting for some kind of signal. Sam knew what the Russians were waiting for and he slowly reached down into his pocket. The metal seemed warm to his frozen fingers after being kept in his trousers. Gently, he lifted the Griffin into the night air. Twirling it in his fingers, he held it out towards the cabins.

"Rövid, you bastard. Bring me the girl."

THIRTY-ONE

SAM'S VOICE echoed around the building site. In answer, both doors of the portable cabins were flung open and out stepped the Russian contingent. The first out were two burly FSB agents, their faces gaunt, hair trimmed close to their skulls. From the nearest cabin a total of four guards walked out to form a line in front of Sam. Rövid stepped out of the far cabin, close behind the first two guards. His silver hair was still oiled and combed flat. Stepping out into the freezing night he stopped to wrap the blue scarf tighter around his neck, one-handed. The other arm was hidden in its sling under a grey coat. The older man looked over to Sam, squinting through his rimless glasses. Seeing the Griffin, he called over his shoulder before moving away from the entrance.

Kate was the last person to leave the cabins. Relief came over Sam to see the pale faced woman. She seemed to be okay, only a bright red mark on one cheek gave a sign of any mistreatment by her captors. Seeing Sam she gave a weak smile, a little light returning to her eyes. He gave her his most reassuring grin. A moment later, the entire Russian delegation was outside, standing amongst the falling snowflakes. A total of seven agents including Rövid now stood ahead of him, but Sam knew there would be more surrounding them in the darkness.

Rövid broke the silence. "Mr Taylor, nice to see you again."

Sam ignored him and spoke to Kate. "Are you okay?"

She nodded. "Yes. I'm sorry Sam, they came from behind and hit me. I should have stayed in the car."

Sam raised his hands to calm her. "Don't worry, it's all okay."

"I see you've brought your brother. Would he be more comfortable outside with us?" Rövid asked.

Jake wound the window down. "It's warmer in here thank you, plus no priceless artefacts to drop."

Rövid's lip curled at the remembered slight. "I hear my men repaid the favour to your friend Bartel's own collection."

Jake's face dropped and a nerve in his cheek twitched.

"You should not have brought dear Klaus into this. Now, because of you, a man of great experience is no longer with us," Rövid lectured Jake.

Jake gritted his teeth but refused to bite.

"Enough of that you miserable little bastard," snarled Sam. "Let's get this over with. I met with Cooper this evening and know all about your games."

Kate's eyes widened. "The Ambassador?"

Rövid turned to her. "Yes, my dear Sam here worked out who was actually behind the USB. Such a clever boy."

Kate looked to Sam, who gave a brief nod. A look of realisation suddenly came over her face. "Then you're here to give them back the Griffin. No Sam, you can't!"

She was cut off as one of the guards grabbed the back of her neck, pulling her back. Sam instinctively stepped forward, but Rövid called out and calmed them all down.

"Everyone stand down, we have an arrangement so let us complete our dealings."

Sam stopped and made the mental note of nine steps now, not eight. How do you want to do this?"

Rövid rubbed his arm hidden under the coat. "You tell me."

"You give me the girl, we all get in the van and I'll throw the Griffin out to you?"

The Russian laughed. "No, that is not how it works young Taylor. You give me the Griffin and then I'll give you the girl."

"Oh for God's sake, get on with it," Jake called out from the van.

Sam looked down at the USB in his hand then up at Rövid. "The girl can give it to you. Release her to me and I'll pass it to her."

Rövid thought for a moment, then agreed. He looked at the agent holding Kate. "Release her."

Kate stumbled forward, rubbing her neck. She gave her captors a look of pure malice.

"Kate," Sam called, calmly.

Kate stood between both parties and looked at Sam. "We can't give it to them Sam."

"Kate, it's not worth your life." She hesitated, so he added, "Trust me."

She looked at him, staring into his deep blue eyes before finally coming to a decision. Kate stepped forward and reached out for the Griffin. Their hands touched as she placed her fingers on the device. He gave a final nod of encouragement and felt her lift the Griffin away. She turned back to her captors and calmly handed it to the Russian agent.

Rövid's excitement was evident to everyone as he took the device from Kate.

"Here, take this and get it to Cooper," he told one of his underlings, handing them the Griffin.

Kate walked back to Sam, her face full of disdain. He took her arm and pulled her round to stand behind him. Arms on hips, he shifted the denim jacket.

"Rövid!" He called out to the Russian, who turned and squinted through his glasses to look at Sam.

"Yes?"

"I take it that's us done now."

The old Russian patted the silver hair. "Of course, until we meet again."

"There won't be a next time."

Rövid shrugged. "We shall see. I think you would be best to start running now."

"I'm not really one for running. I'd rather sit and eat *popcorn* while I watch you and Cooper come to the sticky end you both deserve."

Miklós Rövid shook his head in pity for Sam's perceived lack of understanding. But Sam was already moving. He had felt the movement from behind him, the feeling of the gun being withdrawn from his waistband. Crouching, he swivelled on his heel as the gun fired once, a loud bang in the otherwise silent night. Now facing the campervan, he wrapped his arms round Kate's narrow waist and closed his eyes. Behind him two new louder bangs erupted, the force of the explosions pushing him onwards as he counted the nine steps back towards the van. Around him there were shouts, as light and noise battered his senses. Still carrying Kate he dived forward onto the floor of the van.

More noises could be heard as people became aware of what was happening. Sam could already feel the wheels spinning into gear as they gripped the loose ground to propel the camper forwards. Extracting himself from Kate, Sam knelt and looked back through the rear window. The Russian agents, disorientated by the explosions of two M84 stun grenades taken from Bartel's storage, were beginning to recover. Shots were pinging against the bodywork of the campervan as Jake drove headlong back to the entrance. Sam gave a grim smile at the now prone body of Rövid on the ground. Kate had avenged Otto Schafer.

A scream echoed in the campervan as a bullet smashed the rear window. The Volkswagen bounced violently as it sped across the rough ground towards the gateway.

"Kate, you're okay," Sam called to her before taking the SIG Sauer back from her grasp. He then turned and fired the entire clip blindly back behind them.

"What the hell happened?" she gasped, trying to sit up.

"We borrowed some of Bartel's crowd control toys," called out Jake, "thought they could come in handy. Now hold on."

He floored the accelerator and the van hurtled towards the metal gates, which were being closed by a panicked FSB agent. The blue Volkswagen seemed to fly the final feet as they smashed into the gate, sending it jolting backwards. Jake slammed his foot on the brake and pulled on the wheel to bring the van round to face back down the side street. Taking the pause in momentum to his advantage, Sam turned and pushed Kate into the front passenger seat. Then, seeing her safely fasten in, he grabbed the side door to slam it shut.

"That was a bloody good shot back there," Jake called out to Kate next to him.

Kate was still shaken and did not reply.

"Concentrate on the driving!" Sam shouted as he kept lookout behind him. "Oh, this lot can't take a hint. Put your foot down, we've got company."

Two of the parked cars had followed them from the building site and were accelerating quickly. Sam pressed the release button on one of the small cupboards embedded into the campervan's interior and picked up another clip for the SIG Sauer. More bullets were hitting the campervan's exterior and Sam involuntarily ducked. Up front, Jake had found the main road and forced the Volkswagen into another sharp turn, sending Sam flying into the kitchen unit. He felt his arm becoming wet as warm liquid began to drip down his sleeve. Panicking, Sam ran his hand down his arm, to find no wounds.

"Who turned the tap on?" called Jake. "Hardly the time."

"Honestly, piss off."

Turning the tap back off, Sam returned to his position as rear gunner. The first of the Russian cars had caught up and was now following the Volkswagen as it weaved between the traffic. Crouching behind the bench, Sam waited until the bonnet of the car was almost touching their bumper before rising and returning fire. In his haste, he fired to his left, expecting to hit the driver.

"Damn it, wrong side of the road," he cursed.

The pursuer changed gear and attempted to go around the blue van. Jake, spotting it in his wing mirror, rammed the bigger vehicle into their pursuers' path, forcing it to brake and return to the rear.

"Where are we going?" asked Kate, her wits returning.

"City centre," Jake answered.

"What, why?"

Sam crouched back on the van's floor. "Less likely to be shot at."

Kate looked at the two of them, bewildered. "How will that help us escape?" Then she remembered the Griffin. "Sam, the Griffin, they still have it. We need to get it back."

"It's gone, forget it. Not our problem anymore."

She looked like she was about to argue, but was stopped as the Volkswagen bounced off a taxi which Jake had tried to overtake.

"Seriously?" called Sam, who had been bashed into the van's sidings. "Try and keep it steady."

"Do you want to drive?"

Rubbing his shoulder, Sam climbed back onto to the bench to see their pursuers once again attempting to ram their bumper. This time he knew where the driver would be and steadied himself before emptying another clip into the windscreen. The car veered right into the opposite traffic and into the path of an oncoming bus.

Somewhere, Sam could hear the sound of sirens. The police were coming. The second Russian car was now making its way through the disturbed traffic towards them. They were now on the main SS road which led directly into the heart of the city. To their left train tracks ran parallel to the roadside. Sam went back to the cupboard with the stored ammunition clips. He swore. He had not fastened the lock correctly and the cupboard was now empty. The campervan juddered as the second car rammed into them. Jake, struggling to keep control, drove up to the embankment between the traffic. The whole vehicle bounced as it hit the train tracks.

"Jake!" Kate screamed as a train approached.

Jake, keeping his cool, kept the campervan moving and calmly brought the vehicle back to the road. As the Volkswagen righted itself, Jake forced the engine onwards, increasing their speed as they headed closer to the city centre.

Sam pulled himself round to look at the final Russian car as it returned to its position behind them.

"Jake, have you got any more of the M84s?"

"Passenger footwell."

Kate reached down and handed Sam the stun grenade. Kneeling on the bench he steadied himself and waited as the approaching Russians edged closer. He pulled the pin and gripped tight to the trigger. Waiting until the front bumper of the approaching car kissed their own rear bumper, he threw the grenade at the windscreen and turned back round, covering his ears. He heard the bang rather than saw it. Peering back through narrowed eyes he saw their pursuers had stopped. Smoke was rising from the now stationary vehicle.

"That's uncle Ivan out," he called to his companions.

"Nice to hear it, but now we have the police to deal with," said Jake dryly.

Blue lights and sirens were flashing all around them as speeding police cars were approaching from all directions.

"Where are we?" Sam asked Jake.

"Pretty much in the centre."

"Keep going, I'll think of something."

Kate screamed at them. "What do you mean think of something? We're surrounded by police!"

The brothers ignored her and Jake sped on down the main road. The streets were quiet as they drove on through. Holding onto the rear of the front two seats, Sam looked up through the windscreen to see the Berliner Fernsehturm television tower looming overhead, watching over the entire city.

"They are going to arrest us!" moaned Kate in despair.

Neither brother spoke. They looked out of the windows to see three police cars around them. The officers inside were furiously waving at them to stop. Jake skirted round one car, forcing another of the police cars to brake to avoid running onto the pavement. The remaining police vehicle dropped back slightly as they crossed over the River Spree. Jake increased his speed.

"Now?" he asked Sam.

"Not yet."

Jake shook his head and forced the bullet ridden campervan onwards. The route ahead was clear and they could see far into the distance as the road stretched onwards into the city. Further down they would be in Potsdamer Platz, Kate asked if the plan was to try and get to the hotel.

"There's a plan?" asked Jake in mock surprise.

Sam did not have time to answer. Instead, he pointed ahead. "Stinger, stinger, stinger!"

"What?" said Jake stupidly, before he saw the long strip of metal spikes being laid across the road ahead.

The younger Taylor had no option but to slam his foot on the brake and pull desperately on the steering wheel. The campervan's wheels screeched against the forces being applied by the brakes. The vehicle's occupants were thrown violently. Sam being the only one without a seatbelt desperately tried to cling onto the head rest of Jake's chair. Skidding across the tarmac the front wheel collided with the curb of the pavement and the van flipped over once onto its side, then again, coming to rest on its roof. Sam felt his grasp on the headrest loosen as he was flung about the Volkswagen's interior. Time seemed to stand still as he landed hard on the interior's ceiling amongst a mixture of glass, spent bullet casings, and debris. Somewhere, Kate screamed, but Sam had no real sense of anything but his own predicament.

With a resounding thud the blue Volkswagen campervan, which had started the day as a newly polished top of the range vehicle, came to a halt in the centre of Berlin. Sam lay on his back.

He blinked and stared up at what was once the floor of the van. Pain from all over his body began to register with his brain. He could taste blood. The rest of his senses tried to acclimatise. A high-pitched ringing sound was resounding in his eardrums. Trying to move, he felt his ribs send a fresh jolt of pain through his nervous system. Somewhere near, he thought he heard a dull thud and guessed one of his companions had freed themselves from their seatbelt. He wanted to call out to them, but his voice was unresponsive. The effort of breathing was proving too much.

New signals were making their way to his brain as blue lights began flashing across his vision. The ringing sound was being replaced by sirens and then voices. The voices were shouting, but he couldn't understand what they were saying. He wanted to reply, to shout for Kate, to see that Jake was all right. There was movement close by, but his brain had already made its decision. There were too many signals for it to process, too much to manage. It needed to shut down, to reset. And as the first hands touched his leg, Sam blacked out.

THIRTY-TWO

IT WAS a bright crisp wintery afternoon at the small South London airfield. The January sun shone bright in the cloudless sky, warming the two men who were waiting on the runway. Both were tall and broad shouldered, with one slightly larger than the other. The slightly shorter of the two was dressed in a dark green field jacket zipped up tight. The taller man was dressed in a brand-new denim jacket, a black fur-lined design. His old one had been covered in blood and left in a Berlin emergency ward. Both men were watching the sky as they waited. Having spent the past few days in a wintery Berlin, this deserted airport seemed almost tropical.

Their waiting was interrupted by the arrival of an airport security guard who tentatively walked up to the two brothers.

"Mr Taylor and erm, Mr Taylor, would you come with me please."

The eldest of the brothers sighed. "We might as well get it over with."

The security guard gave a nervous smile and indicated for the pair to follow him across the tarmac to where an open aircraft hangar dominated the skyline.

"I wonder how many guns are currently pointed at us right now?" asked Jake Taylor.

"I couldn't even begin to guess. Somewhere like this will have plenty of hidden security," answered Sam Taylor.

The two brothers walked shoulder to shoulder behind their guide. The whole place seemed deserted, with no planes or ground staff around. Only one thing was amiss, which was that to one side the burning wreckage of a helicopter burnt merrily away to itself. No emergency crews were in attendance to fight the flames. Instead, three body bags were laid on the ground in front of the wreckage.

"Angela Cooper took great pleasure in telling me about this place," Sam told Jake. "Seemed to have almost relished it."

"Well she was right, we did end up here," admitted Jake.

Heading to the large open hangar, they both saw the black cabin with its two doors, exactly as the ambassador had described. At the entrance of the hangar their guide paused and then apologised. "I'm sorry gentlemen, but I must be leaving you here. I'm sure you will understand."

Sam gave the nervous man a warm smile and nodded. "Indeed we do, thank you for your help."

Left alone once again, the two brothers walked forward. The events of the past few days had led up to this moment and neither man had anything else to say. All that was left was to face the music.

"Any guess as to which door?" said Jake.

Sam was saved from answering as the righthand door burst open and a tanned figure walked out to greet them.

"Well, you two have caused us all some real trouble, haven't you?" said a smirking Sir Jeffrey Doyle.

The old diplomat looked far too refreshed for Sam's liking. The grey goatee had been recently trimmed, his face brown from the Caribbean sun.

"You absolute bastard," said Sam, shaking his head. "You love to make an entrance, don't you?"

Sir Jeffrey's eyes sparkled with delight behind his gold-rimmed spectacles. "Because of you I had to fly home early from drinking more rum punch than I could manage."

"Well, we are very sorry about that, perhaps they can have some shipped over?" chided Jake.

"Sarcasm is the lowest form of wit, just remember that. But I suppose I should be thanking you, it's not often we get to find our very own Russian mole. By the way, you two look terrible."

He was right, both Sam and Jake were covered in cuts and bruises from their high- speed crash. Jake's head now had a fresh cut on his face to go with his damaged ear, which after the stitches were removed would leave a deep scar on his forehead. Sam meanwhile was carrying three broken ribs, numerous cuts, a bruised skull and a sprained wrist. All worthwhile injuries for what was about to come.

Sir Jeffrey looked past them, to the main runway. "Talking of moles, here she comes now. I take it you two would like to watch this?"

Jake rubbed his hands together. "It would be my absolute pleasure."

Sam kept quiet and waited for the older man to lead them on. The trio walked to the entrance of the hangar to watch as a sleek private jet came in to land. They looked on as the pilot gracefully brought the plane down onto the runway before taxiing along the tarmac towards the hangar. The noise of the engines deafened the three men as they watched on in silence. Sam, standing slightly behind the other two, wondered if the occupant had even realised what was about to happen. He sincerely doubted it.

The pilot turned off the engines as the door to fuselage opened up to reveal a uniformed hostess who expertly dropped the steps to the floor. Stepping back into the cabin, the hostess disappeared and there was a pause before the plane's other occupants made their way out onto British soil. The first to exit was Ambassador Angela Cooper. Her hawkish face looked up and felt the fresh winter air, refreshing after a flight of stale air conditioning.

Confidently taking the steps she looked round for the expected entourage, but only seeing Sir Jeffrey, she paused. A slight look of confusion quickly became one of concern as she saw Sam and Jake.

"Good afternoon Ambassador," called out Sir Jeffrey to the now frozen ambassador. "I take it you had a good flight?" There was no answer. "I take it you were expecting someone else?" Still, there was no answer to Sir Jeffrey's words. "Come now Angela, I believe you know what will happen next, so shall we get out of the cold?"

Angela Cooper's eyes flashed past Sir Jeffrey to the waiting cabin with its two doors and then to the flaming helicopter wreckage. "You can't do this. I have powerful friends. The Prime Minister."

"Ah yes, the PM asked me to show you this on your arrival. I believe it went out live about ten minutes ago." He reached inside of his coat and pulled out a phone. Showing her the screen he pressed play and the dull tones of the Prime Minister echoed. "It is my unfortunate responsibility today to announce the sudden death of our beloved colleague Ambassador Angela Cooper. As many of you know, Ambassador Cooper was a key figure in the recent signing of the North Sea Energy Deal, which was signed yesterday with our European neighbours."

Sir Jeffrey turned off the phone. "Announced live on the BBC, you should count yourself honoured. I'll be lucky if I even get a mention in my local newspaper."

Angela Cooper's face grew paler as she tried to comprehend what was happening to her. She began to shake.

A still beaming Sir Jeffrey stepped forward and reached out his arm to guide Cooper forward, but she still did not move. Eventually, she realised she had no other choice but to follow as instructed and she tentatively began to move forward.

"There we go," encouraged Sir Jeffrey. "You know the drill."

As Angela Cooper edged towards her fate she paused and

looked directly at Sam. She looked as if she wanted to say something, but Sam stopped her.

He pointed at the cabin and said, "The door you are after is on your left. It's the less comfortable room of the two. I'm sure your imagination can do the rest."

The now former ambassador opened her mouth then closed it again. There was nothing more to be said. The three men watched on as, still shaking, she walked to the waiting cabin.

"I can see you enjoyed that."

The tall figure of John Travers had joined them on the runway.

"You should have heard her all the way here, telling me how she was being invited back to become Foreign Secretary."

Sam laughed and reached out to take Travers' hand. "It's good to see you, John. We certainly owe you a few drinks."

That was putting it lightly. Prior to his meeting with the Ambassador at the Reichstag, Sam had told the old Scotsman everything. From their discussions with Rövid to the discovery of the Griffin. He had laid out everything he knew and suspected about Ambassador Cooper, and eventually the Head of Security had believed him. Once on-side, he had gone above and beyond, sourcing another Griffin from his contacts at the American Embassy. He had switched the Griffin and placed a recording device in Sam's pocket back in the Reichstag as he had frisked the Englishman. It was the same Griffin that Rövid had then sent back to Cooper, but this time the contents were sent directly to Travers' computer, not to the Kremlin. With that and the recording, Cooper's fate had been sealed. Everything else from there had been an act to fool Cooper into a false sense of security and to give Sam chance to save Kate. Even the very public arrest in the city centre had all been a sham.

"To see the look on that woman's face just now made it all worthwhile," chuckled the Scotsman. "That will live with me for the rest of my life."

Sir Jeffrey cleared his throat. "You are more than welcome to stay and watch?"

"Thank you, but no, I need to get back to the embassy. Our American friends will want a full briefing." He looked at Sam. "There's a space on the plane if you want it? I think there's a personal secretary who's quite keen to see you?"

"I think I might just take you up on that," answered Sam, thinking of the brunette beauty and the suite in the Ritz-Carlton.

Travers left to wait for Sam in the plane, leaving him alone with Sir Jeffrey and Jake.

"I guess I'll have to be seeing you."

Jake gave his brother a hug. "I take it you don't want me to come this time?"

"Sod off."

The two brothers stared at each other and Sam gave his brother a gentle tap on the cheek. "You'd better not be a stranger from now on, remember Christmas this year."

Jake smiled and stepped back. "I'll let you go, I want to get a front row seat for Cooper's final performance."

With that, the younger Taylor gave his brother a final wave and walked back to the cabin. Sir Jeffrey, left alone now with Sam, took his arm and pulled him towards the plane.

"You have no idea how happy that makes me."

Sam raised an eyebrow, remembering an old complaint he had with the diplomat.

"I'm not sure I'm that happy with you."

"You're not?"

"No. Why the hell do you think it was all right to hire Jake as one of your Caretakers?"

Sir Jeffrey blinked at Sam. "I don't see why you would have a problem with that?"

"You basically made him a contract killer at the whim of the government."

"And?"

"And it's not right, you're supposed to be a family friend. What would Grandad have said if he'd been alive?"

"Samuel, you of all people should understand this world.

There is good and then there is bad. As for your grandad, have I ever told you how I met Gerry?" Sam shook his head. "It was back in the navy. I was a young officer on my first ship. I somehow found myself in the middle of this bar in Australia, about to be punched into next week by two Aussie sailors. Instead, this non-commissioned officer, a Yorkshireman who I barely knew from the ship, came out of nowhere and punched their lights out. After which, he turns to me and goes, 'Sometimes lad, shit just has to be done.' We were friends for life after that."

Sam understood what Sir Jeffrey was talking about. Jake was just another way of ensuring that the right shit got done. He might not like it, but he understood.

"You will be telling me everything next time we are in Il Conte's, including why you were about to be beaten up in an Australian bar."

The old diplomat gave his most charming bow. "Of course, of course, my dearest Sam, but for now I think there's a young lady waiting for you."

"Indeed, but I need a favour before I go."

"You do?"

Sam tapped his chest. "When you see Emma Read, make sure you tell her just how beat up I am."

"So bad that you will need, say, a full week off to recover?"

"Make it two," Sam grinned then asked, "Now what would you do in Berlin with a beautiful woman, a suite in a five-star hotel and thousands of euros courtesy of the Russians?" he asked his mentor.

"Christ Sam, I'm too old for all that. But I'm sure you will think of something."

ALSO BY BEN BALDWIN

Code Red - A Sam Taylor Thriller Book 1

This time it's personal…

'Wow Unstoppable action, twists and turns… I couldn't put it down.' — **Reader review**

BUY NOW

ABOUT THE AUTHOR

Ben Baldwin is the quintessential Yorkshire man lost down south. Having grown up in the foothills of the Pennines, right in the heart of the Last of the Summer Wine country, he can now be found in Buckinghamshire living with his girls: wife Kimberley and their two children, Ella and Megan.

If he's not writing, working or chasing the kids, he can be found exploring the Buckinghamshire countryside on his bike or hacking holes into it while playing golf.

A management consultant in the professional world, he would be first to admit it is only to fund their adventures in the family motorhome 'Henry.'

His journey into writing has been called 'a hobby that got out of hand' by his wife and the Sam Taylor series is his first foray into the literary world.

He can be contacted at www.ben-baldwin.co.uk.

A NOTE FROM THE PUBLISHER

We hate typos. All of our books have been rigorously edited and proofread, but sometimes mistakes do slip through. If you have spotted a typo, please do let us know and we can get it amended within hours.

info@bloodhoundbooks.com

www.ingramcontent.com/pod-product-compliance
Lightning Source LLC
LaVergne TN
LVHW041622060526
838200LV00040B/1402